He lay there a long time, shaken with wild silent sobs, still conscious of a world, even if it were only made up of birds and squirrels, that must not hear him weep. Must not ever know that a man-child could weep, and could suffer like this.

And then, in an interval of a breath, he heard a light step. Looking up suddenly, his anguished face drenched in tears, he saw a girl, standing quite close to him, looking down. Her hands were full of the wild blossoms she had been picking, and her lovely face was full of startled tenderness and wonder . . . .

Grace
LIVINGSTON HILL

AMERICA'S BEST-LOVED STORYTELLER

THE GIRL
OF THE WOODS

LIVING BOOKS®
Tyndale House Publishers, Inc.
Wheaton, Illinois

This Tyndale House book
by Grace Livingston Hill
contains the complete text
of the original hardcover edition.
NOT ONE WORD
HAS BEEN OMITTED.

Living Books is a registered trademark of Tyndale House
Publishers, Inc.

Library of Congress Catalog Card Number 88-50798
ISBN 0-8423-1016-9

Printed in the United States of America

99 98 97 96 95
12 11 10 9   8   7   6

I

REVEL Radcliffe stood glowering by his father's desk in the library, where he had been ordered to await his father's coming.

His father was even then in the small reception room across the hall talking with a man on business, something to do with printing or engraving. Revel didn't care much. His father's affairs seldom concerned him, and rarely interested him. It had been that way since his babyhood. His few contacts with his father had been to receive commands for the ordinary changes that had followed one another regularly through his life. School attendance, and the standing he was expected to maintain: he was required to be letter perfect in everything or there was a storm. Attendance on certain family gatherings; courtesy in the presence of any member of his *father's* family. His mother's family were seldom around, and never now since her death two years before.

His mother's maiden name had been Emily Revel, and she had lovingly given it to her son against the contemptuous protests of her husband who had insisted on the boy being named Hiram after himself. Hiram R. Radcliffe, he had given reluctant consent to at last, because the doctor had told him that his wife was in a serious state, with fever and lassitude, and needed to be humored. So the baby had been named Hiram Revel Radcliffe. But his mother had called him Revel, and he had always signed his name Revel Radcliffe, without the H. The fellows at school, and even the teachers, always called him Revel. His father was never about the school and didn't know.

He was trying, as he stood there glowering and waiting, to figure out what was coming. He was seldom ordered to await his father unless some change of the present state was in the offing. Perhaps there was a dinner ahead, or some definite prohibition was about to be given. His mind always sprang ahead and tried to anticipate. He liked to prepare himself, so that he could meet whatever was to be with the proper stony indifference. He would not offer interest or joy to meet any crisis, even if it were something he might like. And it seldom was that. He could not hope now that there was anything in the immediate future that would bring him any comfort or peace. Sometimes it seemed to him that his father fairly hated him, and he could recall so many times in the last few months of his beloved mother's life when her wishes were utterly set aside for something his father wanted done, that he bore a bitter resentment down in his heart.

And yet, his father was all he had.

So he waited.

Then he could hear his father escorting the man to the door, his grave cold tones cutting through the dim gloom in the wide hall. That hall that always reminded Revel of his mother's funeral cortege, as she went in state, borne of six of his father's friends. Not a Revel among them all! Not even her own brother present. Somewhere in China, he was, or maybe some other far land, now that there was talk of war everywhere. His father had seen to it that every Revel was well out of his way. Plain and poor they were, though they used to be wealthy. He planned that the grandfather was soon to be banished to an old men's home though Revel hadn't been told that, and the brother-in-law, if he returned, to a training camp where rules and regulations of government and militarism would relieve Mr. Radcliffe of the unpleasant necessity of having to think about him and plan for his absence. At least that was the Radcliffe idea.

Suddenly the front door closed with a final click like the sound of the elder Radcliffe's voice in all conversations. Then a firm self-assured step told the boy his father had entered the room. Revel lifted his eyes with the fleeting glance of sullen recognition that his father always demanded. The boy often wondered if his father recognized the utter rebellion of his young heart as he gave that glance of acknowledgment that this man was his father, and as such had a right to deference and obedience.

"Sit down, Hiram!" ordered the father.

Revel averted his gaze and sidled toward a chair, though as long as he dared, he delayed to actually yield his body to its support.

"Yes, sir?" Revel said with a mixture of obedience, fury and questioning in his voice.

"I called you in here, Hiram, to let you know that I am about to be married!"

The man paused for an instant and let his cold eyes bore cruelly through the tall young fellow with the dark eyes and heavy dark waves of hair that were all so utterly unlike his own vigorous tawny hair and light blue eyes. Revel had heard him almost blame his frail little mother once because her son did not resemble himself, but had the general look of the Revels. It seemed to be an unforgivable thing that his wife had not given him a son who would be a replica of himself. As if she had deliberately willed it to be so.

But Revel was not thinking of this now. The words his father had just spoken had gone deep into his heart, like well-aimed shots, each piercing the vital life of him. Nay, it seemed on second thought that they were great rocks, each word a rock, thudding on his sensitive soul with blows from which he could never hope to recover. And yet he managed to sit steadily without a visible quiver, just enduring those awful words. His father was actually going to wipe out from the home the memory of his mother by putting another woman in her place.

Oh, of course, it was a perfectly respectable thing to do, for his father to remarry, after two years. People would say he was sensible. That it was the only thing for him to do. They would say how nice it was for Revel to have a mother again, and life could go on for them in a normal way. But the boy knew that his life was shattered. So far as his father was concerned, or any memory of his father and mother together which made the kind of dream any boy would like to conjure in his thoughts, it was gone! Dead! Lifeless!

It might have been different perhaps, if he could remember happy days they had had together. But all the happy memories were of his mother, and the rest were of the gloom and sadness that had pervaded the household whenever his father came about. If there had been sunny days and happiness, perhaps even Revel could have felt his father was justified in trying to have a little more happiness for himself. But a man who had made no joy for that precious mother, how had he a right to try for any pleasure in life for himself?

These bitter thoughts chased one another over his mind in rapid succession and yet he sat there and held his face without a quiver, not a flicker of an eyelash. He had had long practice in hiding his innermost thoughts from his father.

"I want you to understand," went on that grim voice, "that I shall demand the utmost deference and courtesy and obedience, the same that you gave to your own mother. The woman I am marrying is a member of an old and noble family, a woman of much character, and she will not brook slipshod manners, nor carelessness of speech or attire. I am telling you this now and I do not wish to have to speak of it again. Do you understand?"

After an instant of utter stillness the boy summoned

courage to lift a fleeting glance fatherward, and grudgingly bow a brief assent to the question.

The father waited a moment, perhaps expecting some other word from his son, but Revel had done all that his tempestuous spirit could do, and not break forth into shocked protest. After a little he managed to get himself to his feet, his glance still down on the floor, controlling by some deep boy-power the awful trembling that was traveling upward from his heart to his lips.

"Well," said his father, "haven't you anything to say, Hiram? Doesn't it mean anything to you?"

Oh, yes, it meant much to him, but Revel could not say it here. Long years of hiding his feelings from his father would not let him speak now. What difference what he would say? It could only bring forth vituperation. He knew that by long experience.

And then, because the silence demanded some reply from him, his cold lips and husky voice stumbled forth with:

"Well, I guess you—had a *right*—to do that, father!"

"Had a *right*? Why of course I did. It is not for you to set yourself up as my judge. Of course I had a right. It seems to me a more pleasant wishful courtesy might have been on your lips."

The boy stuttered, stumbled, turned red and then deadly white again as he lifted almost haughty eyes and managed to say in a clear, contemptuous tone:

"I guess you'll be happy all right!"

"Very well," said the man, having forced congratulations from this unwilling young serf of his. "You may go and get yourself ready for dinner. We are having it early tonight. I have to go out. I hear the dishes being brought in. You had better hurry. Later, perhaps tonight, or in a day or two, I shall tell you the plans I have made for your college entrance next fall."

Without another word Revel went swiftly out of the room, across the hall with silent steps, and up the stairs. He crossed to his own room, and then slid out again down the back stairs, and out a side entrance. Swiftly behind the garage he went, across the fields at the back of the house, straight out of his father's estate, and up a hill toward a woods that had been many times in his young past a refuge when his soul was in agony.

He passed like a shadow through the brightness of the setting sun, on into the shadows on the edge of the woods, and then entered the cool silence of the place he knew. He flung himself down full length upon the soft yielding carpet of moss and delicate spring blossoms. Violets and anemones, spring beauties, hepaticas. He knew and loved them all. They were his friends. How many times he had come here and gathered great handfuls of them for his mother. And unkown to his father or anyone who had been at her funeral, a handful of them lay even now close to her heart, where he had put them when no one was looking. They seemed now to be his only friends, his only touch with the beloved mother who was gone.

So he flung himself down with his face among the flowers, and let his boy tears flow, as he could never have let them go if there had been anyone watching. He had a feeling that not even God, if there was a God, must see him weep. It seemed to him his heart was broken, and there was no use going on.

And yet he had to go on!

The horror of it all rolled over him. He had no mother, never had really had a father, and now his home, what had been left of it, was shattered.

True, he didn't know the woman who was to be his father's wife, had no knowledge of who she might be. He didn't care. It made no difference to him. She might become his father's wife, but she would never be anything else to him. He would not even have the privilege of looking sorrowful any more in that house into which he had been born. The newcomer might be a pleasant woman; he ought to feel sorry for her, perhaps, but he couldn't. Perhaps she would have to suffer as much as his mother had suffered, but at least that had nothing to do with him now. He could not help it. He had to bear this awful shock himself, and find out what to do.

He lay there a long time, shaken with wild silent sobs, still conscious of a world, even if it were only made up of birds and squirrels, that must not hear him weep. Must not ever know that a man-child *could* weep, and could suffer like this.

And then in an interval of a breath, he heard a light step. Looking up suddenly, his anguished face drenched in tears, he saw a girl, standing quite close to him looking down. Her hands were full of the wild blossoms she had been picking, and her lovely face was full of startled tenderness, wonder, and sudden deep embarrassment.

"Oh," she said, "I'm sorry! I beg your pardon! I didn't see you before or I wouldn't have come!"

He gave her a bewildered ashamed blinking stare. He wasn't a boy who was given to tears. He had come away to the woods to hide his misery. And here in the wilderness he was caught, by a *girl!*

She wasn't any girl he knew, and she probably didn't know him. But what difference did that make? Oh, why did this have to happen?

He gave an angry brush at his eyes.

"It's awwright!" he growled, and essayed to arise. Then his misery caught him once more and he bowed his unhappy face into the flowers again with a suppressed groan. "Oh!"

The girl had started to go away, but his action drew her sorrowful glance again, and she turned a little and dropped softly down beside him among the flowers, laying one small hand gently on his bowed head, as lightly as a butterfly might have lit there.

"I'm sorry!" she said gently. "I'm only a stranger, you know, and I don't count of course, but I'm sure God cares."

The boy's tense shoulders quivered and he lifted his head and looked at her in scorn.

"God cares!" he sneered. "A lot you know about it! He's had it in for me ever since I was born! Don't kid yourself. He never even thought of me."

"Oh, yes, He cares," said the girl firmly. "He loves you very much, and He's thinking about your trouble right now and wishing you would come to Him to get help!"

The tense young shoulders quivered again.

He drew himself up and tossed his hair back from his hot flushed face.

"I guess I don't need help. I guess I can take it. A man oughtta be able ta take it—anything that comes—oughtn't he?"

"Why—I don't know that he ought, not all alone. I think God meant us to be dependent on Him, and sometimes only trouble will bring us to recognize that." The girl spoke as if she was working out the thought as she talked. She didn't look like a girl who had been through much trouble herself.

He rested his elbow on the ground and stared at her, trying to look as if there had been no tears, to ignore his own humiliation.

"Well, I don't know about God. My mother used to pray. She taught me little prayers, but that's a long time ago, and she's gone. That's the trouble! I'm a fool of course, because she's been dead two whole years, and dad has a right to do what he likes, only it kind of seems as if dad was dishonoring her, and I can't take that! You see dad just told me he's getting married again, and I saw red. I came off here to be by myself."

"Oh, I'm sorry! And I broke in on your privacy! But truly I didn't know you were here. I didn't see you till you looked up, and even then I tried to get away."

The boy took a deep breath and put out an impulsive hand to hers.

"Don't feel bad!" he said resignedly. "I didn't blame you. Only I just saw red, and I couldn't take it to have that done to my mother. She was a wonderful mother—and it wasn't as if she'd had a good time while she lived, either!"

His strong young lip quivered, and the tears began to blur
into his eyes again, though he blinked them away quickly.
He was gripping her little hand in his now, and looking
down at it curiously, almost tenderly. "My mother had a
hand like yours," he said suddenly, "little and kind of soft,
like silk when you touched it!" He smoothed her fingers
thoughtfully, as if he didn't remember she was hearing him.
And then suddenly he laid her hand back in her lap.

"I guess I'm a kind of a sis," he said shamedly, "and my
mother wouldn't have liked that. But I was boiling mad
when my father told me he was getting married again, and I
couldn't see it. If I could find a job somewhere I'd go away
and he wouldn't ever see me again!"

The girl looked down on him with compassion. She was
wearing a little white dress with tiny rosebuds printed on it.
There were two small bows of rose colored ribbon in her
brown hair, and she seemed so sweet and sisterly there in the
woods looking down on him.

"Well," she said, "maybe that would be a good thing for
you to do. I don't know I'm sure. But I think you would
need to ask God about it before you did anything like that.
God knows what is best for you, and if you would ask Him
He would show you, for sure."

"I doubt it!" said the boy, discouragement written all
over his dejected young face. "But I'm all kinds of sorry you
caught me bawling, and I'm grateful to you for trying to
comfort me, anyhow."

"Well, I wish you'd try asking God," said the girl softly
with a troubled look in her eyes. "I'm going to be praying
that you'll do it. And now don't you worry about my seeing
a few tears in your eyes. I'm just a stranger, and you'll probably never see me again. I'm going away now, so forget it!
I'll forget it too, and you can put it out of your mind forever."

"But no, I don't wish to forget you," said the boy. "You
have been all right. You don't need to go away. I'll pull my

self together. You came here for some reason. Don't let me drive you away." He sat up and dashed the tears away angrily. "After all I'm more than a child. I'm almost eighteen. I oughtta be able to take it."

"Oh, I'm sorry I barged in on you! I only came to pick a few of these flowers, because my mother once came here and picked some and loved them. She told me about them and when I found we were going to stop near here I decided to make a chance to walk out here and find the flowers my mother used to talk about."

She held out a handful of drooping blossoms.

"They don't look like much, do they," she went on, "held in my hot hand so long, but perhaps when I get to the house I can put them in water and they will revive. I want to press a few of them to put in my memory book of mother."

The boy eyed the flowers curiously.

"No, they don't look like much," he said. "You ought to have some fresh ones. But it's getting late and they've mostly closed up for the night, I guess. If I had my flashlight I might be able to find some. Over there there used to be a lot."

He got up and took a few steps, stooping down and feeling around. He brought back a handful of more little drooping buds.

"They aren't much better," he said disappointedly. "The best time to get them is in the early morning. Who are you anyway? Where do you live? I could come up here and get some for you. Maybe you'd like to come along."

The girl gave him a quick grateful look, but shook her head disappointedly.

"I couldn't," she said. "I'd love to, but I'm traveling with my uncle and I have to be ready to leave when he wants to go. So I guess it would be too far, and they would be uneasy if I went away off up here in the morning. They would expect me to get lost or something. No, it doesn't matter. Perhaps some other spring I can come here again and get them. It's probably very silly of me to care about it."

"No," said the boy, "it's not silly!' I had a mother too, you know. Has yours gone and left you like mine?"

"Yes," said the girl, "five years ago. But I've never forgotten her. She was dear and sweet. But look, how dark it's getting! Is there a storm coming up? I'd better hurry. I might not be able to find my way back."

"Don't worry about that. I'll go with you of course. Where is it you have to go? Are you stopping in Arleth, or Chenango, or did you come over the hill? Down Afton way?"

"Oh," said the girl, "I think the name is Sumter Hills, just outside of the town, a big white pleasant farmhouse. I came with my uncle, and we're staying with the widow of an old school friend of his. He had to stop off to see her on some business. He went up to the city this morning to look after it for her. I stayed here to look up places mother had told me about. But you don't need to go back with me. I'm sure I can find my way back. I'd better go at once."

"Sure!" said Revel. "But I'll go with you. I know a short cut across the fields. What's the name of the person you're stopping with?"

"She's Mrs. Martin. Cousin Sarah, my uncle called her, but she's not a real cousin. I never saw her before."

"Oh, sure I know that party. Prim old bird, isn't she? She got me in trouble once when I was crossing the stream back of her house. Reported me to the school superintendent, and got me in wrong with my dad. I didn't fish in her old stream. I was only crossing it when she saw me, but she tried to identify a fish I was carrying and we had all kinds of trouble. You'd better not tell her you've been in my company or she'll haul you to court and have me tried for trying to kidnap you."

The girl laughed.

"I guess you know who she is all right." she said merrily. "I'm sure she would be like that. Though she's been very kind to me. But she is terribly prim, and pretty set in her way. I expect she's awfully upset by this time that I haven't got back yet. I told her I was just going to take a walk. That I wanted to see the old schoolhouse and the church and some of the places my mother used to tell me about. I didn't tell her about the flowers on the hilltop. I thought she might think that was silly. Anyway I didn't want to bring it out in the open. It seemed too sacred to me."

"You're telling me!" rumbled the boy in a low tone. "Don't tell her where you've been. Just say you got turned around and it took you longer to get home than you realized, see?"

"Yes," said the girl. "But I do hope I'll get there before dinner is ready. She went to a missionary meeting of some kind. She wanted me to go with her. She said there was going to be a woman there from China and it would be very interesting, but I told her that I wanted to walk around and think about my mother being here when she was a girl like me, and she finally let me off. But dear me, I don't want to have to have it all over again! My uncle won't be back till midnight. But she's sure to send the farm man after me if I'm very late."

"Well, he won't find you. We'll go another way. You came by the street, didn't you? Till you got to the lane up the hill, and then took to the woods?"

"Yes. But how did you know?"

"Well, I sort of figured you did. You see this is one of my hideouts when I feel sore or something."

"I see," said the girl, and her hand lingered comfortingly on the arm that was leading her.

"Now, we turn here," said Revèl. "You came up that lane to the left there, didn't you? It turns into the highway a little this side of that big light you see in the tower in the valley. That's the town hall in Afton."

"Oh, yes, I remember passing that! And when I get there I turn right, don't I? Oh, I'm sure I can find my way now. I don't need to trouble you any more."

"Trouble, nothing! Do you suppose I'm gonta leave you wandering all over the country in the dark? You a stranger! Not on yer life! But we're going a quicker way than you came. Down here at the edge of the woods we can climb the fence, go cross lots, and cut off a mile or so. See that light away off there to the right? Well, that's on top of the Sumter Hills Bank, and your Mrs. Martin lives out that road, beyond. I'll show you. It won't take long. Come on!" said the boy catching hold of her hand and guiding her down the hill, carefully avoiding the roots and hillocks in their path.

They didn't talk as they hurried down; they were almost breathless they were going so fast. But when they came to the fence at the end of the woods the boy paused.

"Get your breath!" he ordered, leaning against the fence.

"I'm all right," said the girl, "I'm used to running a lot."

"Yes, you're some girl! But you'd better get your breath. You don't want to barge in on old Sarah all puffed. And say, what's your name? Where do you live when you're home? You and I are friends, if you don't mind, and I don't want to lose sight of you entirely. You're the only person I've seen since my mother died that seemed to understand."

"Oh, thank you," said the girl simply. "I couldn't help knowing how *I* would feel if ever a thing like that happened to me. Why, my name is Margaret Weldon, and I'm going out to my aunt's in California to spend the winter and go to school. The address is Linton Lane. Crystal Beach."

The boy took out a pencil and scribbled the address in a small note book.

"Okay," he said. "I'll maybe keep in touch with you if you don't mind, but don't tell old Sallie Martin or she'll tell you what a young reprobate I am."

"Oh," said the girl, "I wouldn't believe her anyway, if she did. But aren't you going to tell me your name?"

"Oh, sure!" he laughed amusedly. "I'm Revel Radcliffe. Just Arleth'll reach me." Then he hesitated. "Ur—that is—if I stay here. I don't much think I'm going to. But I'll let you know if I move on somewhere."

"Oh, yes! Do, please. I'd like to know how you come out!"

"Okay! I'll letcha know."

"Revel is an unusual name," said the girl, "I like it."

"Yeh! Mother's name was Emily Revel."

"How nice that you have her name! And aren't any of her people living?"

"Yeh! Got an uncle in China or somewhere. Or maybe he's over in the English army now. I don't know. He doesn't write to us. An' I've got a grandfather!"

"Oh! A grandfather! How nice! Why don't you go and talk it over with him? Wouldn't he give you good advice on your problems?"

The boy was silent for a moment, staring at the girl in the gathering twilight.

"That's an idea!" he said slowly. "I might. I'll havta think it over. You see, my dad never has anything to do with the Revels. I've lately got in the habit of not thinking of grandfather as a part of the family. Dad doesn't like him. It's some old grudge, I guess. Thanks for the suggestion, though. Maybe there's something in it. It might be a place to go, if he's still there. Now! Have you got your breath? All set? Well, let's go! Take hold of my hand. I know the smooth places."

His firm young hand caught the girl's hand warmly and they started across the close clipped turf where the cows had been carefully mowing the new little grass blades all day long.

Swiftly and silently they sped over the meadow, hearing the distant sounds of the night, the whirr of a siren off in the distance where the sky shadowed forth a flush of brilliant flame, the sound of cars along the highway not far off, the clock on the town hall in Afton striking.

"Mercy! Is it as late as that?" the girl exclaimed. "I certainly am in bad now."

"Sorry!" said Revel. "It was all my fault. I knew it was

dinner time when I left my house. Dad sent me up to get cleaned up for dinner, and I just streaked it out the back door and cut up to my woods. I couldn't see sitting at the table across from dad and having him watch every bite I took, and how glum I looked. He would have talked about it, bawled me out, tried to make me smile and *like* what he told me, and I couldn't see that. I never could eat when I was upset."

"Why, I'm that way too," said Margaret. "Well, I'm just as sorry as I can be for you, but I'm positive God will work out some way for you, and you won't need to be sorrowful all your life. I wish this was my own home I'm going to, and I'd ask you in to eat with me, but you might not care to go to Mrs. Martin's table."

"Not on your life!" said Revel fervently. "I'll take you in if you're scared to go, and help you explain, but I couldn't eat a bite in that old rhinoceros' house. Say, I believe that's her jalopy coming now. Where did she go? Chenango? Because that old car is coming down the Chenango dirt road. See the old style high back? Nothing streamlined about that lady. Say, if we hurry across the next meadow I believe we can beat her to it. Here, creep under this rail. I'll lift this end. Now, let's go!"

They went like two lithe young shadows across the dusky meadow and arrived at the highway before the old jalopy had barely turned the corner into the main road.

"Now," said Revel, "let me help you over the fence. You don't want to fall flat at the end of the race. Here, step on this rail—" He pointed out the spot for her foot, and then reached his hand. "Jump!" he said, and swung her down in a shadowy place by the side of the road.

"Now," he said, "streak it across and slide into those bushes. Then you can get into the house before she turns in at the drive. And say, don't let her know you've just got in, if you can help it. Anyhow just laugh it off. I'm all kinds of sorry I got you into this. It's all my fault. And say, I'm mighty grateful! Maybe I won't see you any more, but—this is to remember me by—" and suddenly he came quite close in the shadow of the tall osage orange bushes that hedged the next meadow, laid his lips shyly, awkwardly on hers and kissed her tenderly, as if it were something very sacred he was doing.

"Now, go! Quick! She's coming!"

He wrung her hand fervently and pushed her forward.

But the girl drew back and turned toward him.

"Listen, Revel," she said in a low vibrant tone, her lips close to his ear, "you *will* talk to God about your trouble before you do anything, won't you? And—I won't forget to pray."

Then she was off like a streak in the darkness, disappearing among the bushes across the road, with just the sight of a small white hand waving farewell.

He watched till he saw her run lightly up the front steps, into the open front door, and give just one glance back across her shoulder into the darkness.

Then the rambling old Martin car came rattling down the road and turned in at the drive, hurriedly, as if the woman driving was almost out of breath with worry. She drew up in front of the steps.

"Is that you, Margaret?" she called in the unreserved voice of the habitual country dweller, who isn't afraid that the neighbors can hear her.

"Yes, Mrs. Martin." Revel heard the girl's voice, clear and sweet. The same gentle voice that had only a few minutes ago been talking so comfortingly to him.

"Well, I'm just ashamed as I can be. I got held up and I couldn't help it. There were two women came over from Chenango way, and they had expected their cousin to meet them at the meeting and take them home, but she wasn't there, and when they telephoned to see where she was the one who drives had a sick baby and couldn't come, so I had to offer to take them home. Wasn't that awful? And when I got to Chenango I found the other woman lived five miles beyond Chenango, and I had to take *her* home. There just wasn't anything else to do, you know. I've been doing some wild driving all the way back. I was afraid you'd be half starved, you poor child! Come on in and let's have supper right away. I declare I don't know when I've been so upset!"

Revel stood there in the shelter of the bushes listening for a minute or two. He heard the hired man coming briskly across the gravel drive to get the car and drive it back to the garage. He heard Margaret Weldon's light footsteps running upstairs. He saw a light spring up in the front room, and the girl standing before the bureau, brushing her hair, patting the two little rose-colored bows that held it. Then the light went out and he heard her running down the stairs again as a little silver bell tinkled a call. He glanced down a dimly lighted hall and could just see a table set for dinner. He saw the girl take her place at one side. Then Susie the maid came and closed the door and he couldn't see Margaret any more. So he turned and made his way slowly down the road, wondering what he had better do now.

2

AFTER Mrs. Martin had muttered through a perfunctory grace at the table, she looked up brightly at her young guest, as she began to serve the chicken from the large willowware platter that Susie had set before her.

"Well, my dear, what kind of a time did you have? Weren't you bored to death? I do wish you had gone with me. The woman from China was most inspiring. I'm sure you would have enjoyed her. But I spent a good deal of my time worrying about you, all alone, trailing around strange country roads. Did you find the schoolhouse your mother used to attend? I was thinking afterwards that I was afraid I didn't make my directions clear, I was really so upset to have to go off and leave you alone that way."

"Oh, but I had a beautiful time, Mrs. Martin. Yes, I found the school all right and walked in one of the halls and peeked in a class room. There was no one of course who would have known where mother used to sit. But it was all right. I saw the building. And then I saw the church and looked in the door there, trying to think of mother sitting in one of those pews."

"You dear child! That was sweet of you to care so much

for your mother's childhood! And what did you do after that?"

"Oh, I took a walk. Mother had described some of the places where she used to go for picnics, and I thought I recognized a lane that led to a hill. I stopped awhile by the way and watched two birds building a nest. And there was a little red chipmunk up on a branch chattering at me, just as if he were scolding me. It was very funny. You know, Mrs. Martin, I've been cooped up in the city for two whole years now, and it's wonderful to get out in the open and watch the birds and the trees and the clouds. It made me glad all through."

"Oh, really, my dear? Well, that's very nice. But I imagine if you were cooped up in the *country* for two whole years you'd be very glad to get a chance to hear a wonderful lady from China tell of what is going on there."

"Yes, Mrs. Martin. Perhaps I would. And I'm sorry if I disappointed you, but you know it was the one thing I wanted to come this way for, that I might see the places where my mother used to be. But I'm truly sorry if it upset your plans."

"Oh, that's quite all right, my dear, if you like that sort of thing. One must expect young people to have their own opinions about what they want to see and do. But didn't you get very tired on such a long walk? You went so *far*. I don't see why you didn't lose your way."

"Oh, I did get a little turned around, and I was afraid I might keep your dinner waiting. But I asked a nice boy I happened to meet and he showed me the way back."

"H'm!" said Mrs. Martin placidly, "that must have been little Joey Wetherby. He's always so kind and gentle. About ten years old, was he, with freckles and a pug nose? Rides a bicycle? I've heard of more kind acts that child has done for people, especially strangers. He's a Boy Scout, you know, and proud of it. Was that near home here?"

"No," said the girl evasively, "it was farther away, up near the woods."

"Woods!" said Mrs. Martin. "And getting *dark!* Oh, no, that couldn't have been Joey. He wouldn't have been allowed to go up to the woods near dark. He's only a child, you know, and there aren't any woods near his home."

"This boy was not a child," said Margaret thoughtfully, "he was almost a young man. He looked like a high school student, and was quite good-looking."

"My *dear!*" said the shocked voice of the lady. "But you shouldn't have asked a strange young man of *that* age. Surely if you had kept on you would have come to a nice farm house where it would be perfectly respectable for you to ask the way."

"Oh, this boy was very polite, Mrs. Martin. He was a perfect gentleman. And I thought it was important to get back quickly before the darkness really came. By the way, Mrs. Martin, when is my uncle returning? Tonight, or in the morning?"

"Oh, he'll be on the midnight train, he said. I'm sending the man down to the station in Arleth to meet him. But—this young man you met, you don't know what his name was, I suppose."

"Why, yes," said Margaret in a clear matter-of-fact tone, "he said his name was Radcliffe."

"Not *Rad*cliffe!" exclaimed the lady, horrified. "My *dear!* I shouldn't have gone off and left you! How wonderful that you got safely home! My dear, if that was Hiram Radcliffe you don't *know* what you have escaped. My child, that boy is a *menace!* He came on my premises once and *fished,* when there is a perfectly plain sign up warning people that it's private property—"

Suddenly Margaret remembered how Revel had told her of the fish this lady was trying to "identify" and a wave of her quick sense of humor came over her and almost choked her. She took a swallow of water and smothered her laughter in her napkin, hoping the subject would change. But Mrs. Martin was not easily turned aside from any object she was pursuing.

"To return to this reprehensible boy, did he say his first name was Hiram? He's named after his father! And he's a shame and disgrace to an honorable name. Didn't he tell you his name was Hiram?"

"Oh, no," said Margaret. "He said his name was Revel. He is named after his mother's family."

"Exactly! There you have it! Disloyal to his father, that's what I call it. His father is one of the foremost business men in town, and everybody defers to him, and yet that boy has the nerve to go around calling himself *Revel*. I never knew the Revels myself. They live in another state, but I should imagine they were kind of a shiftless lot. I know Mr. Radcliffe never had much to do with them. And as for his wife, she was a colorless little thing, never took any part in civic affairs, and kept to herself most of the time. She had an unhappy discontented look around her mouth. I never could stand that. A woman who lived in the finest house in town, and had all the servants she could possibly use, even in that big house! And yet with all that, and new silk dresses every time the season changed, she used to go around with the most forlorn look in her eyes, a look as if she'd been crying all night. Spoiled child, I'll say she was!"

Then Margaret remembered how Revel had told her that his father had made his mother unhappy, and looking at the smug complacent set of Mrs. Martin's lips her heart jumped at once to the defense of the woman whose boy had loved her so. Impulsively she opened her lips in defense of Revel's dead mother, and then remembered that nothing she, a stranger, could say would have weight with a woman like Mrs. Martin. So she closed her lips firmly and set a watch before them. Anyway this was something she had no right to discuss.

Mrs. Martin rambled on with her analysis of young Radcliffe's character, but Margaret said no more, and as soon as opportunity offered she asked a question about some night bird whose call she had heard as she slipped through the hedge. She got Mrs. Martin off to discussing birds, especially the edible ones of which she had a great many in her chicken yard, dove cote, and down at her duck pond. And somehow the conversation drifted away from dangerous topics.

Margaret had hoped that Mrs. Martin would be able to tell her a little bit about the days when her mother lived there, but Mrs. Martin didn't at all remember the little girl who had gone away when she was only in grammar school, and had later married an unknown person named Weldon, so there was not much information to be extracted from her on that subject.

After the evening meal Mrs. Martin got out an old photograph album, and Margaret had to hear long monotonous stories of the people enshrined in it. Her thoughts wandered away from the dreary stories of men and women who had lived and died in that vicinity. Only once did her interest rouse and that was when she caught the familiar face of her mother's old teacher.

"Oh, that is my mother's dear teacher, Miss Hammitt. My mother loved her very much."

"Miss *Hammitt?*" echoed Mrs. Martin sourly. "Oh, yes, Miss Hammitt! I remember her. She was a teacher I never could bear. She never would pay any attention to you if you raised your hand to say something. She said that if scholars would give attention they wouldn't need to ask so many questions. I remember once I tried to tell her that the boy across the aisle from me was spearing a spider with his penpoint, and putting him in his ink well. He said he was pickling that spider. It was horrid, and I thought the teacher ought to know what was going on, so I raised my hand to tell her, but no, she wouldn't recognize me, so I had to arise and call it out to her. I simply couldn't endure it to see that poor spider suffering such agonies. You say she was your mother's teacher? Poor child! I always felt sorry for anyone who was doomed to be in her classes."

"Oh, but mother loved her very much, Mrs. Martin!" said Margaret.

"Well, then, it couldn't have been the same Miss Hammitt, for your mother never could love her, I'm sure. I thought she was utterly unfair in every way. She called me down once for telling a boy who sat in front of me that his neck was dirty. Imagine that, calling a nice neat girl down for advising a boy to wash his neck."

"Well," said the girl quietly, "I suppose it makes a difference under what circumstances you see a person. Mother loved Miss Hammitt very much. But who is this sweet old lady on the opposite page. Was that your mother, Mrs. Martin?"

" 'Sweet old lady?' Who, *that* woman! No, that wasn't my mother, that was my mother-*in-law*, and she was anything but sweet! She certainly made my life miserable while she lived. She had to live with us, and it was most uncomfortable. Fortunately she didn't live long after she came here, but she made a lasting impression while she was here. I don't know why I ever left her picture in the album. My husband put it there, and I've never taken the trouble to remove it. But I don't see how she could look sweet to you, even though she is a stranger. She was a very trying woman. Now there, next to her was a good woman, Mrs. Fordyce." Mrs. Martin pointed to the next picture, a woman with a very determined mouth, and hard eyes. "She ran for the office of poor inspector, and she certainly saved the county money. No one could put anything over on her. She didn't believe in having a lot of whining poor around. She got them all jobs. Of course there was a lot of complaint from lazy people who had been used to being on relief, but she certainly was a worker. She would go around teaching people to do things to earn their living. She taught one woman to hemstitch handkerchiefs and do petit point, till she went blind and had to be sent to the county home. Mrs. Fordyce was my second cousin and I was always proud to own her as a relation."

Margaret was relieved when at last the quaint old clock in

the hall struck nine and Mrs. Martin decided that since the travelers would be leaving early the next morning it was time for a young girl to retire.

As she knelt to pray Margaret thought of Revel, and wondered what he would do. He had seemed so desolate. She wondered if he had found some solution of his problem. "Heavenly Father, show him some way out of his trouble, or else make him very strong to endure it. Please make him happy somehow, dear Lord" she added at the end.

The next morning while they were eating breakfast there came a knock at the side door, and Susie brought in a box neatly wrapped.

"It's for Miss Margaret," she explained to the mistress of the house who was holding out her hand for the package.

"For Miss Margaret?" repeated Mrs. Martin with a bewildered look on her face. "Why, who could be sending *her* a package? You didn't buy anything yesterday, did you, Margaret? Who brought it, Susie?"

"Why it was just that Radcliffe boy," explained Susie. "He said it was flowers and they was all wrapped to travel."

"Flowers! What presumption! The idea of that unspeakable boy daring to give my guest flowers! I wish you had called me, Susie. Go to the door and call him back. I'll make him understand that he can't presume with my guests."

But Margaret was quick to understand. She took the box in her hands and held it firmly.

"Oh, please don't Mrs. Martin," she said calmly. "It's just some wild flowers he knew I wanted, and he has been very kind to get them for me. He knew I was looking for them, but it was too dark to find many."

"How do you know it is flowers, Margaret? It might be some kind of an infernal machine. You can't trust that boy. He would just delight to play a trick on anybody who was staying here. Open it carefully. It might be something that would go off. I've read of such things, and sometimes they go off with quite a noise. Be careful and hold it away from your eyes."

Margaret was very angry, but she rightly judged that the quickest way to end this annoyance was to open the box. It was fastened with rubber bands, and swiftly she slipped them off, lifted the lid of the tin box, and turned back the tissue paper lining disclosing a fine dewy collection of hepaticas and anemones, lying in a bed of maidenhair ferns. Margaret caught her breath with their loveliness, and then she held the box where her hostess could see it.

"There they are! Aren't they lovely? Oh, I'm so glad to have them! Mother used to love them so, and she told me just where to look for them, but it was rather dark when I got there."

Mrs. Martin stepped cautiously around the table to examine them.

"Why, they're nothing but weeds!" she said contemptuously. "I think it is an insult to bring you flowers like that. But it's just what I would expect of that boy!"

"Oh, they are exactly what I wanted," said Margaret, her face wreathed in happy smiles, "and he has brought them with the roots on them. I can set them out and make them grow when I get there! See! He has packed them in wet moss. I'm sure they'll keep. I can open them at night, on the way, sprinkle them, and give them a little air, and I think they'll be all right, don't you?"

"But my dear! You wouldn't cart a lot of weeds like that across the continent. Just because some silly lovesick boy got up early and dug them up for you?"

"Oh, Mrs. Martin! How disgusting! That's a terrible word for you to use! Lovesick! Why, we're nothing but kids, either of us, and I never saw him before, nor he me. Please don't even *think* such things. I told the boy I was looking for some of the flowers my mother used to love, and he was just being polite and getting me what I wanted. I'm very pleased to have them to take with me, and you'll please not say anything more about it. Just forget it!"

"And you are determined to take them with you? You

wouldn't consent to let me return them to him with a proper reproof for his impertinence? I'm sure I don't know what the people of the town will think of you, and of me for *allow*ing this, unless I send them back to him."

"Oh," said Margaret, appalled at the suggestion. "How on earth would the people of the town know anything about it? Unless of course you choose to go out and tell them. Even so I'm sure I don't see what harm it would do! Now, if you'll excuse me, I think I'd better run up and put on my hat. I see my uncle has come downstairs and gone out to the car. I don't want to keep him waiting."

With the box of flowers clasped in her arms she went swiftly up the stairs to her room. And when she came down a few minutes later the box was wrapped in her coat and firmly strapped together with other things.

But Mrs. Martin maintained her air of disapproval all through the farewell ceremony, and as they were about to drive away she remarked, "Well, I still think you are very unwise to hang on to those flowers, and I'm sure I hope that you will have no communication with that boy, not even to send a mistaken 'thank you' to him. That is the only condition under which I could consent to protect that boy and not let the town know what he has dared to do. Remember he is fairly well known in this neighborhood."

Margaret looked at her steadily for a moment, and then said quite quietly: "I'm sorry to have disturbed you, Mrs. Martin. You will have to do what you think is right of course. And now I must thank you for your hospitality. I've enjoyed being in my mother's old home town for a few hours very much, and it was very lovely to see it in the springtime. Good-by!"

Mr. Devereaux the uncle made his elderly adieux and they were presently started on their way once more. Margaret was glad that her uncle, a much older brother of Margaret's father, with a quaint sense of humor, did not seem to have noticed Mrs. Martin's remarks, and there was therefore no need to explain. For Mrs. Martin was his old friend's widow and it would not have been courteous for Margaret to burst forth with complaints of their hostess. So Margaret rode on through the lovely spring day, fairly boiling with rage at the vindictive old woman, and wishing she knew some way to protect Revel Radcliffe from her unpleasant tongue.

But Margaret, try as she would, was unable to keep her thoughts from the boy whose sorrow had so touched her heart. Missing her own mother as she did, it was impossible for her not to know how the boy had felt. She kept wondering what he would do, what he ought to do.

When they stopped at noon for lunch and then to rest a few minutes, she took occasion to slip into the lobby of the hotel and find a desk, and there write a brief note of thanks for the flowers. If afterward any words of Mrs. Martin should reach his ears, at least he would not judge *her* ungrateful.

Dear Revel,

What a beautiful surprise you gave me this morning, bringing those lovely dewy flowers for me to take with me! I thank you from the bottom of my heart. It is just what I wanted, to get fresh ones, with roots.

But I am sorry that you went away so quickly. I would have liked to thank you and to say good-by. I hope you will get this tonight, or at least tomorrow and then you will know that I am grateful.

Now I hope God will show you what to do, and that you will find a happy solution to your difficulties.

I shall not forget to pray for you, and I would be glad to know how you come out with your decision, that is, if you do not mind having a stranger know about your troubles,

Your friend, and well-wisher,
Margaret Weldon

She slipped the letter into the hotel post box, and then told her uncle she was ready to go whenever he was, so they were soon on their way again. But the interval, and the letter she had written, made Margaret feel as if she had been talking with the boy again.

3

AFTER the maid had gone into the house and he could see her no longer, Revel slid through the hedge and made his way by devious brief paths well known to himself. Arriving at the rear lot of his home he stopped to take in the situation. His father he knew had intended going out that evening to a meeting of some business men, and it was long after his usual time for leaving, but Revel was wary. His father might be so annoyed at his absence that he had delayed going. So he slid around the house furtively and watched for indications.

There were the usual lights in the kitchen regions, showing that the servants were still downstairs, probably eating their own dinner. The lights were on at the porch and in the front hall. The big living room was lit dimly, probably with one burner, as usual unless there were guests. He hurried around to the other side of the house, but there was no light in the library. If his father were at home that was where he would likely be. But the library was dark. So were the upstairs windows, except where the upper hall light would penetrate.

It was with relief that he stepped cautiously up the front porch, turned the front door knob warily, and let himself into the hall. There was no sign of his father, and though he drew a breath of relief, still that same desolate lonely feeling came over him that so often came when he went home and found no one there to be glad he had come, no one even to be sorry.

He was well practiced in silent going, but this time he was aware that the doors through the butler's pantry into the kitchen were both open, for there was a sudden cessation of the low grumble of conversation that had been going on, and a sense of intense listening. An instant later Irving the butler appeared shuffling in his slippers.

"Oh, there you are, Mr. Hiram. Your father certainly was upset that you didn't come to dinner. He said he told you he wanted to talk to you."

Revel lifted his young chin defensively.

"Sorry," he said haughtily, "I couldn't come then. You needn't bother about my dinner. I don't want anything."

Revel made a dash for the stairs and hurried up.

"Your dinner's here on a plate in the warming oven," admonished the butler, lifting his habitual formal voice a trifle. But Revel went on to his room and closed and locked the door. The butler came out into the hall and looked up the stairs listening and finally went slowly back to the kitchen shaking his head and mumbling. Then he and the cook held a long grumbling conversation. They had been servants in the house since Revel was a baby and were really attached to him, though they knew on which side their bread was buttered and never dared openly to take the boy's part. But they were set at heart to care for his well-being if it didn't involve any break with the master to whom they gave the utmost deference.

The outcome of the kitchen conversation was that Irving prepared a plate with a tasty little dinner upon it, a bit of chicken and stuffing, some mashed potato with gravy, two biscuits with butter, a glass of milk and a neat piece of apple pie. He carried it up to the young master's door.

"Mr. Hiram, I don't think you should go to your bed without a bite to eat. If you'll just unlock your door I'll set the tray on the table. Then if you get hungry later, why, it'll be there."

Revel drew an annoyed sigh, but the habitual order of obedience prevailed and he opened the door.

The old servant set down the tray, drew up a convenient chair, poked the grate fire and put another stick on it, and then looked at the boy.

"You feeling all right, Mr. Hiram?" he asked anxiously.

Revel gave him a fleeting grin.

"Oh, sure!" he said. "Thank you, Irving. I just didn't want to make you and Mandy any trouble. But that looks good."

But after the man had left with a lingering glance of anxiety, Revel sat for several minutes staring at the door through which he had gone. Here was another who would be affected by the new order of things. Irving had been devoted to Revel's mother. How would he and Mandy stand it waiting on a stranger in her place? His desperate eyes rested meditatively for an instant on the bright flames that were leaping up now in the fireplace. It all spoke of the kindness of these old retainers. The plate of hot food before him with its savory odor was beginning to get his attention and to tell him that he really was hungry. After a little he swung around in his chair and began to eat the dinner, but his mind kept going back to the girl who had come upon him weeping. She was a swell kid. She hadn't laughed at him nor kidded him. She'd been as nice as a mother, or perhaps a real sister would. Never having had one he couldn't know how a sister would act, but he liked her, and he liked her name too, Margaret Weldon. He had a feeling that she was a girl his mother would have liked, and she would have liked his mother, too. It warmed his heart to think about it. To think she had come out to get flowers that her mother used to love, and she had found him bawling at a fancied indignity to his mother. And she had understood. Not everybody would understand, but she had. She was a swell kid. In a way their mothers had sort of linked them together!

Revel lifted his eyes to the wide space over the mantel where in fancy now he felt his mother's picture.

The picture was a lovely portrait, done by one of the great artists of the day. During his lifetime it had hung downstairs in the big parlor. But it was only a few days after her funeral that Revel came upon his father removing it from the wall, and hanging in its place some old warrior ancestor, from the attic. The other picture was of a Radcliffe with a severe turn of countenance, another Hiram Radcliffe, great grandfather to his father, something to be proud of.

Revel had paused in the doorway and watched his father stand the lovely portrait of his mother with its face against the wall, and lift the ugly ancestor high in its place. Then he watched the whole face of the room change into hard severity. It had seemed as though all the gentleness and beauty of the home had been wiped out, and unloving formality substituted. He had stood there dully for a moment staring at the difference, and then as his father had swung around and noticed him he had burst out abruptly with a hoarse young protest.

"What're you doing, dad?" and there was a kind of fierce anger in his tone, a challenge to his father's right to make a change like that.

The father eyed his boy coldly, and answered the challenge with a steely defensive.

"I'm taking your mother's portrait down," he said, "can't you see for yourself? You ought to get over asking such unnecessary questions."

"But—what are you going to do with it?" Revel came into the room and turned the portrait about so that the lovely eyes looked at them like a reproach.

"Do with it? Why, put it up in the attic, I suppose. Or sell it to some museum. After all, it was painted by a famous artist, though I never really liked it. It made your mother look much too childish."

"Oh no!" cried the boy as if something had pierced his heart. "Don't sell it. *Don't! I* want it. I'll get a job, dad, and pay you for it. I *want* it. She was *my mother!*" he added fiercely.

The father looked at him in astonishment. It was not often that Revel showed any feeling.

"Well, of course, if you want it, you can have it. You don't need to pay for it. But I won't have it around the house where it can be seen."

"All right," said Revel. "I'll put it away. You won't need ever to see it. Some day I'll have a house of my own."

"Very well," said his father angrily. "But keep it out of my sight. Put it up in the attic, away back under the eaves, and pull those old trunks in front of it. I don't want it brought out suddenly sometime."

"I'll see to it, dad," said the boy. And he had taken the picture tenderly and carried it upstairs to his own room, where he wrapped it carefully and put it away in the very back of his closet, with garment bags over it, and a row of shoes on the floor in front. No casual observer could possibly dream that a picture was hidden in the back of that closet.

That was the story of the picture. But every night when Revel sat alone in his room before the fire which the old servitor managed to have burning for the young master, Revel sat and looked up over the bare mantel where his heart's desire would have been to see his mother's picture hanging, if he had dared. But he knew if it were there and his father should once discover it that he would stop at nothing until that picture was either sold or destroyed.

So now he stared at the space above the mantel, and thought of the picture. Assuredly if he went away the picture must go with him. He would never leave it, even hidden in the most unexpected place, to the tender mercies of an alien wife, who had not known her predecessor. She would ferret it out, and bring it to his father's notice, or else destroy it herself. Of course he didn't know the woman. He was just reasoning out what might be the natural reaction. No, he would never leave the picture; if he stayed he would have to be constantly guarding it.

Hungrily he ate the supper the servant had brought him, and while he ate he was trying to plan. Where could he go? What could he do? If it were time for college to open he could go there, and arrange to stay there throughout the four years perhaps, but it couldn't be done if he attended his father's alma mater, where his father meant that he should go. He did not want to go there. He felt sure his father's traditions would overshadow him there, and his father would keep a terrible espionage over him. But his college course would be prescribed for him, in ways that his father chose, so that he might follow in his father's footsteps and be what his father was. A country banker, flourishing among his poorer neighbors with whom he dealt harshly, exacting the last ounce of the proverbial pound of flesh. Oh, he didn't put it in so many words to himself, but he knew in his heart that his father was so accounted in the vicinity, and Revel had no desire to be a business man of that type, to grow rich on borrowing and lending among those who ought to be his friends and were not.

As he thought this over he came to the firm conviction that he must go away, and at once, before a new mother should be introduced to the scene. But where could he go that his father would not search for him and bring him back, if but to work out his own desires in him? His father had never cultivated any sort of friendship with him, never asked him what he wanted to do, but always told him what he *must* do, and no amount of protest gave any relief from that absolute *must*.

Then while he considered possibilities of running away and hiding, the words of his new acquaintance came to him. She had practically made him promise that he would ask God before he did anything in his perplexity.

There was something about the girl's memory, brief as the contact had been, that lingered and left a pleasant comforting presence. She was like his mother. Yes, he would pray, if only to keep his promise to her, though he hadn't much idea that it would do any good. Yes, he would pray before he went to bed.

He thought of the girl as she first appeared to him in the dusky edge of the woods, and he burned hot at the thought that she had found him weeping. Yet somehow it did not shame him as it would have done if she had been some girl he knew, or even an older woman. She had gentle eyes, remembering eyes for her mother, and she had come to that sweet quiet woods where he loved to go himself, to find some of the flowers her mother used to love. She had intended to get them by the roots to take with her, and he had kept her there with his troubles till it was too dark to get them. She had only lingered to try and help him. He owed her a lot. She had helped to tide him over that first impossible place where he couldn't get his bearings in a world that seemed to have turned utterly against him, and upside down. He wished he could do something for her in return for her clear common sense and her gentle sympathy. Why didn't he tell her he would get the flowers she wanted? Would there be time now? She had said they would start early the next day. What if he got up at daylight and went to the woods and got the flowers? He could pack them in a box with wet moss, and they ought to keep till she got where she could give them light and air and water again. *That* was what he would do!

He glanced at the clock on his desk, the little clock his mother had got for him on his last birthday before she died. It was getting late and his father would be coming in soon. It would be well for him to be asleep when he came. And in the morning he could slip away very early, and be back in time for the regular breakfast hour.

He gathered up his dishes and took them down to the

kitchen. His mother had taught him to be careful about such little things to save the servants. But he found Irving dozing in his chair over the newspaper, and he took the dishes from him, and smiled grimly at the murmured thanks of the boy.

So Revel went back to his room and got ready for bed. But after his light was out he knelt in the moonlight by his bed and kept his promise to that girl, asking God to show him what to do in this trying situation. Then he got into bed with a sense of having done all he could to make things right, and was almost instantly asleep, his little clock on the bedside table carefully set for early rising. He did not hear his father when he came in very late, did not know that he paused before his door and hesitated, frowned, and then went on to his own room. Other nights he might have been broad awake listening and have felt the disapproval, the scathing lecture that was in reserve for him next morning. But he had trusted his future to God, and he slept calmly on.

Mr. Radcliffe was still sleeping when the little clock in his son's room buzzed softly and was instantly stilled by an alert hand. Five minutes later Revel stole out of his door, which he always kept well oiled, went silently down the stairs, and out the front door, and was soon speeding across the meadows on his way to the woods. Even the servants were not awake yet to hear or see.

He had taken a box with him in which to pack the flowers. It was a beautiful tin box that his mother had treasured. Her young brother, David Revel, had sent it to her a year or two after she was married. It had been the outer covering for a box of delicious candy. How often Revel had stood beside her as a little boy, and heard her tell the story of that morning, her birthday morning, when that box had come, surprising her. She had not told how her husband had sneered at the brother, without a job, spending money for foolish expensive candy. But Revel did not need to be told that. Without explanation he had sensed the attitude of his father toward his mother, and especially toward her family, even from mere babyhood.

So he knew that the box was very precious to her, and therefore was precious to him. Yet so the more it seemed a fitting carrier for the flowers to the girl who had comforted him in his dire dismay. It seemed that he would like to remember it as having gone to her. He had brought some paper. There was a brook in the woods, and plenty of moss. He could wrap the roots of the flowers in wet moss, and cover them close. He was sure they would keep.

When he knelt in the woods in the very spot where she had stood, and gazed down on the wide open blossoms of blue and white and pink, all fresh and dewy with the early morning, he was filled with awe. It seemed as if he never had seen such beauty in the little flowers before.

Suddenly he put his face down and laid it in the coolness of those little living blossoms, letting the dew touch his hot eyelids that were so near to tears, and waited so for a moment, with his lips against them in almost a caress.

Then he lifted his head and set about gathering them, digging close about their roots with his pocket knife, and selecting the very best plants.

It did not take long. He had stopped on the way to gather the moss from the roots of a great tree at the edge of the woods and wet it in the brook, and now he packed the roots softly and close in the moss and laid them in place in the box, till it was full. Then he laid the tissue paper over the tops, gently as if they had been human, sprinkling it over with fragments of wet moss, closed the cover sharply, and fastened the little metal clasp. His work was done, and it had not taken long. Now, if he could get them to Margaret before she was gone!

He sped down the hillside, and across meadows of dewy grass, arriving within sight of the Martin house just as the breakfast bell rang sharply through the house.

It was early, even for a breakfast in the country, yet of course it would be when people were journeying far, and wanted to be well on their way in the freshness of the morning.

He was glad Mrs. Martin was not in evidence. He stole silently up to the door and rang the bell, reassured as the grim old servant took his box and nodded that she would give it to the girl. "Miss Weldon" she called her. Revel turned and hastened silently down the steps, out the gate and across to the screen of shrubs, before the owner of the house could appear to identify him, for instinctively he felt what her reaction would be.

Then, too, he began to remember his father, and that it was near breakfast time, and he, Revel, had been quite absent from dinner the night before after having been told that his father especially wished to talk with him when the evening meal was over. There would likely be a lot of irritation over that. His father would be fairly furious, and he must go home and meet that. Yet he had the memory of that quiet wooded place and dewy flowers. He was glad he had that. It would carry him through the hard things of the day that were before him. For he was sure there would be hard things.

As swiftly as a swallow might have sailed over the bending grass he made his way across the road, and hidden by the great hedge, stole entirely out of sight of the Martin house, lest his enemy should pursue him.

And then across the clean air he heard a light laugh, with a lilt in it, and looking furtively through the leafy branches of his hiding place he saw Margaret Weldon come out of the house, with his box in her arms, held firmly. He could hear the sharp voice of Mrs. Martin imploring her, though he could not hear the words. But Margaret's happy laughter rang out again with reassurance, and he saw her get into the car, holding his box in her lap. Then the car started on its way into a far country, taking the girl who had so unexpectedly touched his life, and taking his flowers with her.

He watched until the car was out of sight around the bend by the old mill, and then he sped straight to his home.

4

REVEL came in by the kitchen way and anxiously searched for Irving.

"Has dad come down yet?" he asked in his lowest tone.

"Your father had his breakfast an hour earlier than usual," said the old servant stiffly. "He found that he had business in New York that might keep him a couple of days, and he was greatly disturbed not to see you before going. He said he had some orders to give you, some things he wanted done while he was gone. He did not understand your absence both last night and this morning."

Revel lifted his chin with almost the haughtiness of his father.

"I had some things to attend to," he said reservedly. "I expected to be back by our usual breakfast time. I did not know he was going away."

The old servant looked at the boy curiously. There was something in the boy's manner that reminded him of his dead mistress, the quiet dignity with which she had sometimes been able to give her orders and keep her reserves.

"Well, your father left you a note, Mr. Hiram," said Irving with a more respectful tone in his voice. He handed

Revel an envelope containing several papers and a hastily scribbled note.

Revel took them and went out on the porch to read the note. It wasn't long, but the very angularity of the script looked like his father's severe countenance, and demanded instant obedience.

> Son:
>
> I was much annoyed at your absence from dinner last night, especially as I had expressly told you I wished to talk with you afterwards. Much more I am offended that you went away before I could see you this morning. Such actions are unprecedented and inexcusable. And now I am called to New York, and may be a couple of days. Don't leave the place while I am gone, except to go to school and see that you occupy all spare time on your homework, and in filling out the enclosed papers and studying up on the subjects herein named, relative to your examinations for college entrance.

Revel examined the papers disinterestedly, then slowly folded them back into the envelope and sat staring off at the hills in the distance thoughtfully. Did he have to do this? He had no heart for it now, although he had expected of course to go to college. But this was not the college of his choice, and it would make no difference if he tried to protest and urge another. His father would never listen to him.

Well, he had to go to school in a few minutes now, that is if he decided to stay here and face the thing that his father was bringing to pass. But his whole soul was still in rebellion, and as yet he had got no light on what else he might do. If he could only hear of a job, far enough away so that his father would not find him for a while at least. And yet his mother's teaching had made him feel that he did not want to do anything in an underhanded way.

That girl had told him to ask God first before he made any decisions, and he had asked God last night. God hadn't answered him yet. Would He?

He went slowly upstairs to his room, locked his door, knelt down again and really prayed.

"Oh, God, if you are interested in me, won't you show me what to do? I can't stay here. My dad doesn't understand. If You understand won't You please make a way somehow for me to get away. My dad doesn't care anything about me. He never did. You know that. Please show me what to do."

Then he took the college papers his father had left and glanced over them apathetically again, but finally laid them in his desk. There was one thing he must do, whether he went away or stayed, and that was to put away his personal things, in compact form, so that if he had to stay, and that strange wife did come, she would have no opportunity to pry into them, and perhaps order them to be thrown away. They were not many, but they were things that were connected with his childhood and his beloved mother, treasured toys and old keepsakes. His fierce young heart rebelled at the thought of an alien looking them over and perhaps despising them.

He heard Irving driving out the driveway, on his way to do his morning marketing. It would be some time before he returned. He could hear Mandy rattling pots and pans down in the kitchen. Now would be a good time to look after this when no one would be likely to come upon him unawares. There was no telling how soon changes would come here, and he must be ready for anything. What he had to do must be done quickly, or it might never be done at all.

He stood a moment considering, and then unlocked his door and went silently over to his mother's old room. His father did not occupy it now, and the door was usually closed.

He went in and shut the door, locking it against interruption, and opened the closet door. There hung his mother's dresses, just as she had left them when she was taken ill. There was the soft gray silk that he loved, and the pretty blues, and greens. The simple dresses she had worn about the house. How he had loved her in them! And that stranger should *not* have possession of them! He must take them down, hide them! His father would never care. He did not take thought of such things. Jewels, yes, he would notice their absence, that is, the ones he had bought for her, more for ostentation than for love, he felt sure. And yet, why had he married her? Not for money, for he had often referred bitterly to the fact that she had not been wealthy. She was beautiful of course, but he hadn't cared for her beauty except as it would reflect glory upon himself, and give him a mistress for his home who would be admired. Thus the seventeen-year-old boy reasoned it out bitterly.

Then he set to work swiftly, folding the simple house dresses first, and laying them carefully in a box. Then the silk frocks, and dinner gowns. Somehow he couldn't remember her very clearly in those. She seldom wore them; only when she was ordered to go out to some function which the master of the house felt would further his standing in the business or the social world.

He was not skilled at folding delicate fabrics, sewed into intricate forms, but he was so determined that these things of his mother's should not be left for her successor that he went at the business with great care and precision, and finally had them folded and stowed in a small trunk he found in the attic. He transferred it silently to his own closet, hiding it behind boxes and garments, where old Irving or Mandy would never think to look, even if the new mistress should be seized with a sudden desire to clean his room. As soon as there was opportunity when he wouldn't be seen he must get the trunk and other things out to the garage and hide them in the haymow.

There were things in her bureau drawers, neat piles of lingerie, and laces, a few ribbons. He handled them almost reverently, feeling nearer to his mother than he had since her death. His father, he was sure, would never think of these things, and would not know what to do with them if he did. He wasn't entirely sure what he meant to do with them himself, but he would find out. There were also some bits of quaint old jewelry that he knew his mother had possesed before her marriage, and carefully he took the boxes containing them and put them in with his own things, making sure that the bureau, and her desk, where he found only a few letters and notes from friends, were empty of everything. He even took care to dust out the drawers. His father, if he investigated, would likely think the servants had cleared away everything.

He was so deep into his work that he was startled when he heard the clock chiming the hour. It was getting late. He was going to be late to school if he didn't hurry. The opening exercises began at half past, and he would have to hurry to get properly dressed and arrive before the last bell rang.

He cast one anxious glance about his room. Perhaps he really ought to miss school and get everything ready for a possible exit in a hurry. He *must* have the work done before his father came back. But the mischief would be to pay if he cut school, so he made a very hasty toilet and started on the run. As he sped along the highway he reflected that if he found he had to stay here for the present there wasn't any point in getting into trouble about being late to school, and Irving would be sure to report it if he dared miss school. Irving was a good friend, but he was afraid to go against his master's orders.

Revel slid into his seat at the last sound of the gong and was studiously bent over a book when the teacher looked his way. He had made it in time. But he was trying to plan how he could save time when he got home.

There was a possibility that his father might return that evening. He often did return unexpectedly from his short trips. He seemed to like to take them all unawares.

It was well for Revel that his first hour that morning was a study period and he had a chance to compose his mind and make a few brief plans.

He remembered that it was Friday, and the afternoon period would be given over to public speaking. The senior class were taking turns in giving commencement orations, and it was not his turn this week to recite. He would be merely one of the audience who were appointed to criticize, and maybe he could be excused from that. He seldom asked to go home early. So at recess he went to his teacher.

"Miss Grandon," he said, "I'm not one of the speakers this afternoon. I wonder if you would mind excusing me from the last period. I've got some work I ought to do at home, and I'm afraid I won't get it done before night unless I can have a little more time."

Revel didn't often ask to be excused, so Miss Grandon gave a pleasant assent, and Revel went back to his seat and began to write out notes of some things he must be sure to remember to do. Getting ready his clothes to pack for a possible flitting was only a part of it. His main anxiety was to get everything that had been a personal possession of his adored mother into such hiding that a new wife would not come upon it, nor desecrate it by even so much as a tone or a look.

And there would be things of his own that must be planned for. Why, even if he stayed at home to protect them he would be going away to college in the fall, and a stranger would very likely think she had a right to haul out everything in the house, attic and cellar and all. Of course he had fishing rods, and skis, and things like that in the attic, and all kinds of traps in the cellar. But to heck with those things. He had bought them with his own pocket money, and in the same way he could buy more if he needed them. They had nothing to do with his mother, or with his present trouble. But there were other things. Books of his own, gifts from his mother, in a special bookcase she had chosen. Could he possibly manage to seclude them where they would not be interfered with? How about the loft above the garage that used to be a haymow when the garage was an old-fashioned barn instead of a garage. Certainly they would be safe up there, if he could get wooden boxes to pack them in. At least for a few days, or maybe weeks, until he could devise some other hiding place. And they were not things whose absence his father would notice, he felt sure.

While he was studying his mathematics for the next period occasionally a thought of something he must remember would flit into his mathematical calculations and he would write down a word to bring it to his remembrance later. So when noon came he had quite a list of notes.

At noon he made short work of his lunch, not taking time to go home, and wrote out more notes, so that when he finally got free and hurried home he had it fairly well in mind what he was going to do first.

And then, just as he was turning from the highway into the big gate of the driveway at home, the delivery car from the postoffice stopped beside him.

"You Revel Radcliffe?" questioned the delivery man, although he had known Revel since baby days. But he showed by the quirk of his mouth that he didn't altogether approve of him, much less of his having a special delivery letter. That was too much importance for a lad of that age to have.

Revel turned and looked startled. Was this something from his father that would perhaps upset all his plans?

"Got a couppla letters fer you. One's a special delivery," said the man grimly. "Sign here!" and he indicated a smudged line, and a stubby pencil.

Revel accepted the pencil and paper and signed his name. Then he took the letters in a hand that had hard work not to tremble, but he managed to smile nonchalantly at the mail man as he swung his car around and started back to town, just as if receiving special delivery letters were an every day matter with him. Then he slid inside the stone pillars at the side of the driveway and slipped into a little grove of spruce trees where he often took refuge if he wanted privacy. Here he felt no one from the house could see him. He did not want to be questioned about his letters until he knew their contents, and especially who they were from. Irving had orders to keep watch on him, he knew, for he had overheard his father giving them, so he made all his plans not to be spied upon. Revel did not get many letters, only advertisements of cameras and airplanes, and now and then a college catalogue, and these were always inspected by his father before he was allowed to have them.

But neither of these envelopes had any revealing line of advertising at the top. Whom could they be from? Neither was written in his father's high scrawl. Could one be from the lady he was going to marry? If he thought it was he would be tempted to tear it up unread. The special delivery letter was more like a man's writing. A good strong hand with quiet character in it.

With fingers that were cold from excitement he tore it open, reserving the one with the more feminine writing till afterwards. If that was from the woman who wanted to be his stepmother he needed time to be fortified to read it.

5

MARGARET Weldon, during the first day of her ride west, began to think ahead to the place where she was going. She had never been there before, and it had been many years ago when she was a very little girl that she had last seen the aunt to whom she was going. The aunt was her mother's sister and much older than Margaret's mother. She had been married when Margaret's mother was a mere child, so the two sisters had not grown together. Margaret felt she was going into a great experiment making this journey west and promising to stay for a whole year. Now that she was started on her way she began to wish that she had stayed where she was, a boarder in the home of one of her mother's friends, who had been most kind, but who really needed the room she had been using. So when the invitation had come from her aunt, Mrs. Gurlie, it seemed best for her to accept it, at least for a year.

Her uncle, Mr. Devereaux, with whom she was traveling, was very kind, but a man of few words, and hour after hour went by in utter silence. Only when they came to something as notable as Niagara Falls or the Grand Canyon did he seem moved to speak and explain what it was. Margaret grew woefully tired of the monotony of silence, and now and then broke out with questions.

"Uncle, tell me about my aunt Carlotta. What kind of a looking woman is she? You know it is a great many years since I have seen her, and I can't remember her at all."

"Mrs. Gurlie? Why, yes, let me see. I think she would be considered a fine appearing woman. She's not so young any more of course, but she's well-preserved. Rather stoutish, with gray hair very smartly arranged, my wife says. She has style, and is very kindly, a bit imperious perhaps, inclined to patronize religion and the arts, frequently has musicals at her home on Sunday evening for the benefit of some poor lad who needs a college education, or something of that sort. A fine bridge player, and much in demand on committees of every sort. She really is a fine woman, and I'm sure you will have a wonderful time in her home. She'll be apt to have a regular procession of dances and parties for you, and you'll be pretty gay."

"Oh!" said Margaret with a little catch in her breath, and then after a thoughtful pause, she added:

"But I shall be in school, you know. I'll not have time for parties and things of that sort. I want to be ready for college by the end of this year."

Old Mr. Devereaux looked at her indulgently.

"Well, my dear," he said with a comical little smile, "I don't imagine Mrs. Gurlie would be one to take the thought of your education too seriously. At least your classical education. She will be much more likely to stress your social education. At least that's my impression of her."

"Oh!" said Margaret with a sinking of her heart. Was she going into an atmosphere that would be hard for her? Would there be a lot of worldliness? That was not to her taste. Her home had been a plain sweet place with quiet ways and simple amusements. Margaret sat thoughtful for a while over Mr. Devereaux's description, and then she reflected that she was to go to school, and probably things would not be as trying as she feared. At least it would not last forever. A year would soon hurry along, and she could return east to friends, till time for college. So she cheered herself and took heart of hope. Her uncle might be partly joking.

The box of flowers lay at her feet, and now and again she would lift the cover and the wet paper to see if they were carrying well, and would think of the boy who had gone to the woods so early in the morning to please her with them. More and more her thoughts went out to him, wondering how he was coming on with his problem, and what his father said to him when he got home.

She tried to think how she would have felt if her dear father had lived after her mother died, and had told her he was bringing another in her mother's place. Only she couldn't think of his doing a thing like that, not in the way this father had done it at least. Her father had always been so loving and kind, and if he had felt after the years had passed, that he should marry again, he certainly would have gone about it in a sweeter spirit than Revel's father appeared to have done. He would have felt he should carefully and gradually make her acquainted with the new mother, to be sure that they could be fond of one another, before he brought any such announcement. But of course if it was something that had to be, and there was no way for Revel to go away without making trouble, it would be right that he should stay and try to make a happy thing out of it, not a blight on his life. But somehow it did seem that Revel's case was a hard one. A father who had never been kind and loving, but always hard and grim as he described him. Perhaps, of course, the boy might be wrong about that. Perhaps his father only had an unfortunate way of expressing himself. But anyway, if he had no happy memories of life with his father, how hard it was going to be for him to take on an unknown mother also. Of course she might turn out to be one who would make the home over, and bring some happiness to him, but he was rather old to accept a new mother now, when his own mother's memory was so very precious! But he was a nice boy, and he certainly must have had a nice mother. Presently she found herself quietly praying in her heart:

"Oh God, please arrange something happy for Revel, and help him to bear this in the right way."

And then she remembered how she had stepped into the woods and seen him cast down there among the flowers, his head bowed low, and real tears on the startled face he lifted when heard her step. And yet she was glad she had come. He surely needed someone to speak just a word of sympathy, and to remind him there was a God. Well, it had been a precious little experience after all, leaving her with a sense of having at least relieved a trying moment, and perhaps tided him over the worst, where he could look his shock in the face and realize that there were other things left, even if a dear mother's memory did seem in danger of being desecrated.

Of course a stepmother was not always an unhappy presence. She might turn out to be a wonderful woman, and make the home a pleasanter place. But yet she could understand what the boy was suffering, and felt great pity for him. She wished that she might do something to help him. As the long hours went by she kept going over that experience on the hillside among the sweet little spring blossoms, and remembering the look in the boy's eyes when he had discovered her standing over him.

And then the walk home. They had seemed almost like old friends by that time, as he fell into step beside her, guiding her over the rough places, helping her over the fences. Even the memory of his good-by kiss seemed quite a natural thing. She wasn't a girl who liked that sort of thing generally. But this was different. Almost a holy kiss. Sealing a little incident between them. It was as if God had sent them together for that short time to be a help to one another. It was something she must put away in her memory and never forget. She likely would not see him on earth, perhaps ever again, but she must always count him a real friend, even if she never even heard from him in her life. Because when they got up to Heaven, with life all past, they would surely come together sometime and talk over that day when they had found each other in the woods, and got a little bit acquainted.

Margaret fell asleep for awhile, thinking all these things, and when she awoke suddenly at the sound of Mr. Devereaux's voice asking for more gas at a filling station, she realized that she had been feeling the touch of the boy's lips upon hers. She must have been dreaming about him. Yet it did not appear to be an unseemly thing. He was just one of God's children having a hard time and needing a friend.

So during the rest of that journey she traveled more or less in the company of the nice boy of the woods. For she found that it did no good to try to get the old uncle to be enthusiastic about the lovely view along the way. He just didn't enthuse. He would lift dreamy eyes toward whatever she pointed out and say: "Yes, very nice," and that was all. There wasn't much sociability in that. So she kept her eagerness to herself, and began to think what Revel might have said. Revel who had seen beauty in the little wild flowers, and had cared to get up very early and bring them to her!

There were old friends, schoolmates she had left behind several days ago. Frannie Bruce, and Alton Cole, Carolyn Comfort, and Minnie Waters, Jimmy Ellery, Foster Heath, Gail and Albert Rathbone, and a lot of others. They had all been in her class in high school. But that was over. She had said good-by and it seemed final, a closed chapter. If they met again after years they would be grown-ups definitely, and she wasn't breaking her heart about leaving any of them, except perhaps Carolyn Comfort. Carolyn had been her best friend, and had cried when she left. Carolyn of course would write her. Perhaps she would go back east and visit her sometime. That is, if she decided to stay in California. She wasn't at all sure she would. That would depend on where she decided to go to college. But for the present she seemed cut off from all her old friends, and this boy who had taken the pains to get some flowers to remind her of her mother, seemed nearer to her thoughts than any of the others she had left.

Her uncle stopped to telephone Mrs. Gurlie early on the morning of the last day of their journey, telling her they would arrive in time for dinner. And Mrs. Gurlie went promptly to work summoning a crowd of young people to greet her niece. It was her idea of making Margaret feel at home. So when they drew up in front of the elaborate bungalow, the front terrace was filled with a gay crowd, in all sorts of bright array, and they flocked around her and proceeded to take her in according to their own modern ways.

Margaret rallied to her best and sweetest, but she did wish her aunt had waited a few days until she had got acquainted with her, and had adjusted herself to the change in her life. However, her aunt had arranged it for her pleasure and she must make the best of it.

So she smiled and tried to appear pleased.

"Why, how lovely of you all to come and greet me right at the start!" she said graciously. "I'm sure we shall be the best of friends." Her eyes wandered from one to another of the sharp sophisticated faces, and she wondered if they would. Somehow there was an air of boredom about them, a savor of smart sayings and little sympathy in the conversation that did not tend to make her feel at home.

And yet of course there must be some delightful ones among them. She must not judge them at first glance when she was tired and a bit excited.

Aunt Carlotta had the maid take her to her room at once with an admonition to hurry into something gay and fresh and come down immediately, for supper was to be served on the terrace right away. The maid stayed to help, but only bewildered Margaret the more, and gave her a feeling of sudden tears behind her eyelids. Aunt Carlotta had only given her a very formal kiss, and then had rushed her off with a servant! It gave her a sharp feeling that she was alone in the world. Aunt Carlotta was not a loving soul who would cling to her because she was a dear lost sister's child. It was nothing to her that she had come all those miles to be with her. It was only an occasion for a party!

Well, perhaps she mustn't think that, she told herself while she blinked the tears back, and tried to insist that the maid should not unpack her simple belongings.

"No!" she said wildly, "please don't open that suitcase! The dress I wish to wear is in the other one. Let me get it! I know just how I packed it!"

She drew the smaller bag to her side and knelt beside it, bringing out a box from the very bottom.

"It will be horribly mussed," said the maid. "I shall need to get an iron and press it. Or suppose you give me the box and I will take it downstairs, and have it back for you presently."

"No," said Margaret, with a dignity all her own, "it will be all right!" She opened the box and drew out a soft little uncrushable crepe, so packed amid tissue paper that its freshness was not creased at all. She slipped it over her head. A bright soft rosy garment, well selected, with lovely lines and of a becoming shade. Margaret had been most careful in her choice of the simple garments she had prepared for this first coming to her unknown relative, and even the maid recognized that everything was all right.

"Well, say. You are some packer to be able to carry a delicate little frock like that all this long journey and have it look as fit as a daisy," said the maid. "And now would you like me to dress your hair?"

"Oh, no," said Margaret with a pleasant smile, "I'll just fix it as I always do, and I'll be ready in a minute."

The maid stood in admiration as the girl's swift fingers arranged her lovely brown hair in its natural waves.

"Well, you certainly are fine at it," said the maid. "You need just a dash of color in your cheeks, and a bit of lipstick. Everything is here in the case of your dressing table. Shall I put it on?"

"No thank you," said Margaret firmly. "I would rather not have it."

"But madam, I am afraid, will be upset! She expects me to turn you out all right."

"Sorry," said Margaret with a little lift of her independent chin. "I never use it. Now, shall I go down the way I came up? I feel quite fine and rested after that shower. It's nice to feel clean again after the dust of the way. Thank you. Yes, I'm quite all right!" and with a bright smile she went quickly out to the terrace, reflecting that she would probably hear from this later, perhaps tomorrow, when Aunt Carlotta and she had time for a heart to heart talk.

When she stepped out of the doorway like a bright young flower, all the crowd of gay young people turned to stare at her. But Margaret smiled and went and stood by her aunt quite easily as if she had been accustomed to such staring all her life. Why should she mind what they thought of her at first? They would judge her by the cut of her clothes, and the lack of make-up on her face. If she could win them to be her friends, later, when she got to know them, that would be something worth while. But just this first judgement of outward appearance wasn't really worth worrying about. That was a philosophy that her mother had drilled into her as a small child, and at intervals all across the continent the young woman Margaret had been thus fortifying herself for this occasion. Although of course she hadn't expected a horde of young people to be present as audience. But she carried it off very well, just being her natural self, and presently they were seated about the terrace in great willow porch chairs, and waiters were passing dishes of delectable food, and everybody was chattering wildly, and furtively watching her to see just what she was going to turn out to be.

"Where have you been all my life," said a fascinating youth entitled Bailey Wicke, a youth with deep mahogany hair and great brown eyes, drawing up a chair beside her, and handing her a plate piled high with sandwiches.

Margaret looked up with a twinkle in her eyes.

"Oh," she said innocently, "do they say that out here too? I've practically been raised on that phrase!" And then suddenly the group around her turned, surprised, and burst into a laugh of quick appreciation. Margaret Weldon had taken her place among them as a person with wits of her own. She might be worth cultivating. At least she was not afraid of them.

6

SUDDENLY as Revel turned the letter over in his hand his eye caught a glimpse of the postmark. Ah, he knew that postmark! Linwood! How he used to watch for that as a little boy, to take any letter that bore it to his mother! But it was a long time since he had seen that postmark. Not since his mother had died! Linwood was the place where his mother was born, and where his grandfather still lived when he had last been heard from. He often wondered why his grandfather never wrote to him. Always there used to be a little letter enclosed in his mother's letters, for him. But nothing came any more. At least if it did he never had been told. His father always sorted over the mail before anyone else saw it. Irving had orders to take the mail from the postman, put it in the library, and not give any of it to anyone. He had heard his father tell Irving that.

But now Revel was trembling, as he unfolded the letter. It wasn't his grandfather's handwriting. Had something happened to him? His heart sank as he slid down on the ground and began to read the letter. Of course he hadn't seen much of his grandfather, ever and not for years now. But it was sort of comforting to know that he was alive. His mother's father!

"Mr. Revel Radcliffe," the letter began.

Revel turned the envelope over to see his name written there, "Revel," and had a passing gratitude that it had not fallen into his father's hands. Certainly if it had he would never have seen it. How his father hated to have him called Revel! Then he went on reading the letter.

> Your grandfather, Mr. Allan B. Revel, has been very sick and may only last a few days more, the doctor says, or even only a few hours, for he is very feeble. I am the nurse who is caring for him, and he has asked me to write you and ask you if you will kindly come and see him before he dies. Or if that is not possible, will you send him a few words of good-by? He says he loves you very dearly, and your mother Emily was his precious daughter, so for her sake as well as his own he wants to see you and talk with you before he dies. Enclosed is a check to pay for the journey.
>
> He says you have never answered any of his letters since your mother died, but please, young man, I earnestly beg that you will take the time to come to your grandfather before he leaves this earth forever. If you could see how eager he is I am sure you would be sorry that you have not done so before. He wants to give you a blessing, he says, before he goes.
>
> Yours truly,
> A. B. Stetson, nurse

As Revel read this letter the tears came to his eyes. Letters! So there had been letters and they had never been given to him! And the poor old man had thought he did not care!

He read the letter again, and then started angrily to his feet. So, this separation from his grandfather had been deliberate and intentional! He must go quickly before his father could return. For surely if his father found it out he would stop him! He would be already angry with him for not being on hand before he went away, and this would be the last straw. What must he do first? Wait, he must not bungle this!

He looked down at the check in his hand. The bank. He must cash this check! And he must draw out some of his own savings too, that had been intended for college days, for in case he did not want to return he would need more than fifty dollars. He must hurry, for the bank would close in three quarters of an hour more, and he had a great deal to do besides. It would be better if he didn't go into the house now for Mandy would be sure to question him about being home earlier than usual. And Irving, if he was about, would make a terrible to do, and probably tell his father, even wire him if he found out in time and get permission or an order to stop him from going. He must not tell the servants till the last minute. Or perhaps, if he could possibly get by without it, he need not tell them at all. Just leave a note for his father. That would be it. But he must hurry. He mustn't run any risks at all.

He stuffed both the letters into his breast pocket. The other letter didn't matter now. He hadn't time to read it. Anyhow it bore a strange postmark he didn't know. He slid out the gateway and down the road, taking very long steps, thinking fast as he went. There would be the things he had packed, the little trunk with his mother's clothes. There would be her picture. He must not forget that. There would be his small bookcase filled with books. He would have to provide a way to get those all to the station, and that part ought to be managed before dark too, so he could arrange about their being shipped. He needn't put his own name on them, he could send them to his grandfather. No one would think to tell anything about that. The picture he would carry by hand. He couldn't trust that any other way.

If only he could have managed to get that trunk and the books out to the garage before he went to school!

Presently he sighted a boy driving a truck. He used to be in Revel's class, before he quit school and went to work.

"Hi, Bud," he called, "going to be busy all the afternoon? I'd like ta get ya ta take some things down ta the station for me. Any chance?"

"Yep. I might," said Bud, sporting a discouraged looking cigarette. "Want I should go up that way now?"

"No, not yet. I got some errands, and I've got to do some more packing before the things will be ready. It's some books I'm sending away to somebody, and a trunk. Suppose you make it four-thirty. I'd like to get them off on that five o'clock train."

"Okay!" said the lad, eyeing him thoughtfully, "Say, Rev, you ain't thought any more about that proposition I made ya ta buy yer old bicycle, have ya? I want it fer my little brother."

"Oh," said Revel, with a quick flash in his eyes. "Well, I might. I'm thinking of getting a new one some day. What was it you wanted to pay?"

"I said I'd give ya fi' dollars."

"All right," said Revel. "If you help me get these things off on that train I'll let you have it for four-fifty, but you've got to make it snappy or nothing doing."

Bud's eyes lighted.

"Okay!" he said. "I'll be there on the tick."

"Well, say, suppose you drive around the back street, and stop behind the garage. The wheel is in the garage, and that'll save lugging it around. I'll have the other stuff down there too. I'm sort of cleaning up and making more room. But say, keep your mouth shut about this, will you? I don't want any other kids in on it. And you needn't go telling anybody you bought my wheel. There's several other fellows might come around and make trouble if they knew I was selling."

"Okay," said Bud, "I getcha!"

Then Revel sped on his way.

To the bank first, where he got his finances in good shape. Then to the station where he made sure about the hour of trains, and buses. There was a bus to the near-by city at quarter to five connecting with the first train for Linwood. If he got done he could take that. He hurried back home. He had a great deal yet to do, and very little time in which to do it. And he must not miss that bus. He could ride down to the station on Bud's truck, and arrange to ship his things, and then he would get away before his father could possibly arrive. There wasn't any train from New York until six, so he was fairly safe till them. But he must write a note to his father. It would not do for him just to disappear. His father would very likely put it into the hands of the police if he did, and it would be broadcast all over the vicinity. He would be hunted and perhaps jailed, surely sent back home. For he wasn't of age yet. And it wouldn't be because his father cared so much for him either, but just that he had been defied. His father never could bear to be defied. No, the best way was to write him a very brief note.

It was only half past three when he slipped into the house stealthily as he could, not to stir up the servants. But Mandy heard him.

She opened the pantry door and stuck her head into the dining room, looking sharply through into the hall just as he was opposite the wide doorway.

"Thet you, Mr. Hiram? Ain't you earlier'n common, boy? You ain't sick, are you?" She stared at him alertly, as if searching for some kind of trouble, she didn't know what. Although Revel was not a boy who often got into trouble at school.

"No, not sick, Mandy," said Revel, giving her an understanding smile. "I just had a chance to get excused a little early, and as I had a couple things to do I thought I'd cut baseball practice and do them. Got any cookies, Mandy?"

"Yes, I reckon."

Revel went rooting in the hall closet for his raincoat and his tennis racket and baseball bat. He probably wouldn't need them at his grandfather's, but there was no point in leaving them around for any stepmother to mess with.

By the time Mandy came back with the plate of cookies and a foaming glass of milk, topped off by two huge chicken sandwiches, he had gathered out all of his own things from the closet, rolled them together and was ready to go upstairs.

"Thanks awfully, Mandy," he said accepting the lunch with gratitude. "That looks swell. They had a rotten lunch at school and I didn't eat much. That cook at the cafeteria can't cook one, two, three with you!"

Mandy grinned cheerfully and said, "Aw, now, you, Mr. Hiram. Don't begin on your flattery! I ken always tell when you is hungry."

Revel recognized a certain freedom in her speech that usually denoted the absence of Irving.

"What's become of Irving?" he asked casually. "He taking a nap?"

"Nap!" sniffed Mandy. "You get that Irving to takin' a nap an' you ketch a weasel sleep. Irving, he's drove down to the garage ta get the oil changed in the car, an' git sompum done ta the brakes. I reckon he won't be back afore dinner time. He was plannin' on stoppin' at Sauter's farm ta git some more p'taties an' napples. We's jest out, an' we wantta be all stocked up afore your daddy gits here. He said he might be here late this evenin' or sometime t'morra! You want something I kin git fer ya, Mr. Hiram?"

"Oh, no, Mandy, thanks. I don't need anything. I was just wondering where he was. It seemed mighty still in the house."

"Yes," said Mandy thoughtfully, "Irving, he makes a heap o' noise, times when he gits riled. Well, Mr. Hiram, you just call out if ya need anything else."

"Okay, Mandy!" and Revel went cheerfully upstairs to his room reflecting that now he was going to have ample time for his operations. It would be easy to keep Mandy busy somewhere looking for something, when he wanted to carry the things out to the garage, and he could get all his things ready for Bud to take, without having to answer Mandy's many questions.

But, he reflected, it wouldn't do to count too much on Mandy's ideas of when Irving was returning. He had better get his things out of sight before there was any chance of his coming.

So, taking a hasty swig of the cold delicious milk, and stuffing a few cookies in his mouth, he went at once to work, getting out his two suitcases, folding and packing his clothes without regard to the neatness of their folds, just any way to get them in in a hurry. He could repack in the train if necessary.

He hadn't many clothes. His father didn't believe in having a lot of things around at once. There were two pretty good suits, some old trousers, a lot of sweaters to choose from, dating back several years. Swiftly he selected the ones he would need, folding them firmly.

A few of his possessions he stuffed into a chest in the attic. It took him a very short time to pack his personal belongings.

A visit to the attic brought some good strong corrugated cardboard boxes, in which he stowed a lot of his unimportant things, old shoes, baseball togs and the like. He could send those on ahead with the books and the trunk. Some heavy cord, and some labels and the whole was ready. He locked the door, cautiously took out the screen of his side window and by the help of a rope that was one of his cherished possessions, he let the boxes and suitcases down to the ground, where they were safely hidden from view behind a group of tall lilac and syringa bushes. Then he locked the strong little bookcase, wrapped it in a great piece of burlap he had found in the attic, roped and labeled it and let it down from the window. It was only a child's bookcase after all.

It was getting late, and he still had a lot to do.

He slid downstairs and called to Mandy.

"Mandy, do you remember what was done with my old bicycle?"

Mandy appeared.

"What you goin' ta do, Mr. Hiram?" she asked perplexed. "You can't ride no baby bicycle. You with your long legs."

"Why, I was going to sell it. It's too small for me any more. I know a fellow who wants to buy it. Where was it put? In the attic?"

"Seems ta me it was," said the old woman.

"Well, would you mind seeing if you can find it, Mandy? I told a fella ta come and look at it."

So Mandy plodded up the stairs, and while she was gone Revel carried his things from the bushes to the back of the garage and hid them behind some more bushes.

He had most of the heavy objects transported when he heard Mandy clumping downstairs, and he hurried in.

"Did you find it, Mandy?"

"No, Mr. Hiram," said Mandy with a troubled look. "Seems like maybe you give that away sometime back. Or maybe it's out ta the garage. Want I should go out and look?"

"Oh, no, Mandy! I'll look!" and Revel hurried out the door and to the garage. Then he came back.

"Yes, it's out there all right, Mandy," he called, putting his head in at the kitchen door. "It's out in the garage. Sorry I made you go up all those stairs for nothing."

"Oh, that's all right, honey boy!" said Mandy, half under her breath, from the habit of never showing any kindliness to the boy at a time when his father or Irving might be around, to scold her for spoiling him.

"Well, thanks a lot, Mandy," said Revel, with a sudden feeling of the approaching separation, an almost guilty feeling that he wasn't being fair to the faithful old servant and friend by stealing away unawares. Yet he knew that neither Mandy nor Irving would dare leave undone anything that could hold him from going before his father got back if they knew his intention.

"Now, I've got some writing to do, Mandy, but if anybody comes for me, call me, will you?"

Mandy promised, and Revel went back to his room to write that note to his father. Looking at his watch he found it was almost time for Bud to come, and he must hurry, so instead of studying over his words as he had meant to do, he wrote hastily, the main facts only.

> Dad. I just had word that my grandfather Revel is very sick, and about to die. He wants me to come and see him so he can talk with me a few minutes before he dies. The nurse wrote for him. He has sent me money to come, so I'm going right away. I thought this would be the right thing to do. Mother would have wanted me to. I'll let you know how Grand is.
>
> Hastily, your son

This note he put in an envelope addressed to his father and went and laid it in his room on his bureau.

Then he heard Bud's old truck rattling down behind the garage. He gave one wild half-frightened look around his room and hurried down the stairs.

Mandy appeared in the front hall.

"Where ya goin', boy? It's goin' on toward dinner time."

"Why, I'm going down to the village on an errand," said Revel with troubled impatience. "Don't wait dinner for me. I've got some things to attend to."

"What if yer dad comes back afore you get here?"

"Why, I've left a note for him up in his room. He'll understand. Don't you worry, Mandy."

But Mandy stood watching him go down to the garage with trouble in her eyes.

Bud and Revel made short work of stowing the things in the truck, and were soon rattling down the back street with the small-sized bicycle in evidence, if Mandy appeared to question again. But Mandy didn't come. She had seen a look in Revel's eyes that was something of the quality his father could assume at times and she decided she had gone as far as she dared in trying to restrain him.

Revel was white with excitement now. So far all had gone well, but suppose Irving should appear on the scene, or his father should arrive by plane or private automobile with a friend? Even now at this last minute his plans might go all astray.

But Irving had met an old friend, and lingered longer than he had intended, and Mr. Radcliffe was still in New York. Revel, feeling that perhaps he was under the protection of the God who had made a way for him to go, went on with what he had to do. At last the packages were all on their way to their destination. Bud bore the bicycle away in triumph, and Revel, dodging around the back way, caught the bus to the city and was started on his journey. His old cap was pulled down over his closed eyes. His head was back; he was getting a much needed rest. He found he was so tired that it felt good to rest, and it wasn't long before he dropped to sleep.

7

IT was very still in the sick room. The invalid lay white and stricken, scarcely seeming to breathe sometimes. The nurse in an easy chair was keeping close watch. Her heart was very much in this case. She felt deeply sorry for the old man who seemed so alone in the world. She sat there wondering whether the young grandson to whom she had written would ignore her letter as he had ignored all the other letters his grandfather had written with his own hand during the early part of his illness.

The afternoon shadows were growing long upon the grass out in the yard. She kept a close watch out the window and down the road for a possible telegram or special delivery letter, but no one was in sight, and she sighed softly.

Then the old man opened his eyes.

"Your're sure you sent the letter, nurse? Special delivery, you know?"

"Oh, yes! I sent it. I gave the postman the money for the stamp as you directed."

"And you put my check in?"

"Yes, I read the letter to you before it went. Don't you remember?"

"Yes, I remember. But nurse—" the old man was short of breath and paused. The nurse gave him a spoonful of medicine and he went on again. "I think—if the lad—does not come—it is not *his* fault."

"No, of course not," agreed the nurse. "He maybe didn't get the letter. Or he may be away at school."

"He—has a—*hard* father—" said the old man breathlessly.

"Yes, of course, it wasn't his fault. He wasn't ever that kind of a heartless boy. From what you've told me about him I *know* he wasn't."

"No, he wasn't—" murmured the old man.

"Now," said the nurse, "you'd better not talk any more. You mustn't use up your strength before he comes. He might get here in the morning."

The old man smiled, the kind of smile that might dawn on an angel's face at the threshold of Heaven.

He knew she was trying to help him over these hard facts that were attending his last hours.

So he took the medicine obediently, and then just as he was settling to close his eyes and rest again, the telephone rang. It was in the next room, but the old man opened his eyes and there was about him a glad eagerness and a joyous impatience. He waited breathlessly. He heard the nurse's clear voice. "Yes? Yes. *Yes!*" A pause. "Yes." He could almost hear the scratching of the pencil on the pad as the nurse took town the message. Then she slowly came back to him, a glad light in her eyes, which the old man's eyes were not too dim to see and understand.

"It was a telegram, sent from the train," she said. Then she read from the paper.

Am on my way. Shall be with you in the morning. Cheer up Grand, and try to get well for my sake. I love you and need you.

Your loving grandson,
Revel Radcliffe

Ah! what a light came into the old eyes, what joy into the face that had been expecting to step away into Heaven the next few minutes.

"Read it over again, nurse," he said, and already his voice sounded stronger.

She read it several times, each time the fleeting joy in the invalid's face quivering brighter, more assured. Then he asked for the paper and held it in his hand. When the doctor came he held it out to him mutely.

The doctor read it through and nodded, a light in his eyes also.

"That's great!" he said. "I thought little Emily's son wouldn't fail you."

He touched the frail wrist with its fluttering pulse, and nodded to the nurse.

"Just a trifle firmer," he murmured to the nurse.

After the doctor was gone the invalid dropped into a gentle sleep.

All night the faithful nurse watched him anxiously. It would be so dreadful for that fine boy if he should arrive too late. "Grand" he had called him, as if he really loved him. But why hadn't he ever answered the letters? Of course young people didn't like to write letters. But he might have written *once,* at least. However, maybe he didn't realize.

So she got the invalid ready in the morning, and they waited quietly, the old man with his eyes closed, and a semblance of a smile upon his lips.

Revel walked all the way from the near-by city, out to Linwood, because it was too early when he arrived for any taxis to be about, and he could not bear to sit and wait till the early bus went that way, so he walked. And sometimes ran. For his heart was almost light thinking about his grandfather.

And yet, he thought, as he drew nearer to the old farmhouse where he remembered having gone with his mother once, suppose the old man had not survived the night?

Suppose he was already gone, and it was too late for him even to put his face down to his and whisper in the dulling ear, a love message for him to take to Revel's mother, over there! How could he bear that?

His young face grew graver, and his step swifter at that thought. But he must not think of that possibility yet. He could not, *would* not believe that Grand was dead. Not when he had come on the very first train to answer his summons!

But the keen old ears of the sick man heard Revel's step on the walk even before the watching nurse. He opened his eyes with eagerness, and lifted one frail hand. "There!" he said, and a kind of peace went over the worn face, as if the height of his desire had been attained.

The nurse saw, and went swiftly to open the door. Then she was back, with Revel standing in awe behind her, his eyes wide with apprehension.

"Revel! My dear boy!" said the quavering old voice, and the old man tried to lift his hand with a welcoming gesture, that went to the boy's heart.

Revel's eyes lighted with an answering gladness, and with a long stride he was beside the bed, kneeling, his grandfather's frail hands in his, softly, tenderly. They felt so like his own dear mother's hands! And then he lifted his young lips and kissed his grandfather.

"Grand!" he said. "*Dear* Grand!" and suddenly knew what he had missed not having been much with this old man.

He bowed his head gently over those wrinkled hands he held, and the quick tears stung into his eyes, for somehow he seemed to feel his dead mother was near.

Presently the nurse came near with medicine, and Revel rose and stood beside the bed, looking down eagerly, studying the dear face, recalling its memory, line by line.

The nurse could see that the boy's eyes were questioning her, yet she could only answer him with a grave smile.

"I'm glad you've come," she murmured later when the

doctor had come in and she and the boy were on the other side of the room for a moment. "He's wanted you so *much!*"

"Oh," said Revel fervently, "if I had only known it. I didn't have any idea he cared. He didn't write to me."

"Oh, but he *did!* He wrote a good many letters!"

Revel looked at her in astonishment, and shook his head. "I never got them," he said sadly.

The doctor called for the nurse then, and Revel stood thinking it over. Was it possible that his father had deliberately kept the letters from him?

When the doctor had completed his examination he smiled down at his patient.

"You've got your wish, old friend," he said, "and now you must take a little rest. Close you eyes and go to sleep."

The sick man's anxious eyes sought Revel's.

"Don't go, Revel," he pleaded.

"No, Revel won't go," said the doctor. "He'll sit right over there in the willow chair where you can see him as soon as you wake up. Won't you, Revel?"

For answer the boy came and sat where the doctor indicated. The old man's face lighted with pleasure.

"Nearer. Come nearer," he whispered.

So Revel moved the chair nearer to the bed, where he could put out his hand and touch the old one, and the patient finally closed his eyes and drew a deep breath of satisfaction.

So Revel sat that morning beside the sick man and watched the gray shadows creep about his lips and under his eyes, and his heart cried out to the God he was just beginning to believe in again. "Oh, God, save Grand! Let us have a time to know each other before you take him away!" Over and over his heart pleaded, as the old man slept, and finally Revel, worn out with the unusual excitement of the last few hours, slept too.

It was the nurse, stirring about with medicine and a spoon who awakened him, and then he saw his grandfather's eyes were open, and a slow smile was dawning on his lips.

"I dreamed you were gone away—" he murmured in a whisper, "but you're here yet. Emily's baby—is here—yet—!

"How—long—can you—stay?" the words were almost inaudible, but Revel answered them clearly with a glad ring in his own voice.

"Just as long as you want me, Grand!" and wondered in his heart why he was so sure of that. What would his father say to such a proposition? And how much power would his father have over him legally if he should take a notion to exercise it? He was not of age yet, of course. And yet Revel knew in his heart that he would never desert this beloved old man as long as he needed him. Somehow he would accomplish that. How he didn't know. But perhaps the God who sent that letter of summons just when he was wondering what to do, would manage this staying for him too, so long as he was needed. Then a stab of pain went through his heart as he realized how very near the border this dear invalid was drawing, and it seemed now that he had found him again, he could not bear the thought of giving him up. Not while he was living, anyway.

Each time the doctor came in, and his visits were frequent, he would slip in silently with the awe of one who expected to find the patient gone. But the old man held on his way, his pulse slowly keeping up the rhythm, that seemed sometimes so near to stopping that no man of science could reasonably expect it not to stop very soon. And Revel standing across the room watched, and prayed in his heart, and stood so face to face with the possibility of death that it seemed as the hours went by that he had lived several years since he arrived.

As soon as his grandfather slept Revel wrote a brief note to his father and sent it special delivery.

Dad:

I reached here early this morning, and found my

grandfather still breathing, but that was about all. The doctor says he may go any minute. He does not think that there is likelihood of his rallying much, though he seemed greatly pleased at my coming, and the nurse says his pulse is somewhat steadier. I will keep you informed how things are going here. I am glad I came. As ever,

Your son

He addressed it apathetically, and put it in the postbox at the gate for the postman to get when he came, and then he went back and sat by his grandfather, his young strong hand firmly clasping the old wrinkled one. And as he sat so he thought again how very frail and hot and unearthly that hand seemed to be. How like his mother's before she died, when he had held her hand in just this way. Again his heart contracted with sudden fear.

That afternoon Revel wrote to his father again. He told him that the doctor thought his grandfather might linger for several days more, or even a week, just on the border, and that it was very important to have the grandson stay here. Then he added:

"You just go ahead with your plans, dad. I'll stay here. I wouldn't want to be there anyway, and I'm sure the lady you are marrying will be just as well pleased to have me out of the way."

That evening there came a telegram:

Have just returned. Find your communications. Insist you return at once! This is all nonsense that a man so sick would know. I despise a sis. Take the next train home. These are orders!

Your father

8

THE night that Revel left home for his grandfather's, Mandy began to be anxious as twilight drew near. She knew that Irving was to be late because he had intended stopping at one or two places on the way back, and then meeting the nine o'clock train from New York, in case "the Boss" as they called Mr. Radcliffe when he was not around to hear them, decided to return that night.

But Mandy was most uneasy. She had a nice dinner prepared for Revel, and she wanted him to eat it before Irving got back to see it and tell her she was pampering the boy, and if the Boss found it out there would be thunder to pay.

But Revel did not come. The darkness came down, and there was no sign of anyone coming down the road, though she watched diligently.

When the telephone rang Mandy jumped, and waddled so rapidly across the floor to the instrument that she was all out of breath when she got there. And then it was only Irving to know if she wanted him to get more butter in case the Boss should be there for breakfast.

Mandy got herself together and recollected several other things she needed at the store, and then she said breathlessly:

"Young master ain't come home for dinner yet."

Irving, true to his role, gave Mandy a good scolding for not keeping better track of him, and then asked a number of questions about when he went out. Finally Mandy hung up on him, and went to answer the door bell. And then it was only that "Bud" boy, the truck driver.

"You 'Mandy'?" he demanded, holding out a crumpled and soiled envelope.

"Yeah, I am," said Mandy, with the air of one being summoned to court for stealing.

"Well, here's a note fer ya from Revel. He said ta be sure ta give it to ya when nobody weren't around."

Bud departed with the air of one having performed an international mission, and Mandy, after squinting in the dark hall at the invisible envelope, betook herself to the kitchen, hunted up her spectacles, and spelled out the letter which Revel had written most plainly.

> Dear Mandy:
>
> I certainly hated to go away without telling you, but I thought it might be easier for you if I did, because you would have thought you had to stop me, perhaps, and I couldn't be stopped.
>
> You see I got a letter this afternoon saying my Grandfather Revel was about to die, and wanted to see me before he went, so I had to hurry. I left a note for my dad, and I guess it'll be all right. Anyway, I've gone. Thank you, Mandy, for all you've done for me, and you needn't tell anybody about this note unless you want to. It wasn't your fault I went. Give my love to Irving sometime when he gets over being angry, and take care of yourself,
>
> Revel

Mandy barely finished reading the note before she heard Irving drive into the garage, and she folded it carefully and stuffed it safely in the ample bosom of her kitchen dress. She hadn't decided yet whether she would tell Irving tonight, or wait until a more favorable time. Anyhow since the boy had written a note to his father why not let it rest at that?

So Irving came in and stormed around and blamed Mandy in all the ways he knew, which were many, for having let the boy escape so near meal time. Then the two settled down to a gloomy evening, Irving to worry, look out the windows, call up the station, call up several of Revel's friends; and Mandy to grin secretly, that for once she knew more than Irving did about the perplexities of the household. More and more it appeared to her that she must not tell about the letter Revel had written her. At least not until his father got home and had seen his own letter. Then if she wanted to show it she could. Nobody would know when it reached her. It had no date on it, and she need only tell that some strange boy left it at the door for her. So Mandy set out Irving's dinner, listened to his worries, and hugged the note inside her dress, thinking how nice it was that the boy had remembered to thank her for the little no-count things she had done for him. It began to be like a little tune singing itself in her heart. Mandy hadn't ever had very many things in her life to make her happy, but she cared a lot for the boy who had grown up in the house under her ministrations, though since his mother died she hadn't been allowed to show much tenderness toward him. She came as near to loving him as anything else in her life.

But as she watched Irving's uneasy state she began to feel sorry for him. For Irving knew he would be called to account most severely if Mr. Radcliffe came home and the boy was not there. He sat down in his usual place with the evening paper spread before him, but he did not read. He only sat frowning across the room at the face of the clock on the mantel, trying to think where the boy had gone. He went went over in his mind all the places in their vicinity that would attract a boy of the age of Revel. There were the pool rooms. A lot of the young fellows hung around them, but Revel had always been kept close to his home. His father required evening study of him, homework, and then early to bed. Perhaps Revel, knowing that his father was to be away several days, was feeling his freedom, and trying out some of the things the other boys did. Though there had never been any show of rebellion in such a way. He would never suspect the lad of playing pool. His discipline had been too long and severe. Still, perhaps he ought to go and see. Perhaps it would be expected of him.

He glanced at the clock. It was getting on to ten o'clock. He wasn't as young as he once was. He dreaded the thought of getting out the car and going back to the village, sneaking around to see if he could find Revel. He tried to think of somewhere else he might have gone. The drug store for soda, or candy. To meet the girls? Though Revel had never been a lad to have much to do with girls. Perhaps there was a girl now, and she had asked him to her home. But Mandy said he had not been home for dinner. Maybe he had been invited to someone's house to dinner! Well, perhaps— But there was no end of things he might have done. He hadn't been in the habit of going out to parties, not even high school parties. His father hadn't favored such things. But perhaps all the while he had wanted to go. It wasn't right to keep any lad as close as this boy had been kept, thought Irving. Sometime there was bound to come a reaction. Just hedged about with laws, the boy had been. But there was nothing *he* could do about that. His father was his father and would never brook a word of remonstrance. Certainly not from a servant.

With a great sigh Irving rose and wound the clock, just to make a little more time before he had to go out and get the car. He might of course talk it over with Mandy, but what would Mandy know about it? She would just get excited and worry about his going out so late. No, he'd better say nothing. So he wandered out to the back door, and Mandy followed him, calling sharply:

"Where you going, Irving?"

"Oh, I just thought I'd go outside and look around, see if I could any sign of Mr. Hiram." He said it as casually as he could.

Mandy caught her breath and felt guilty. She opened her mouth to speak about Revel's letter to her, and then closed it again. If she told Irving where Revel had gone he might think he had to telegraph his father, and Mandy had a strong feeling that Revel's father had never been fair to him. It was time he found it out.

But by the time she caught her breath again and decided she *must* tell Irving, she heard the car driving out and knew it was too late.

Irving came home very late, later than he had been out in many a year. He had dragged his respectable self from pool room to pool room in the neighboring villages, from tavern to tavern, even from roadhouse to roadhouse, and made a thorough survey of all the disreputable places he knew. Not that Revel had ever manifested any desire to go to such places, but Irving knew that Revel's father would be sure to think of them first and ask if Irving was sure about them. He always expected the worst of his son, and Irving wanted to be able to say that he had not been in any of those places. He came home more worn and weary than he had been for years, and Mandy would have felt deep compunction and probably would have hurried to divulge her secret of the letter, if she had been awake. But Mandy, not having the burden of responsibility upon her that Irving bore, was sleeping soundly and did not hear him come in, and Irving was too disheartened to waken her and hear her outcry of distress. For he was sure that was what it would be if Mandy should thoroughly comprehend the situation. For Mandy was very fond of Revel, and womanlike was the frequent haunt of fears of various kinds.

So Irving went to his bed and tried to think what he should do in the morning in case the boy had not yet returned. At last he fell into an uneasy doze, from which he awakened at a most unearthly hour. He stole from his bed and out to the car to try and look up one or two other places he had thought of to search for Revel.

Mandy awoke at the sound of the car going out the drive and hurried to the window too late to call. Now what was Irving going to do next, and what trouble had she brought upon herself by not telling Irving about that letter?

Still, if she had told Irving he might have thought it his duty to drive to New England and bring back Revel before his father got there. Mandy had no idea how far away New England was and her reasoning seemed quite sensible to herself.

So she read her letter over again and gloated a little all by herself, that whatever should happen she had a little word all her own from the young master himself. And she needn't tell anyone about it if she didn't want to. Most of the time she thought she wouldn't ever tell it even to Irving. Not so long as they were working under Mr. Radcliffe.

So she went to work and got herself a nice breakfast under the impression that she was getting it for Irving. But Irving didn't come back to eat it, and after a while she got to worrying about him. The boy was safe with his grandfather by now, and perhaps having a nice comforting talk with him before he died, but *what* was she going to do about Irving? Suppose something had happened to him? Maybe he had a smashup, and was lying in a hospital somewhere, nobody knowing who he was nor where to telephone. She was too utterly ignorant of licenses and such to know there would be something about the car to show where he belonged if he had an accident. But she began to think what a faithful, even though sometimes cranky, husband he had always been. What a perfect record he had as a servant! How exceedingly respectable he was! How he came from a fine race of butlers and servants of high degree. And although he was often hard to live with, it was mainly because he always put first the interests of the man for whom he was working, no matter how wrong and hard that man might be.

Thinking of all these things Mandy got out a bitter salt tear or two and let them roll down her ripe-apple countenance. And then she brushed them meticulously out of sight, washed her hands, and set out to supply the house with some of the viands of which the master and his servant both were fond. She baked cakes and pies, almost as if she knew that a new mistress was coming soon to inspect the house and everything concerned therewith. Somehow Mandy always seemed to have a sixth sense to be prepared for unexpected happenings before they came. And so when Irving finally returned late in the afternoon with a drawn gray look on his face and his eyes wild with weariness, Mandy had a tasty dinner well under way.

"Boy come yet?" asked Irving through white set lips.

Mandy shook her head with an almost cheerful grin.

"You didn't find no sign of him?" she asked.

"Not a trace nor a word," said Irving dejectedly. "Seems like he's disappeared off the earth."

"Well, ef you hada stayed home and tended to your business you mighta been saved a lotta trouble. I cud of helped ya out a lot ef you'da been here."

"What do you mean Mandy, *you* helped? What do *you* know about this business?"

"Well, I know cause I had a letter from the young master," said Mandy with a toss of her head.

"A letter from Mr. Hiram?" exclaimed Irving. "Came in the morning's mail? Mandy Hollister, you mean you went and looked over the mail when you know Mr. Radcliffe said I wasn't to let anyone see the mail but myself."

"No, I didn't look over your old mail," said Mandy sharply, "and the letter didn't come in the mail. It come by messenger boy."

"A messenger boy? You mean a special delivery from the postoffice?"

"No, it wasn't no postoffice letter. It was just a boy brung it to the door, and he wasn't any boy I knowed. He jes' handed it ta me an' made off as fast as he could run. He said Mr. Hiram sent it to me, and I was too took up studying' the letter without any glasses on, to notice the boy till he was gone."

"Well, get on, won't you?" said Irving impatiently. "What did the young master say? Where is he?"

"The letter sayed there had come a message that his grandfather Revel was a'dying, and wanted his gran'son ta come quick. An' I reckon that boy just made off soon as there was a train."

"To his grandfather's!" exclaimed Irving, turning a white face toward her. "And a pretty state of things that'll be. I stopped at the postoffice and found a telegram from the Boss. He's coming home on the six-thirty tonight, and he may be bringing a lady with him!"

"A *lady!*" said Mandy, and now it was her turn to turn white. "What's he bringin' a lady fur? He gointa git married again?"

"I don't know what he's going to do, but I know what he'll be if he finds his son's gone. Especially when he finds *where* he's gone. He hates those Revels like poison, and I don't mean maybe! And it'll be as much as my job—*our* job—is worth that I didn't stick around and keep him from going. Where *is* that letter you got?"

Mandy produced it from the bosom of her dress, and Irving read it.

"That young scamp! He knew what his father would say!" said Irving with greatly troubled eyes. "Now I've got to tell him, I suppose."

"I don't see why you gotta tell him nothing," said Mandy, "only just thet the boy's gone. He wrote a letter to his father. Let him read that. You got no call to get inta this with both feet. You ken blame it all on the boy. He ain't here ta suffer, so it can't do him any harm."

"You say he wrote the Boss a letter? Are you *sure* of that?"

"Yes, I'm sure. I went and looked where he put it on his father's bureau. I saw it there. All sealed up nice, without no stamp on it. You're not supposed ta look out fer that room, why do you say anything at all about it, just that Revel ain't home?"

"Yes? You know what he'll say. He'll be *raging*."

"Well, you can't do nothin' about it. Jes' tell him he left a letter for him, that Mandy found it when she was dustin' up."

"Yes? You want to lose your job, do you?"

"Well, ef there's another woman comin' here mebbe I'd jes' as soon," said Mandy with an independent swag of her gingham skirt.

"*Woman!* What's that to you? She might be all right."

"Yeah? Well I ain't sa anxious ta say. I'm tired of this here bein' feared ta call yer name yer own. What did yer telegram say anyway?"

"Oh, just said he might be home tonight, or he might stay some place on the way. Then he said he might bring a lady with him, and to get the guest room ready. If she didn't come with him she might come a day later, but in any event get the house ready for company."

"Ummm!" said Mandy with her arms akimbo, and her head irate. "I thought that would be comin' ta this house some day, an' now it's come! Say, Irving, do you reckon that boy *knowed* about this lady? Do you reckon that's the reason of all these carryin's on?"

"What carryings on, Mandy?" snapped Irving crossly.

"Why, his not comin' to meals, and his kitein' off ta his grampa's?"

"Certainly not!" said Irving. "You think that kid would make me up all that story about his grampa being near to death? He's no liar, that kid. He never was. You know that, Mandy. He'd never get all that story up!"

"Well, I don't like this lady comin', an' I don't reckon the boy would either."

"Well, hold your horses, Mandy, she isn't here yet, so

don't start judging her before her time. She might be some aunt or other."

"Well, I ain't goin' ta stand fer no aunt, neither!" said Mandy irately.

"Mandy, whatever you do, you've got to get this house in order before the Boss comes, and you know that, so get to work."

"The house is *always* in order," said Mandy with a toss, "an' I gotta big chocolate cake, like what the Boss likes, an' a rhuberb pie, an' a napple, an' fresh bread an' rolls set. What more do ya want?"

Irving subsided, and Mandy stalked away upstairs and subjected the guest room to a thorough going over, putting on clean sheets, and even washing the curtains. She put out the best bureau scarf and fresh towels, as she used to do for her dead mistress.

Irving spent a lot of time making the lawn fine, and scrubbed the garage floor, and washed the best car, but his thoughts were greatly troubled. He knew that for at least the first few minutes after Mr. Radcliffe's arrival the storm would break over his own head, no matter what happened, and he almost prayed, much as he dreaded it to happen, that the lady would arrive with the master. He certainly wouldn't carry on quite so much in her presence as he would if he came alone.

But after all when the six-thirty train came in Mr. Radcliffe came alone. He told Irving that the lady would appear the next afternoon. And then after Irving uttered his usual deferential "Yes, sir!" the Boss began.

"Is my son at home?"

"No, sir, that is, he wasn't when I left. I came down right early to get a few things that Mandy wanted."

"Not home yet? I thought I told you to tell him not to stay out so late again. Has he been at home every night on time?"

"No, sir, not since you've been away."

"Well, where has he been? What explanation does he offer?"

"Well sir, I believe he left you a note. Mandy found it on your bureau."

"A note!" frowned the father. "What did it say?"

"I couldn't say, sir. It was a sealed note. Mandy didn't open it, of course."

"Oh, I see, of course not," said the father, growing angrier every minute. "But Irving, something has got to be done about this. It seems to me if you had been watching this could have been avoided. You know I gave you strict orders."

"I know sir, quite right, sir. But everything seemed to be all right sir, going on as usual, and you know I had your orders to be away at the farm getting produce, and there were several errands you gave me. Besides, the car needed attention, and you told me to take it to the garage, and wait for it, and watch the man and see what was really the matter."

"There, there, Irving. That will do," said the man. "I told you those things of course, but I expected you would use common sense and do those errands when it did not interfere with watching over the house and my son. However, we'll get together and sift this thing down. Hiram has got to understand that I will be obeyed."

"Of course, sir! You're quite right, sir! And I felt quite badly when I got home to find the lad was gone. But now, Mr. Radcliffe, about this lady you're bringing tomorrow. Was it the green guest room you meant we were to prepare? And is she to remain long, or only for the night?"

They were driving in to the Radcliffe place now, and Irving cannily stretched his questions to fit the time as they drew up before the steps.

"I'll tell you later about the lady," said Mr. Radcliffe, stepping out of the car and slamming the door. "Where did you say my son's letter was?"

"In your own room, sir. On your bureau, I think, was

where Mandy found it when she went in there to put clean towels."

The master of the house stamped up the steps and disappeared inside the door, and the rest of the evening was fully as stormy as Irving had expected. The telephone grew noisy with the message for Western Union, as the Boss shouted into the receiver. Mandy was greatly distressed because she knew she would be blamed that the dinner was spoiled on account of taking so much time over the telephone. And she was. But then she was quite used to it and she had the letter from Revel still in the bosom of her dress.

But though the master lingered long after he had finished eating, asking questions, giving directions, and thundering orders to both Irving and Mandy, still they didn't learn much about the lady who was coming.

And then, it was the lady herself, the next morning, who called up and said she couldn't come for a couple of days longer, which gave Hiram Radcliffe more time to devote himself to harrowing the feelings of his son by more messages.

"I shall expect you back on the late afternoon train today," was his first communication and he pranced around the house irately, scolded everybody that came near him, went down to his business and gave a good round of faultfinding there, and then returned to snarl at Irving because there had been no reply yet to his telegram.

He went himself to the late afternoon train, but there was no repentant son arriving. He came home to indite a lengthy letter which he sent by airmail, special delivery, making plain to the boy what he was doing to his own fortunes.

I had arranged to put you in my own alma mater, where you would have the prestige that my son would carry. I had reserved the pick of rooms in the best dormitory, and because of gifts of mine to the new fraternity building you were to be voted into the most exclusive fraternity without a question. Your path from the start would be smoothly paved, and your college course a success from every point of view.

I have looked forward to bringing you into my firm when your college course is ended, and putting you in the way of making a fortune! And now for the sake of a poor little runt of a man who happens by unfortunate circumstance to be related to you, you are putting all this in jeopardy!

I had no idea before this that you had inherited your mother's unfortunate temperament, holding grudges, and being stubborn for your own way. I thought I had trained all that out of you. And now can you not see what sorrow and humiliation you have brought upon me, your father, who surely am nearer to you than any grandfather, even if he wasn't such a dismal failure as a man.

You are too young to understand what a foolish thing you are doing, too young to have good judgement about character, and to understand what a mistake I made when I married into a family who cared so little for appearances, and were so narrow and fanatical that there was no peace in the family. And it is just because I made this mistake and was taken with a pretty face and winning ways, without looking ahead to see if she had the character to become a fit mistress for a man who was going to succeed in this world, that you had a mother who has given to you this vascillating character that moves you to yield weakly to each whining request from a foolish old man who will stoop to any lengths to win you away from your own father.

Now, my son, I have tried to make plain to you what you are doing to your life. If you do not immediately respond to my command, I shall have to withdraw all this that I have outlined to you. I shall have to cancel your entrance to one of the most renowned colleges in this part of the world, to withdraw my support from you entirely, and just allow you to grow up a country hoodlum, whom I shall be ashamed to call my son. You speak a great deal about what your mother would like, do you think she would like that for your future? Consider, my son, and be quick about it. For I mean what I say! Also, I demand that you come home to meet and welcome the woman I am to marry.

The letter would have been much longer and more bitter had not the clock suddenly announced to him that there was barely time to get it to the office before the mail closed.

Then he waited through a bitter night when his own ugly temper made a black background for his forthcoming marriage.

The truth of the business was he did not wish his new lady to know of the trouble between himself and his son. He had told her very little about his child, and he did not wish to introduce a rebellious member of the family to her. He wanted his boy to come home and give her the courteous reception that his son should naturally yield to the woman who was to be his future stepmother.

When Revel received this letter he barely read it at all, for there had come a relapse in his grandfather's illness, and he was lying at death's door all that day. But later, when the doctor had brought a specialist, and his grandfather had rallied again and seemed to take a feeble hold on life once more, the boy wrote a sorrowful brief little letter.

Dad:

I couldn't answer sooner. This has been an anxious day. Grand has been very low. For a time the doctor felt he might leave us any minute. But we got a specialist from Boston, and now he has seemed to rally again and I am very thankful.

Dad, I'm all kinds of sorry I have to seem so

ungrateful to you, for the home you've given me, the standing in the financial world that was mine, the prestige you were arranging for me while acquiring a superior education. But not for all that, dad, could I leave Grand now. And all I can say in answer to what you have said about him is, you do not know him really or you never would think all that about him.

About that request of yours that I come home and try to be courteous to the lady you are going to marry, I ask you to put it up to her. I am quite sure she would prefer not to have me there. At least not now. If you are marrying soon, it will not be thought strange that I am staying by my dying grandfather's side. So I am asking you to put this up to her entirely.

And dad, one thing more. If you should carry out your threat of withdrawing your support from me, that's all right by me. I'll go on and *work* my way through, and I'll promise you I'll get a good education, too, so you won't need to be ashamed of me.

So now, dad, you and the lady talk it over, and I'm sure you'll begin to see that I'm right in staying here. At least for the present.

Your son

He did not sign his name, because he would not sign Hiram, and he knew that Revel would only anger his father more, so he sent the letter unsigned.

The morning it reached his father, the lady herself arrived on the scene, to help in the solution of Revel's problems.

9

THE lady was tall with a well set-up figure, and a handsome rather overbearing face, that well knew how to hide her unpleasant feelings on occasion. She was delicately made up, and looked younger than she was. Mandy saw that at once. There was nothing soft and sweet about her to remind of the master's former wife, although she had regular features, and hair that was in the very pink of beauty-parlor order, giving her a smart stylish finish that belied her height and bearing. She had very red thick lips and a well-applied flush on her smooth cheeks. She wore a number of sparkling rings, reminiscent of her past marriage, and her nails were deeply tinted. Mandy fixed her eyes upon them at once as one fascinated. Hiram Radcliffe introduced her to the two servants at the dinner table when they came in to serve the dinner, as Mrs. Temple of Rochester, New York.

And it was just as they were sitting down that Revel's special delivery airmail letter was brought to his father.

Mandy saw the Boss frown as he recognized the handwriting, and her heart quaked. That would be from the young master of course, and what would he be saying now to bring such a black look on his father's face? Her heart ached for the poor lad.

But the master had no opportunity to read the letter until the meal was concluded, and they had withdrawn to the front piazza to enjoy the coolness of the evening after an unusually hot May day. Mandy made a hasty errand to the coat closet by the front door that had a little high window overlooking the piazza, and she presently returned to tell Irving about it.

"They're settin' there as big as life, holdin' hands right out on the front porch!" she announced breathlessly.

"Well," said Irving meditatively as he put away a large portion of the gala roast into his mouth, "it's his porch. I guess he has a perfect right to do what he wants on it."

"Yes, but *her!* The shameless huzzy! It ain't her porch. Not yet, anyway!"

"Well, I guess there's no one around looking at them!" said Irving with a shrug of his shoulders. This wasn't the stage of the game yet for him to take sides.

"My dear," cooed Mrs. Temple, "you're looking troubled. Is there something that worries you?"

"Well—ur—yes! There is! It's that boy of mine!"

"Oh, yes, the boy!" murmured the guest. "I'd forgotten about him. Is he here?"

"No, he isn't, not just now!" said the father irately. "I told him distinctly to be here. I told him I wanted him to welcome you courteously. But no, he had to rush off, and be stubborn. Naturally he's rather upset at a new order of things."

"Oh, is he? Well, I suppose he would be somewhat upset. But he'll be going away to college very soon, won't he? I thought that was what you said."

"Well, yes, of course. He will. That was the plan. However it is only spring and college doesn't open until fall."

"Yes, of course," said the lady, a coolness in her tone. "And where is he now?"

"That's the trouble. He's gone off to his grandfather's. The grandfather is a cagey old fellow and he has staged an illness, with death in the offing, and worked on the lad's feelings—he's quite an emotional fellow—and begged him to come and hold his hand while he dies. So the lad went, and I've been very much mortified not to have him here to welcome you when you came. It doesn't look right."

"Oh, *Hi*," —that was the lightly fantastic name she had invented in place of the old fashioned Hiram which she told him was all out of date— "Hi, I don't think you ought to be so upset about that. It's just as well for him not to be here this first time we are here together. You know it's much more cozy without any outsider."

"Yes, of course," conceded the usually peppery Hiram. "But yet, on the other hand he's my son, you know, and it's discourteous to you that he isn't here."

"Oh, well, I don't mind, really," she smiled. "It's much pleasanter this way for now. You ought not to worry."

"But I do worry. I've ordered him home at once, and he doesn't come! Yesterday I wrote him my ultimatum. I told him to come at once or I would cut him off from his inheritance. I would not finance his college course, nor look after him financially any more unless he obeyed me at once."

A sudden glint of avarice came into the cold eyes of the lady. "Oh, Hi! Don't you think that was rather severe?" she drawled. "And what does the boy say to that?"

"Well, I don't know. He hasn't said anything all day, and I rather looked for him on the six-thirty train, but he didn't come, and now there has just come a letter from him, handed to me as we sat down to dinner. Perhaps I had better find out just what he does say. Will you excuse me if I read it?"

"Why, of course!" said the lady. "Just light me a cigarette, please, and then take as long as you want to."

A few minutes later Mandy made another excursion to the coat closet and placed a wily eye behind the folds of the master's raincoat where she had a full view of the scene. When she went back to Irving she gave a full account.

"Well, what d'ya think they're doin' now? Just settin' there as neat as two clams, him readin' his letter you guv him at the dinner table, an' her holdin' his han', an' both of em's smokin' *cigarettes!* Ef that don't beat all! That settles it. Ef she's goin' ta be mistress here, I'm done! Yes, *done,* Irving!"

"Now Mandy, don't you go saying what you won't do and what you will. In fact you haven't been asked to stay yet, not by her! And she may not be so bad. Wait till circumstances develop."

"All right fer you, Irving. You talking like tat. How would you like *me* to take to smokin' cigarettes? That's what it would likely come to, ef I have a mistress who smokes. You ken stay ef you likes, but I know my upbringin' an' I don't serve no smokin' lady."

But on the piazza Hiram Radcliffe was having an argument, and for the first time in years he had met his equal. Oh, she didn't storm, nor talk loudly, nor beat the air with gestures. She was very soft-spoken, but most persuasive. Her large eyes pleaded, her jeweled hands made passes at his big hand, and her voice was sweet and drawly.

"Why, Hi, what does your boy say that angers you so? Let me see his letter. Are you afraid to have me read it? I assure you I won't judge him harshly."

"No, I'm not afraid to have you read the letter. There it is. Read it! Just a silly boy that doesn't in the least know which side his bread is buttered. But he'll find out he can't defy *me.* I think I'll send the police after him in the morning. He'll find out that he hasn't the *right* to say where he's going to stay, and what else he is going to do."

The lady was silent while she read Revel's pitiful plea. A close observer might have seen that sinister gleam in her eye again, but as she finished the letter she handed it indifferently over to Hiram Radcliffe, and said in a casual lazy tone:

"Do you know, Hi, I think you're making entirely too much of this matter. He's only a youngster, you know, and hasn't found himself yet. Why not let him stay there awhile and find out for himself that things are not what they seem to him. If the Revels are what you say he'll find out. He can't help it. And you know it will be a great deal better for the young man to *find out* he has made a mistake, than to be ordered home and come because he *has* to. He'll always be sore at you for it, and never discover he was wrong. If I were you I'd tell him to go ahead. Tell him you've changed your mind, and he can stay as long as he sees fit. Let him put himself through college if he thinks he's so smart. Then it won't be long before he'll come crawling to you to help him out, and then you'll have him just where you want him, and you can make your own terms."

"Own terms!" exclaimed the man. "I shall *make* my own terms, of course! And I won't wait for him to crawl, he'll come because I *say* so."

"Oh, no, Hi! That's not good psychology. That's merely spoken by a man who wants to flatter his own ego, who is determined to impose his will upon a mere child! Wait until he has had even one year of college at least before you attempt to force him into anything. He isn't a babe in arms. He is old enough to choose what he thinks best, and find out for himself. If he doesn't trust you enough after the years in which you have brought him up to let you decide his order of life you certainly cannot *force* him to trust you. He must find out for himself that you were right."

"Natalie, my dear, you do not understand. I am trying to plan for our almost immediate marriage, and what would my friends, my neighbors, my business associates think if my son were not present at his father's wedding?"

"Oh, that's silly!" laughed the lady. "Your son has himself provided the excuse. What is more wonderful, more self-sacrificing than that a son of a former marriage should quietly give up the privilege of watching his adored father married, in order that he may stay by the dying bed of his dead mother's father? I think myself it is a very noble reason, and very charming in a young fellow to be so faithful to his mother's kin, even though that kin may be not worthy of so much devotion. Come, now, Hi, your son has put it up to me to decide this question, and I am very willing to be the arbiter of this matter. I think your son is *right!* He should stay where he is, at least for a while. His reasoning is good. And most of all is his suggestion that you ask me what I would like. He must have keen perception to realize, young as he is, that you and I can have a far happier time during the first of our marriage months, if we are by ourselves, and not hampered by the presence of a son who is not my son. Can't you see that, Hi dear? If you really care for me in the way you have told me, will you not be persuaded to let the boy alone, and keep us apart, at least until such time as he shall *desire* to be with us, which may, or may not come in the future?"

The man drew his heavy determined brows down fiercely and looked at her.

"But surely, Natalie, you do not object to the presence of my son?"

"Yes, I do," she said firmly, in a very low clear voice. "I do very decidedly object to his presence in our home. He represents a portion of your life in which I could not possibly have a part, and he reminds of a time when I had no part in your life. It could not be a pleasant thing for me to come into a household thus divided. I certainly do object."

"This certainly is a strange time to bring up a matter like this, Natalie! Just two weeks before the date we have set for our marriage. Do you realize that you have never said anything of this sort before?"

"Do you realize, Hi, that you have never mentioned your son to me but once, and then very casually. You spoke then very casually. You spoke then very finally of his going at once to college, and probably being there four years. I supposed of course he had other young interests, and would not be a factor in our lives at all."

Her voice was low and very sweet. Her fingers were smooth and most vital as they curled about his hand, and occasionally moved softly up and down his wrist. Mandy from her point of vantage, watched at intervals, and returned to the kitchen to tell Irving.

"She knows her onions all right! She'll make it! An' he won't get wise, neither, not'll she *get* him good and tight! Me, I'm goin' out an find me 'nother place, just as soon as ever she leaves ta get ready fer her weddin', and I hope that'll be soon."

"Now, you Mandy, you hold your horses! You can't tell what won't happen yet."

"Keep yer own shirt on, Irving. I know one thing ain't goin' ta happen, an' that is the Boss ain't agonta get wise ta her till it's too late."

But the lady left that night, after all, on the midnight train.

"And I didn't needta get that gues'-room cleaned after all!" sulked Mandy watching the taillights of the master's car disappear down the drive, as he drove his lady to the midnight train.

The lady had conquered. She had made it plain that she wanted to be alone with her bridegroom those first few months, and she had done it so winsomely that the man was actually pleased over the idea. It wouldn't of course make much difference in his plans for his son. Let the boy remain with his grandfather until college opened. He could arrange for his entrance all right, he was sure. A little money, a hint of more, and the authorities would fix things up for *his* son. He had always been generous in his gifts to his alma mater. It looked well, and all such things "told in the end," he told himself.

So he went on with his preparations for his marriage.

He did not write to Revel at once. Let the boy realize that he had meant what he said. And since he didn't come home, and he didn't reply immediately, let him take the consequences.

So Revel was left in doubt as to what was to happen to

him next. But indeed he was so anxious for his grandfather
that his mind did not dwell much on what was going to happen to himself. He only hoped that no police officer would
arrive to remand him home while his grandfather was lying
so low. What he would do in such a case he didn't know.
When the law came in it was no longer his to decide. But he
prayed continually that nothing would happen to hurt his
grandfather.

One day he was going through his coat pockets looking
for his pen which he was sure he had had with him on the
train on the journey, and he suddenly came on the two letters, the nurse's, and the other one which arrived at the same
time, and which he now remembered stuffing into his side
pocket that terrible rushing day he came. He pulled the letter out now and looked at it. Yes, strange writing. That must
be from the woman his father was marrying next week, and
he might as well read it now and get it over with.

So he opened it and began to read:

Dear Revel:

"Dear Revel:"
But—*Revel!* Why did she call him that? Surely she
wouldn't know that name! Or would she? Was she somebody from the home town who already knew him?

With a heavy frown on his brow he turned to the end and
saw the named signed, "Margaret Weldon" and suddenly
his heart leaped up with a glad thrill. This was Margaret, his
friend. This was the lovely girl who had come to him in the
woods when he was in despair, the girl of whom he had got
the flowers! He hadn't expected ever to hear of her again,
and so many things had happened since the evening in the
woods that he had almost put her out of his thoughts, but
now a great glad peace came to him, like a gentle hand on
his brow. *Margaret!*

Then he read the letter, a flush coming on his cheek, his

eyes shining. This was one friend he had to whom he could tell what had happened, and who would be glad for him, and sympathize. She would not find fault with him for coming to his grandfather. She had practically suggested it herself. Of course she didn't know God was going to send him. She didn't know that he had followed her suggestion and taken his trouble to God and that God had answered in this way. She didn't know anything about all this, and he must write and tell her. That would be one person in whom he could confide. His grandfather wasn't well enough to hear anything of the details of his coming or his life. His natural reticence made it impossible for him to confide in the nurse, but he could write to Margaret! He would do it right away! The doctor was with the patient now and he was not needed for a few minutes, so he sat down at the desk, that used to be his mother's girlhood desk, and wrote.

Dear Margaret:

I was all kinds of glad to get your letter, and to know you liked the flowers. I hope they keep for you, but if they don't perhaps I can get some more for you later.

A lot of things have happened since I saw you. I prayed as you told me to, and right away the next day God answered. I got a letter on my way home from school, a special delivery, from a nurse who has been taking care of my grandfather. He is very sick, and is not expected to live, but he had asked for me to come to him before he dies. He wanted to talk with me. It seems he had written me a lot of letters before he was sick, but I never got them. I guess my father didn't want me to have them. The nurse begged me to come at once as Grand might not live but a few hours. So I started right away on the first train. My dad was in New York so I packed up and left. I wrote him a note explaining, and left it for him. I knew he wouldn't like it, but I couldn't help it, I had to go.

When I got here Grand was very short of breath. He couldn't speak much, but he let me know how glad he was. His eyes shine with joy when he looks at me, and he has frail hands, soft and warm like my mother's. Like yours when I touched them. I sit and hold Grand's hands a great deal. He has a queer thing the matter with him, a clot in the heart, and he has to lie very still. They won't even let him speak to me any more, so I just sit and hold his hand. Sometimes I pray. I was wishing you knew about it and would pray too for my Grand. He's a swell person, and I'd like to keep him here if I might.

I don't know what dad is going to do about all this. He has ordered me home, but I didn't go. Grand was too sick to leave. The doctor said my being here was doing a lot for him, and he maybe might get better if I stayed. So I'm staying.

Dad will probably do something about this, maybe send the police after me. Won't you pray that nothing will come that will hurt my dear Grand?

Please forgive this long letter. I have no one else to talk to about it. It is a comfort to call you a friend, but don't let me bother you. If you get time write me a little letter sometime.

Your friend of the woods,
Revel Radcliffe

After that letter was started on its way, the boy thought much about the girl to whom it had gone. It seemed as if a long time had passed since he had seen her, so much had happened to him in between. Perhaps she had almost forgotten him. Perhaps she would think he was presuming to write to her, a stranger. And yet she had been so kind!

And that night when he was sitting by the sleeping invalid to let the nurse rest, he was startled into realizing that he had been remembering Margaret Weldon's sweet lips against his when he had kissed her good-by. Would he ever feel them there again?

The next morning he thought it over and decided that he was a sap, and that it was time he did some real work of some kind instead of just sitting around mooning.

His father's next communication was a brief note:

> Very well. Have your own way. But you'll have to expect to take the consequences.

This communication filled the boy with great relief and a kind of exhilaration. Whatever "the consequences" might mean, at least he was free from that terrible dread that the law might appear in some form and snatch him from his grandfather's side while he still needed him. And then the next day there came a formal engraved announcement of the wedding of Mrs. Natalie Temple and Mr. Hiram Radcliffe.

It was over, then, and he had not had to attend. He felt unspeakably relieved.

It was a few days later that the doctor told him he had hope that his grandfather might be going to get better, and Revel sat hour after hour holding the feeble hand, and smiling when the old man smiled, and just being happy. In fact he was happier than he had been since his mother died. His grandfather *might* get better and then he would have somebody who cared for him. Of course his father might rise up and make trouble again, after the wedding was over and he was back at home settled down to living. He knew his father well enough to realize he didn't ever give up his will easily, and he would surely pursue this subject of college, for he had always been very determined about that. But why worry now? It would be enough if Grand got better, and they could have a good talk.

But through those long hours that Revel sat patiently watching with the invalid, sometimes reading a few paragraphs to him when the doctor said he might, Revel was thinking out a future for himself, trying to plan so that he wouldn't ever have to go back to his home and watch an alien mother take the place of his own.

He found among his mother's things in her desk in the room he occupied, a lot of papers and catalogues, and some bits of diary records about her own college life, in a college quite near Linwood. He knew from the stories she had told him of her college life that there had been men as well as girls in that college. Why couldn't he go to that college, if it was still in existence? He would ask Grand about that when he got well enough to really talk with. If there was a college near by, *any* kind of college, he would go there if he could get in, at least until Grand was well and able to be left. But oh how great if it was near enough for him to stay here with Grand and walk to college every day, or maybe get another bicycle and ride there! Well, that was something to put aside and think about. Perhaps that was another thing he ought to ask God about before he decided. This idea of living as God guided, that Margaret Weldon had suggested, had taken great hold upon him, because the first prayer had worked out so wonderfully well. Even his father seemed to have subsided for the time being, though of course that couldn't be expected to last long.

How he wished that Margaret Weldon lived in this part of the world, and that he could talk things over with her sometimes.

Then when he got to feeling that way he would go to his room for a few minutes and read Margaret's letter over, and wonder if she would ever write to him again.

Then one day another letter came from her.

Dear Revel:
　　It was grand to get your news about going to your grandfather's and I hope your father will let you stay there. And I hope so much God will let your grandfather get well. Both of my grandfathers and grandmothers

are gone to Heaven and sometimes I feel very much alone, not having any. I only knew two of them, my Grandmother and Grandfather Weldon, for the others died when I was very small, but I loved Grandmother Weldon especially, for she lived longest, and used to read to me and play games with me when I was little. I am certainly glad your grandfather wants you. It is so nice to be *wanted*. Sometimes I feel terribly depressed that nobody really needs me, nor wants me so awfully much, although everybody is very nice to me.

Of course I am praying for your grandfather to get well. I began right away as soon as I read your letter. What a splendid name you have for him! Grand! It just expresses what he means to you, doesn't it?

I think it is so sad that you never got the letters your grandfather wrote you. It was nice that the nurse's letter came as an answer to your prayer. I am glad you have found out that God does answer.

I do hope the police will not have to get into your affairs. But if they do, keep on praying. If God is with you you will not mind what happens, will you?

I want to tell you about my flowers. In the first place I had a sort of a fight with your Mrs. Martin to keep them. She pried right into things when they came, and wanted to know who sent them, and how I came to know you, and she was true to form. She threatened to tell all around the town that you had insulted a guest of hers by scraping acquaintance and daring to give a strange girl flowers. I just couldn't make her understand.

Well, you know how she can talk, and I'm only telling you this because if you should go home, she *might* carry out her threat. I don't want you to think I had anything to do with the story.

I still love my flowers very much. They speak to me of my precious mother. And they remind me of you, my friend of the woods. I have planted them in a little shady corner under some trees, so they will think they are in the woods, and they are growing beautifully. I wish you could see them.

This is a very gay place to which I have come. I don't feel at all at home here. Maybe it will seem better when I get really acquainted.

Please write me again soon, for I'm honestly quite homesick, and somehow you seem like "home folks," perhaps because we've both lost our mothers. Besides, I shall want to know how things come out, whether your "Grand" is getting better, and if you are being allowed to stay with him. I shall be hoping and praying. May God keep you.

Your friend
Margaret

When that letter came, Grand was really getting much better and Revel as he read it over many times thought how he would some day show it to his grandfather, if he got well enough to read it.

The letter gave Revel great comfort, as he read it over every time he got sad and discouraged. It was like a pleasant talk with a friend. And it often comforted him that the little flowers which he had arisen so early to get for Margaret were really growing, and pleasing her.

IT was at breakfast that first morning after her arrival at her aunt's home that Margaret broached the subject of the flowers.

"Aunt Carlotta, I've brought some flowers with me from a place where my mother used to gather them in her old home town. They have roots, and I've been wondering if there is a little shady spot in the yard or garden, where I could plant them. Do you mind?"

Aunt Carlotta looked up from her morning mail and smiled.

"Flowers?" she said absently. "You mean you carted plants all the way across the continent? Oh, my *dear!* How very *silly!* As if we didn't have flowers enough in California, without bringing little uncultivated weeds from a country woods! Yes, of course if you want to, put them out, but they'll never live. It isn't their native climate, you know, and you can't expect them to survive here, especially after a journey like that. Packed up tight. No air!"

"Oh, but they weren't packed tight! They were lying comfortably in a nice tin box, their roots wrapped around with wet moss, and I kept the cover of the box open most of the way, so they had air nearly all day, and of course I set the open box in the window at night. They look quite sprightly this morning, and I would so love to set them out somewhere, where I can attend to them and keep them growing."

"Why, my dear, of course if that will give you pleasure. Go out and look around till you find a suitable place. Would you like the gardener to set them out for you?"

"Oh, thank you, no, Aunt Carlotta. I'll enjoy doing that myself. I'll find some little place under a tree where it is woodsy, and maybe they won't know they've moved." She laughed shyly.

"Dear me!" said the aunt amusedly, "how quaint of you! But what are these flowers that they are so unusual, and demand such personal care?"

"Oh, they are just spring blossoms, anemones and hepaticas and spring beauties. Just the common little wild flowers of mother's home town. She used to tell me about them, how she loved to go to the woods for them, and she described the place to me so well that I went by myself and found them."

Margaret didn't mention the nice boy who had got up early and dug them for her, and then packed them so carefully. She had learned her lesson from Mrs. Martin about telling such things.

"How extraordinary!" said the aunt smiling. "You're a romantic child, aren't you? As I remember it that is like your mother. She used to get me out of all patience when she was a child, being so romantic about things. Birds and squirrels and flowers, you know. Insisting that they had feelings and would be hurt if we were thoughtless with them."

"Yes?" said Margaret smiling dreamily. "Mother always had such beautiful imaginings. That was why I wanted just these flowers from the very place where she used to pick them."

"I see!" smiled the aunt indulgently. "Well, that is a harmless little hobby to follow. Suit yourself about where you want them put, and if you find you need the gardener's help just tell him I told you to ask him. But you know, my dear, soon you'll be so engrossed in swimming and boating and dancing parties that you'll have little time for fussing with plants, and the poor little mites will die a natural death. However, put them where you like and let the poor things have a fighting chance if you think they can weather it."

Margaret gave her aunt a startled wide-eyed glance, and the young eagerness was quietly subdued in her eyes. She was quick to sense the lack of understanding and sympathy in her aunt, and it was a great disappointment. Didn't her aunt used to love her mother dearly? She couldn't quite make it out.

She went out into the yard searching for a place to plant her flowers. She couldn't bear to put them where they would be trampled down, or carelessly uprooted, and finally she found a shady little nook in a corner behind some wide-spreading trees, and planted them carefully. It was not a place where others would likely notice them, and she went and asked the gardener if it would be all right to put them there. He was very helpful, suggesting some rich woods earth he had, and he spaded up a place for her. So the little wild plants found a quiet place where they would not be disturbed, and sometimes their young owner sought refuge among them, when the constant crowd of gay young people wore upon her nerves, and she was sore perplexed about the right and wrong of things.

Somehow in this new world to which she had come, there seemed to be no such thing as right and wrong. If you suggested that it wasn't right to do something the only answer would be, "Who says so? I guess we can do it if we *please* to. Anyway I'm *going* to."

This was the general code of Bailey Wicke, who continued to infest the house at times, until Margaret wished she could run away. It wasn't that she did not like him, so much as that he went against all her inborn principles, and it troubled her greatly to be always saying no to his propositions.

He wanted to do such crazy things. Apparently the whole crowd was ready to do anything that occurred to any one of their wild brains.

But these troubles came slowly, one at a time.

The first clash came just after lunch that first day. Aunt Carlotta had spent most of the morning with her secretary, going through the mailing list of her club, calling out names of those she wanted invited to a certain social event she was planning in the near future, dictating a few letters, and writing the menu lists out for the next week. Meantime Margaret fluttered about the lovely house, examining beautiful pictures, statuary, fine old furniture, and best of all the wonderful old books in soft-toned rare leather bindings.

Then the delicious lunch was served, and as they were getting up from the table Aunt Carlotta remarked, "Well, now, Margaret, suppose you and I get to work. First what do you like to be called, Mag, or Margo, or Marge, or just plain Peggy?"

Margaret looked at her aunt in astonishment thinking this was some new kind of a joke.

"Why, I like my own name, Aunt Carlotta. I prefer to be called Margaret, the name my mother gave me. I've always loved it."

"Yes?" said the aunt with a lifting of her eyebrows. "Well that's odd! A girl that's satisfied with her name! Most of the girls I know have chosen some outlandish nickname."

Margaret smiled wistfully.

"Mother never liked nicknames," she said shyly. "I would rather you called me Margaret."

"Oh, very well," said her aunt, "but I fancy you'll find the young mob changing it pretty soon."

That was the beginning.

Aunt Carlotta took her to her own room, arrayed herself in a charming negligee and then said, from the vantage point of her chaise lounge, "Well, now little girl, I think we'd better get at your wardrobe first. Just what do you need? Tell me all about it."

"Need?" said Margaret, wide-eyed. "Why, I don't think I need anything, thank you. I bought my winter's outfit just before I came away. I think I have everything that I shall have any use for this winter."

"But my dear, you wouldn't be supposed to know just what you need out here. This is a different land, you know, from the small suburban place where you have been attending school for the last two years."

Margaret gave her aunt an astonished look.

"Isn't life about the same everywhere?" she asked gently.

"No, indeed it isn't. And I really don't think a girl of your age would have the experience to select wisely the most useful, and becoming, and the smartest things for a winter here. Besides, little country towns don't ordinarily have very smart goods on display, and of course the customer has to take what they have."

"Oh, Aunt Carlotta, I didn't get my wardrobe in a village. I went to New York to the regular places where mother used to get them. They were quite smart shops, what they call 'exclusive places.' Mother had a friend who owned one of those places. She has two such shops now, on Fifth Avenue, and she advised me what to get. She knew what we liked and she used sometimes to find something abroad with me in mind. She always gave us the benefit of low prices, besides."

Aunt Carlotta opened her eyes wide now, although there was still an incredulous look in them.

"Really? Why, that is quite extraordinary. Suppose you run and get a few of these garments and let me see if I agree with you in your ideas of what is smart."

Margaret gave her a steady look, that had dignity as well in it, and went out of the room. Presently she returned with a few really lovely garments over her arm.

The cold eyes of the aunt surveyed them. She shook them out one by one, examined the material, the cut, the finish.

"Well, they're not bad," she admitted after a moment.

"Awfully conservative of course, but not half bad. What else have you?"

Margaret was trying to smother the anger that she felt rising in her young breast, but she managed to control her voice as she said quietly:

"Would you like to come into my room and look my things over?" She was trying with all her might to keep resentment out of her voice.

"Why, yes, that might not be a bad idea," she said. "Those three dresses you brought in are a good start, but you'll need a lot of other things if you are going to keep up with the other girls here."

"Oh, do I have to?" asked the girl.

"Well, yes, of course you have to, if you want to get on, and be a success."

"What do you mean, a *success*, Aunt Carlotta? I'm not sure I want to try to be a success."

"But you do, of course. That's why I sent for you to come out here. I felt that it was my duty to make you a success. Socially, you know. You've got to be popular, and have loads of invitations, and a gay time, and then in the end you'll be a success. You'll make a brilliant marriage!"

"Oh!" said Margaret aghast, in a tone that was almost like a moan. "But why should I make a brilliant marriage? I don't think I would want to make a brilliant marriage. It doesn't sound like a happy thing, a *brilliant* marriage."

"Nonsense!" said her aunt sharply. "Of course it is a happy thing. A brilliant marriage means that you will have plenty of money and an adoring husband, and can go anywhere and do anything you please. Live on the top of the world, you know. Buy anything you like and have the entree simply *everywhere!* Of course you want to make a brilliant marriage."

"But all those things would not make up for the lack of love," said Margaret thoughtfully.

"What nonsense! Why shouldn't you have love too, you romantic little idiot? Of course you'll have love. You are beautiful, and if you just know how to take care of your beauty, and enhance it, you'll have all the love you want. That's what makes men fall in love with girls, beauty. And dress has a lot to do with your appearance."

The aunt had thrown open the closet door and was looking at Margaret's wardrobe, taking out a dress now and then on its hanger, suveying it and then hanging it back, realizing that Margaret's selections were not only lovely, but surprisingly sophisticated.

"But you haven't any slacks or shorts or pajama suits, and simply *every*body is wearing those now. You won't be in it at all without them. We'll have to attend to that at once."

"No, please, Aunt Carlotta. I don't like those things, and wouldn't want to wear them."

"But that's ridiculous!"

"I'm sorry you feel that way," said Margaret lifting her chin with a grave look in her eyes, "but I really wouldn't care to wear them." She took her dresses and hung them quietly in their places. "Of course if there is any place you wish me to go for which I do not seem to you to be suitably dressed, I can always stay at home."

She said it very quietly, but her aunt, giving a swift glance at her face, was reminded of the gentle firmness of Margaret's mother. She was still for a minute, shutting her own thin lips and flashing her dark eyes. Then she said with a disagreeable little laugh, "Oh, well, if you want to be stubborn of course, there is always that refuge. But I fancy after a little you will learn to do as others are doing."

Silently Margaret hung away the last dress and closed the closet door.

"And now," said her aunt, glancing at her watch, "I think it would be a good idea for us to run down to the beauty parlor. I had a tentative appointment for you this afternoon, and there is plenty of time before people begin to run in for tea time. I want madame to look you over and see just what needs to be done to you."

Margaret had a sudden frenzy of anger rise in her, but she took a deep breath and was silent as her aunt went on.

"There will be your hair and your nails of course, and you'll need a facial, before madame selects the type of powder and rouge for you."

Margaret was standing by the window now, looking off at the great mountains in the distance, and the bright sea spread out on the other hand, trying to gather strength from them before she answered. Then she turned, struggling with the smarting of tears behind her lashes, and smiled sorrowfully at her aunt.

"I'm sorry, Aunt Carlotta, that I'm going to be such a disappointment to you, but I really would rather not go. Those are some more things I would rather not do. I don't like long red nails the way a lot of girls have them, and I don't want to be all made up. I know you think I'm a queer little country girl who doesn't know what the world's people think, but I don't want to be like the world, and I *can't*. If that disappoints you so that you do not want me to stay here with you this winter I can go back to where I was living. I was very happy there, and they liked me the way I was. I came out here to you because you were my mother's sister, and I thought you would be like her. But she would never want me to do these things. And I want to go on being as my mother taught me!"

"But your mother is not on earth now, my dear, and her ideas were far behind the times!"

Margaret was almost in tears now, and her aunt saw that she was not getting on very fast in her attempt to bring about a fashionable change in this sweet natural girl. Suddenly Margaret put her face down in her hands, and let the tears come for a minute.

"Oh, for Heaven's sake!" exclaimed the annoyed aunt, "don't be a cry-baby. If it's so much to you as all that, go on and be old-fashioned. Only if you knew what an impression you are making I'm sure you would change. Especially when one of the best prospects we have in this part of the country is interested in you. I don't suppose you are really matured enough to realize what that means, but I do, and it's more than I could have hoped that you would make a hit with him the first time he saw you."

"What do you mean?" Margaret lifted her tear-stained face and looked in wonder at her aunt.

"Well, I mean Bailey Wicke, if you must know in plain English before you will understand. Don't you know that he is worth millions in his own right, and he'll be of age and come into full ownership within a year and a half?"

Margaret looked at her aunt with a puzzled frown.

"Honestly, Aunt Carlotta, I don't understand what you mean. What has being worth millions got to do with it?"

"Now don't be so naive. You can't be as dumb as that. Does it mean nothing to you that a boy who is rich as Croesus is crazy about you, and you could have him just as easy as turning your hand over?"

"Have him? Oh, Aunt Carlotta. How *dread*ful! You don't really mean that you want me to dress up and try to attract somebody to *marry* me, *now,* when I'm nothing but a little girl! Oh, please don't talk like that. It seems awful to me. I am not thinking of marrying anybody yet, and if I were I certainly wouldn't pick him out!"

"You *wouldn't?* Why, you crazy child! He's handsome as a picture, and every girl in this part of the world is just wild about him. What can you mean? Don't you think he is stunning looking?"

"Why, I suppose he might be called sort of good-looking, but I don't like a 'pretty' boy, do you? He looks like a *sis!* No, I don't admire that kind of looks in a man. I like him to look as if he had some character, and did something in the world besides just play around!"

"But he doesn't *need* to do anything, child. He has enough without it. And think what it would be to be his wife, with all the money you wanted!"

"No, please, I don't want to think of that. I never could

love a man for a reason like that. I *couldn't!* And marriage without love would be terrible. It would be a *sin!*"

"Oh, heavens and earth!" said the aunt, springing to her feet. "You are hopeless! You are the most fantastic piece of fanaticism I ever saw. It is just useless to try to do anything for you if you start out with such abnormal prejudices. You are trying to pattern yourself on what you imagine your mother was like, and you don't seem to know that even when she lived she was considered old-fashioned. You forget entirely that she is dead, and the times are changed. You have simply *got* to live up to the times or you will never get anywhere! Don't you know that?"

Margaret was having a hard time to control the tears again. She felt it was cruel of her aunt to speak that way of her mother but she knew it was useless to argue about it. They simply didn't think alike, that was all. But she was hurt, terribly hurt! It made her feel that her life was worse than useless. Then suddenly she looked up with one of her almost blinding smiles that shone through her tears like a ray of glory, like the sun bursting through black clouds after a storm.

"I think," she said very softly, very tenderly, "that I might get to *Heaven*, even if I am all those things you say!" and there was such a look of sweetness and humility in her eyes that her aunt with suddenly strange reaction, put out impulsive arms and drawing her close kissed her on her sweet lips and on her wet eyes.

"Oh, you quaint funny little thing!" she said, a kind of compunction in her voice. "Well, go on! Try it out and you'll see. You may get to Heaven with those ideas, but you'll have mighty slow going on this earth. And it's on this *earth* we have to live *now anyway*. You can't just walk into Heaven when you want to."

"No—" said the girl wistfully, and sighed.

GRANDFATHER Revel was getting better. There was no question about that. Revel saw it himself in the little gleams here and there, in the look of the tired old eyes, the curve of the wrinkles about the kindly old lips when he smiled, the gradual steadying of the trembling hands. He caught the assurance of it from the light in the nurse's eyes as she administered the morning medicine, and brought a more generous breakfast to tempt the fluctuating appetite. He saw it in the doctor's face, even read it in the sound of his step as he came into the room with more and more confidence. He read it in the sound of his grandfather's voice.

And then one morning, after a thorough examination of the patient the doctor told him in so many words.

"Well, my boy, your Grand is getting well. He's going to get up again and go about with you. And I lay his cure to you. If you hadn't come when he called for you I am sure he would have been gone long before this. He needed *you!*"

"Yes, sir!" said Revel with a clear ring to his voice, "and *I* needed *him!* You don't know, but *I did!* Some day perhaps I'll tell you both about it all."

So there was great joy in the dear old farmhouse by the

roadside, joy that walked softly, and did not presume because of what it had been through. Joy that grew day by day more sweet and precious, as the two who had been separated so long grew into a closer and closer fellowship, youth and age together under a shining glory that was life to both their souls.

The doctor was coming less and less often now, sometimes staying away for several days at a time, and the nurse was only staying by courtesy to "get a bit of rest," and keep her eye on the two to be sure her patient didn't overdo.

And then one day in middle summer, when the old man was feeling stronger, and said he'd like to go out and plant a field or something, they began to talk.

"Suppose you tell me a little more about things, boy," said the old man. "You came here under what conditions at home?"

"Well," said Revel thoughtfully, "my dad had just told me he was getting married again, and I saw red. I had to go *some*where and if you hadn't sent for me I don't know what I would have done. I'm sure I wouldn't have stayed at home, anyway."

"Yes?" said the old man after a long pause. "That was to have been expected though, in the natural order of things. Were you sure you were right to come away?"

"Absolutely."

Another pause. Then, "What effect did your action have at home?"

"Well, you see, I left while he was away. When he got home he found my note and he was very angry and ordered me home. I said I couldn't leave you then. He threatened to disinherit me, and he wouldn't support me, nor pay for my education if I didn't come at once. You were so sick then I couldn't even take time to think about that, so after a few days I wrote and told him to talk to the lady he was marrying about that, and ask her if it wasn't better for me to stay away."

"Yes?" There was the semblance of a grin about the old lips then. "And what was his answer to that?"

"A wedding announcement! And yesterday an order to go to the college he has selected for me to attend and make arrangements at once about taking entrance examinations."

"You didn't do it?"

"No, sir."

"Why not?"

"Because I don't mean to go to that college. I never did want to. I'll tell you my reasons later. It's a long story. But I thought perhaps pretty soon you would be able to let me talk it over with you. I would like to go to some college close by if I can get in. Is the one my mother attended possible?"

A light grew in the old eyes, as he nodded emphatically.

"Grand, I thought perhaps there would be a way I could work my way there!" went on the boy. "I'd rather do that than have my father pay for something he doesn't like. In fact he wouldn't, of course. He would put his foot down good and hard and *command* that I should obey him."

"What would your father say to your going to our college?" asked the old man after a minute of thoughtfulness.

"Oh, he wouldn't like it. But I'm not sure he would stop me. He's a great one for saving, and perhaps he would think it would make me independent. But my strongest bet is the lady. I don't think she wants me around, any more than I want to be near her, and naturally she'd be willing to save their money, and not spend it on me."

The old grin deepened again.

"You have anything to prove that theory, Revel? Or is that just a clever hunch?"

"I don't know about the cleverness, but I guess it's all hunch. I haven't any 'clippin's to prove it.' "

"Well, that's a clever guess," said the old man.

There was silence for quite a few minutes while the two

sat thoughtfully staring into the summer day, and then the old man spoke.

"Revel, my boy, when you were born I thought the matter over carefully, and finally I entered your name in that college you speak of, the college that is over beyond Linwood here. I knew it was a good sound college scholastically, and that it had a firm Christian faith behind it. I always was a great believer in small institutions of learning. I felt that it was a healthier atmosphere in which to study, and to form a young mind, than a great big overgrown institution where there were so many students that the scholar never had personal contacts with his teachers. So on that I made my decision. Of course I knew your father was a man of very strong will, and that he would not be likely to make any of his decisions to please me, or because of my advice. In fact I was sure the very opposite was true. And it was altogether likely that my plans would never be possible to carry out. But I knew that time brings changes, and there are always possibilities. So I began to pray for you, boy, that you might be led in the right way. Also, I began to put by, year by year, a little money into the bank, stipulating that it was for your college expenses should you be allowed to come to this college, or should other need arise for you to use it. I have taken great pleasure in accumulating that money. I saved it a little at a time when things with me were going hard, and always I felt that somehow it might be made to benefit you. The money is there in the bank now, Revel, and if you want to use it, or are permitted to use it, I shall be very glad. It is not a great sum. There will be more, not a large fortune, but more to give you when you are of age, and some more when I am gone. You will not be wealthy, but you will not suffer. But the college money is yours now, my boy, if you will accept it. It would give me great joy to have you here, near me, during my remaining days of course, but you must not be guided by my wishes. You must do what you think is the *right thing* to do. And of course till you are of age, what you are *allowed* to do."

It was very still out there on the broad piazza where they were sitting. The great pine trees down by the white gate were whispering and nodding to one another about it, the birds interpolating a sharp sweet note of persuasion now and again, and a snappy little chipmunk chattering antagonistically to represent the other side of the family.

It was a very precious picture, those two sitting there, heaven and earth holding their breath about the great decision. There was the humble offering of the dear old man whose latter years had taken their joy from saving this gift that he had not been sure might ever be given, and there was the lad with the light of youth and wonder in his eyes.

And there was something else. Revel got quietly up and went and knelt beside his grandfather's chair.

"Grand," he said, and his voice was husky with feeling, "can I ever thank you enough for this wonderful thought of me, before ever I was old enough to know you, while I was still carelessly going through my days without forethought or knowledge! Oh, I thank you, Grand! Yes, of course I'll take it, if it is not robbing you, and try to be worthy of the education you have planned for me."

He was still a minute, and then, lifting his head and looking earnestly into the old man's eyes, he said:

"I guess you understand, Grand, how I've felt about my father. I don't think he cares about me except to have me do what people will think is the right thing for a son of his to do. But I'd do what he wanted me to if I thought it was right, even if I hated it. I'd have even stayed there and endured having another person come to take mother's place, if I thought it was right, though I was very bitter about it. But mother taught me that, and I can't go back on her."

He was still a minute, with the old hand on his head, and then he went on again:

"But Grand, there's something else, something I haven't

told you. I went to the woods that night dad told me about getting married. I was there alone. It was almost dark. I thought nobody would see me, and I was *bawling*. And then I heard a step. I looked up and there was a *girl!* A strange girl I didn't know! She apologized and was going away, but asked if there was anything she could do for me, and I like a fool blurted out what was the matter. She was swell. She told me not to worry, she would forget it, and she told me to tell God about my trouble. Not to do anything till I had told Him. So that night when I went home I knelt down and asked God to show me what to do. And—the next day, your letter came! Then I knew God had made a way for me. And—Grand—I guess maybe He's keeping on making a way. Thanks awfully, Grand. Of course I'll take your gift. It was swell of you to plan for me."

And then, after a minute, with his face against the older hand he added:

"I have a hunch my mother is glad now."

There were tears on the old man's face, like dewdrops in the sunshine, as he smiled, and something like a natural surge of love went through the boy's heart. A minute later, he spoke again.

"Boy! I've got a *family* at last!"

That afternoon Grand took a long nap, with the nurse keeping it very still all about, so that even the birds and the katydids put the mute on their conversation. For Revel was taking a long walk over to Linwood College. He was carrying a note that Grand had written, introducing him, and he went to find out just what entrance requirements he would have to have.

But the old man was doing more than napping while he was gone. He was lying on his bed, it is true, and his eyes were closed. His pulse was going steadily, for the nurse tested it after he had been still for a little while. But Grand was praying for his boy, thanking God that Revel had turned out to be what he was.

Revel was fortunate to find the president and several of the professors at leisure, and he had a long talk with each. When he walked back with the promise of sunset in the sky, the thrushes were spilling their evening songs about among the tree tops, and there seemed to be joy in the air. Revel looked up to the glory of the rosy sky and smiled. And suddenly he thought of Margaret, and wished she were there that he might tell her all the professors had said, and how the old president told him that he looked like his mother, that that was the nicest thing he knew to say.

"Oh, dear God, don't let my father barge in and spoil all this happiness, please!" he prayed quietly in his heart.

He came in with bird songs all about his head. The old man watched him from the big chair on the piazza where the nurse had established him, in time to watch his grandson arriving down the road.

"It's all right, isn't it boy?" said the eager old voice as Revel came up the steps.

"Yes, Grand, it's all okay. Say, but they're a fine lot of people. Yes, Dr. Anderson was there, and his brother Will Anderson, and they were *rare.* Then he brought Prof. Gunnison, and Prof. Fairley and I like them too. Yes, they sat me down and asked me a lot of questions, a regular quiz it was. First they wanted to know how far I'd gone in math and Latin and all that stuff, you know, and what my standing was. And when they heard I was exempt in all of my studies I could see they were really interested. They said they would write the high school and see whether I could be given a diploma, but in any case they require entrance exams and they feel it would all be okay. They lifted their shaggy eyebrows and nodded at one another, and Doc Anderson said to his brother 'He's like his mother, isn't he?' Boy! That made me feel good!"

The grandfather smiled happily. It was what he had dreamed and hoped, a little, yet had feared would never happen.

And presently the watching nurse, who had a great deal of romantic common sense, arrived with a tray with supper for two, and set it out on the porch table between their two chairs, which she had made sure were in place before Revel had even returned.

So they had a beautiful little supper there, with the thrushes spilling their liquid notes all about them, the evening stealing softly down, and a throaty cricket putting in a cheerful note now and then. The end of a very happy day for Revel.

That night he wrote a letter to his father, for he still was fearful that something might stop his happy prospect. His father would of course be very angry at having his plans frustrated, would likely resent anything his grandfather was doing for him. In fact his grandfather had told him not to say anything about the college fund, merely to tell his father he had made arrangements for his tuition, and his grandfather was helping him out a little, what he couldn't do himself. Somehow the old man, in view of past experiences with his son-in-law, was pretty sure that Revel's father would do his best to get the boy away from his influence if he suspected that he had presumed to arrange as he had about his education. Mr. Revel was a wise old man, and a patient one, and he would not encourage the fear and distrust already in the boy's heart for his father, much as it might have been justified.

So Revel wrote.

Dad:

I've been having a talk with the doctor, and it seems important that I should remain here at least for the present. Grand is better, able to sit up a little. Still has to be very careful. He seems very happy at having me here.

Dad, I'm all kinds of sorry to disappoint you in your plans for my college, but it seems right that I should stay here for a while at least. So this afternoon I walked over to Linwood College and arranged to take my entrance examinations tomorrow. I like the president and the professors I met, and as it is an accredited college I am sure it will do for the present. Later, if it seems best, I can of course be transferred elsewhere. But, dad, this won't cost you anything. I have arranged to take care of all this myself, and Grand is helping me out. I am to board with him of course, and the college is near enough so that I can walk in pleasant weather, and there is a bus near-by.

Please present my apologies to your wife for not being home when she came, but I am sure she will agree with me that I have done the right thing, and that you will both be happier for it.

Hoping you will agree.

Your son

After that letter was dispatched Revel felt like one who has burned his bridges behind him, and wondered what might be coming next.

For several days he waited, watching every mail breathlessly, but went about his plans, nevertheless. He took his examinations when he no longer had hanging over him the possibility of a father barging angrily in to question his teachers minutely. He realized that he had all through the years been nervous about anything that was connected with marks and records that would be sent home. And now that he had actually taken the initiative and made decisions of his own he felt so much more free, and at ease. It was probably a matter of nerves, and he ought to have controlled them better in the past of course, and not have allowed himself so to dread the outbreaks of anger and questionings that were sure to come if ever there was a mark that was less than perfect. At least that was what his mother used to tell him.

One day President Anderson came over in his car to call on Mr. Revel who was an old friend of his. He took him and his grandson out for a ride, and Revel began to feel quite as if he belonged to the new future which he was trying to work out for himself.

Finally, at his grandfather's suggestion, Revel wrote to his father again. The letter was brief and to the point:

> Dad: I thought I should let you know that I passed all my examinations and am entered as a student in Linwood College. As ever your son.

And still it was several days before any response came. But when it came it was just what might have been expected.

> Am not surprised at your headstrong decision. Have it your own way. But let me warn you that when you fail, and come crawling back to be helped out, you will find no help. You are *on your own,* absolutely. Now take the consequences!

Surprisingly, when Revel read this heartless letter tears sprang stinging into his eyes. Of course he had not done what his father told him to do, and he had not expected sympathy nor interest, and yet, perhaps he had unconsciously been looking for a little commendation at least. Some fathers would have been proud at what their sons had done, even if it wasn't their own choice. Revel took the letter and showed it to his grandfather. The old man read, and then looked up with a sympathetic smile as he said: "Well, there's your challenge, boy. Now do your best."

12

IT was an all-day meeting of the Ladies' Aid in the Sumter Hills Trinity Church, and Sarah Martin was parceling out the sewing to be done. They were making an outfit for a poor family whose father had recently been killed in a mine disaster. Mrs. Martin was also largely director of conversation.

"There, Mrs. Apsley, you better take this dress and sew up the seams. I know that seam where the goods had to be pieced in the front breadth don't quite match the plaids, but it can't be helped. That's all the goods there was in that piece and it *had* to do. Besides, a mine-child wouldn't likely mind that. Anyway she ought to be glad to get something to cover her. Frizzie Cutler, you oughtta reinforce those buttonholes you're making in that petticoat. A child'll tear 'em out in no time, and I don't want it to get out that Sumter Church doesn't do reliable work. You know those people that get something for nothing are awfully critical. We have to be careful for we have the best reputation for sewing in the country."

"Say, Mrs. Martin, how much hem did you allow for this little pink dress? One inch? Don't you think that's rather scant?" asked Mrs. Osborne anxiously.

"That's plenty!" said Mrs. Martin crisply. "You know

these days when we ought to economize. One inch is *plenty*."

"Say, Mrs. Martin, are you sure the minister's wife won't object to that? I heard her say all children's dresses ought to have a deep hem for letting down. She said that was true economy," said Minnie Marlin with a worried look.

Mrs. Martin's lips pursed thinly.

"Well, if Mrs. Castor wants to dictate about hems she better be on hand when the work is being done. If you ask me I think it's rather late for the minister's wife to come to an all-day meeting. It's almost time for lunch and she's not here yet. Of course she's rather new here, only been in the parsonage four months, but that's not long enough for her to dictate. Not about hems, anyway, especially when the material wasn't donated by her."

"Why, she's got a sick child. Didn't you know it, Sallie Martin? She's probably got her hands full without trying to get here at all," said Mrs. Bowen.

"Yes, I know it. That smallest child of hers is *always* sick," said Mrs. Martin. "If you ask me I think she's just a spoiled baby, always demanding her mother."

"Shhhh!" said Mrs. Green. "Here comes the oldest daughter. Her mother's likely sent her in to take her place."

"Take her place! Humph!" said Mrs. Martin. "That little high school whiffet take the place of a minister's wife? Well, not if the minister's wife herself was the right kind of a woman, she *couldn't*."

"Sh! She's coming in, I tell you!" said Mrs. Green.

Rose Castor entered sweetly, breezily, carrying a large platter covered with a napkin.

"Good morning, ladies. Mother sent me over with these hot biscuits. She said you were to sit right down and eat them now, that she'd be over in a minute or two."

"Oh!" said Mrs. Martin with a somewhat mollified air. "Well, that's nice. I suppose we can appreciate the biscuits even if we don't appreciate her being away all the morning, and *work* here to be done."

Rose's cheeks were the color of her name.

"Oh," she said, her sensitive lips quivering, "mother was sorry not to be here. She had to stay and wait for a telephone call for father from New York about the arrangements for a funeral. And he had to go to the Tanner funeral this morning, you know."

"Oh! Was *that* it? Well, of course that couldn't be helped," said Mrs. Martin in a conciliatory tone.

Rose went on into the church kitchen and put the biscuits where they would keep warm, and when she came out she was talking with Mrs. Green's daughter Luella who had been making the coffee for the lunch which was soon to be served.

"And oh, Luella, I forgot to tell you!" said Rose. "I heard the nicest thing about Revel Radcliffe. You know he went away to be with his dying grandfather, and now the grandfather is getting well, but Revel is staying on with him, and has entered Linwood College."

"You don't mean it!" exclaimed Luella Green eagerly. "Isn't that perfectly grand for Revel! You know how he used to say he didn't want to go the University, he wanted to go to a smaller college."

"Revel *Radcliffe!*" exclaimed Mrs. Martin, swinging around on the two girls. "You don't mean to say that two respectable girls like you have any acquaintance with a young reprobate like that Radcliffe fellow. Why, he's a young *bum*, and nothing else. He's heading to be a gangster I'm sure. I certainly am surprised that you know him. Of course the minister's daughter hasn't been here long enough to be expected to know, but *you*, Luella, you certainly have no excuse like that!"

"Why, Mrs. *Martin!*" said Luella in astonishment. "What can you mean? Revel Radcliffe was in my class in high school, and he was a perfectly grand student. He led the whole class, and he was even exempt from examination in every one of his studies!"

"I know nothing about his scholastic abilities," said Mrs. Martin severely, "it is his morals of which I am speaking. The rudest, most unprincipled boy I ever knew. A boy that would actually dishonor his own noble father by refusing to be called by his name, and taking instead the name of his mother's family! A boy that would deliberately absent himself from his own father's wedding! No one could know those two things about him and *not* know that he was un-principled, even if there were no other things against him. I happen to know several! He is dishonest and rude in the ex-treme."

"Why, Mrs. Martin!" exclaimed the two girls in chorus, "how can you talk that way about him? Why he always had an A in deportment."

"Yes? Well you may be sure it was a hypocritical A then, to hide other things. I have no doubt that he is quite slick in getting around his teachers. But *I* happen to *know!* You see it was on my own property that he was poaching, catching fish, and actually daring to go by the house carrying them away. I *saw* him *myself,* and when I charged him with it he tried to lie out of it. And here, just recently, he was very rude to a young girl who was visiting in my home for a few hours. He picked an acquaintance with her up near the woods some-where, when she was all alone and no one about to protect her, and he actually presumed upon that acquaintance to send her a lot of flowers, *weeds* they really were, just nothing short of an insult it was. I tried to get her to let me send them back with a fitting note, but she was so kind-hearted that she wouldn't let me, and she actually took them with her! But I have never forgiven him for insulting her in that way. A guest in my home! And such a sweet charming girl, so unsuspecting that anything was wrong."

"Oh," said Mrs. Hopkins who lived up the road on the way to the woods, "was that the little girl I saw walking down the hill past my house with a boy when it was almost *dark?* I *won*dered. And do you say that Radcliffe boy actually chased her and picked up an acquaintance with her. At *dark?* Oh, my dear! How un*for*tunate! Who was she, anyway? She had a very attractive way with her, and she seemed to like his company well enough, for she was smiling up into his face as they went by my house. I guess he's the kind of boy who gets acquainted with strange girls very easily, isn't he? He looks like a boy who is sweet on all girls."

Suddenly Luella Green spoke:

"Mrs. Hopkins, Revel Radcliffe is *not* that kind of a boy in the *least*. He never had anything at all to do with girls. He never went to dances, nor took girls to movies and things, nor even went walking with them. And *we know,* for we were in the same class with him, and I at least have been going to the same school and in the same room with him ever since we were in kindergarten. He never *looks* at a girl if he can help it, except to be extremely polite to them when it is necessary."

"Oh," said Mrs. Martin, fixing Luella with a pale cold eye, "I suppose you mean he never gave *you* any attention! Is that it?"

"And yet he looked at *this* girl who was Mrs. Martin's guest," put in Mrs. Hopkins in a nastily significant tone.

"Well," said Luella with a grim look at Rose, "I'm certainy glad I'm not old enough to belong to the Ladies' Aid! I never heard such mean cruel gossiping tongues in my life. I thought you all pretended to be Christians! Come on, Rose, let's get out of here!" and they went out the side way and slammed the door.

"Hoity-toity!" said Mrs. Hopkins. "They must both be in love with him! And one of them is our minister's daughter! Imagine *that!*"

"So, *there,* you can see what kind of a boy he is!" said Mrs. Martin with a significant nod to her audience.

"I wonder," said Mrs. Hopkins, taking a pin from her mouth and sticking it in the back hem of the petticoat to mark the next buttonhole, "I wonder if our minister's wife knows what kind of a boy her lovely daughter is going with. Rose is *so* sweet!"

"Hush! There comes Mrs. Castor now!"

"Well," said Mrs. Hopkins defiantly, "what's the difference? Somebody really *ought* to tell her, anyway, don't you think?" And then all those women settled back to a dead silence as the minister's wife entered the Ladies' Parlor.

"Why, I thought you'd be already at the table. I told Rose to tell you to be sure to sit right down and eat those biscuits while they were hot," she said. "They're not so good when they begin to get cold!" Then those women lifted cold critical glances, and laying aside their sewing arose as one woman.

"We were waiting *for you,* of course," said Mrs. Martin who considered herself the acknowledged spokeswoman of the company, and she led the way down the stair into the basement dining room.

It was only a few days after that that Revel Radcliffe, a good many hundred miles away, coming out from an afternoon class during his first week of college was approached by a couple of seniors, still strangers to him.

"Hi, there, Radcliffe!" one said. "How about coming to one of the meetings of our Fellowship tonight and seeing if you'd like to join us?"

Revel turned and met the cordial glances of the two seniors whom he had noticed afar.

"What kind of a group?" he asked. "What's the idea?"

"Come and see," smiled the tallest man whose name was Jim Gray, and who introduced his companion as Bill Pentecost. "We'll meet at seven o'clock in the first class room to the right of the Assembly Hall. We'd like you to come among us and see if you feel that you belong."

"I'll come," said Revel with a smile. "I may not be able to join whatever you have, because my time belongs first to my grandfather, who has been very sick, but I'll try you out anyway."

And so Revel went to the first meeting and found it was a

group of students who met each week for a few minutes of prayer and Bible reading. It was something new to Revel, and he talked it over with his grandfather when he got home, who promptly suggested that Revel invite them to meet at his house for their next meeting, taking a whole evening to it to get acquainted if they liked. And so in a few weeks, this group grew to center their interests around the old farmhouse, where the few minutes of prayer and Bible reading blossomed into an occasional whole evening, with some doughnuts to top off before they went back to college. Life began to open up to Revel in a richer fuller way. Surprised indeed would some of the women of the Ladies' Aid in Sumter Hills have been if the next time they talked over Revel Radcliffe and his misdeeds, they could have been gifted with television, could have looked into the big farmhouse living room and seen the subject of their subdued whispers, kneeling with the rest around the great open fire, and praying! Revel Radcliffe was learning really to pray! But, would that have meant anything to Mrs. Martin and her group?

That night after the pleasant company were gone quietly back to college with the hush of the hour of prayer upon them, Revel wrote another letter to Margaret. He found he was thinking a great deal about her in these busy days, in spite of all he had to do. She had come to seem so much a companion of his thoughts that he wanted to tell her of the sweet experience he had had that night.

Dear Margaret:

I haven't written you sooner because a lot of things have been happening, and I've been pretty busy, but I've thought about you a lot and been wanting to tell you.

In the first place Grand is better. He is able to sit up now, and even walk a few steps from his bed to his chair. The doctor is still careful with him. That makes me very glad. He is a swell companion.

Next, my father got married two weeks after I met you. He had telegraphed me to come back, and I said I couldn't, not yet, anyway, it might make Grand worse, and his next word was an engraved announcement of the marriage!

Next, I'm a student in Linwood College, going strong and I like it fine.

When Grand got well enough to talk I told him dad had sent for me to go to the University, but I didn't want to go. I asked him if the college where mother went wasn't for men as well as girls, and did he think I stood a chance of getting in and getting a part-time job somewhere so I could work my way through.

Grand just smiled and said that he had entered my name there when I was born, hoping there might be a chance I would want to go there, though he knew pretty well my dad wouldn't favor it. He said there would be no trouble about my entrance. He could fix that, and then he told me that when I was born he began putting little sums of money in the bank for my education, and it was there in the bank ready for me if I wanted it.

Well, I went right over to the college that day and arranged to take entrance examinations. Then I came home and wrote my dad. I couldn't leave Grand yet so I had entered Linwood College, arranged for my entrance exams, and it wouldn't cost him a cent. Grand was going to help me some but I was on my own.

Well, dad didn't like it of course, but he just warned me that when I got stuck and wanted help I wouldn't get it. I think maybe his wife didn't care for my coming home. But anyhow that's how it is, and I'm here, and in the college, and I like it fine. So far dad hasn't done anything about it. And that's because of your prayers I'm sure, because mine had very little faith behind them. I've learned that faith is something you need when you pray, and I'm getting more of it every day. You couldn't be around Grand and not see Faith, and what it does.

But there's something else around this college you would like. I never heard of it before in a college, but it's swell. They call it a Fellowship, and they meet every week to study the Bible and pray. It's not a part of the curriculum, it's a thing the students got up, and I like it a lot. They are swell fellows in it, and they really mean what they say.

Grand likes it too, and he's invited them to meet here at the house real often. We have a big fire in the fireplace. Grand comes to the meetings too; they asked him. He just sits quietly, and now and then he prays. He's a great guy. I wish you knew him.

They tell me the girls have such a group in the college, too, and are doing good work among the students, all on the quiet. So you see I am beginning to learn how to really pray, and to know the rules. It seems there are a lot of rules in the Bible to show how to be sure of an answer. Here's the one we learned tonight. "Delight thyself also in the Lord, and He shall give thee the desires of thine heart." That sounds like a pretty good one to try. I think Grand does that one well.

Grand is being great to the fellows and they like him a lot.

Boy! I never thought I'd get a college like this one. Am I thankful to God for fixing things this way for me, and I hope He lets them stay so. You know, it's an education in itself just to live with Grand.

I'm sorry if you don't feel happy out there. But perhaps by now it's getting all right. I think you ought to have the nicest kind of a home. I hope it gets better every day. I wish you could have it as fine as I have. Maybe God will fix things for you some day. I'll pray about it for you. You ought to have things pleasant, you're so kind yourself, but I'm sure I never rated what has come to me.

Now I've got to stop and do some boning for my morning class, but I'm all kinds of glad you are willing to be my friend and let me talk to you sometimes.

I'll be letting you know if anything new turns up.

Yours,
Revel

He paused as he signed his name, and had an odd little impulse to put one of those little rings his mother used to make for him on his grandfather's letters when he was a little kid, and call them kisses. And then he used to solemnly stoop and press a kiss on the paper. He wanted to do that now. *Sap!* He'd better get to work and forget this silly business. He was just lonely, that was all, and Margaret reminded him of his mother, the way she talked and thought about things.

13

THE winter that followed was one of unmitigated joy to Revel. As he grew daily into the heart of his grandfather, and they companioned together, he felt that he had never been so happy except when his mother was living. And even then he was daily distressed because he knew that she was unhappy. His father had contrived to keep the household in a ferment whenever he was in it, and to keep his hand upon every thing connected with their lives, overruling all their plans and desires and bringing disappointment into every day. But now he not only was relieved of that constant unhappy espionage, but he had the added joy of his grandfather's companionship.

Also, he was growing in the knowledge of the Lord, and of his Bible, and that meant a great deal to him. So that, with the exception of occasional fears that would arise lest his father might suddenly spoil all this, Revel was very happy.

On the other hand, Margaret Weldon was most ill at ease. She was as unhappy in her new life as such a sunny nature as hers well could be.

Aunt Carlotta, though yielding gracefully where she saw she could not conquer immediately, was nevertheless just as much on the warpath, determined to make this niece of hers just as much like all the other nieces about her in the world as could be, and this attitude did not make for peace.

They would be preparing to go out together to some concert or evening entertainment, and Margaret, though the evening's program was seldom of her choosing, would come down obediently, dressed for the occasion charmingly, and would be met by her aunt's cold critical glance. Aunt Carlotta said no more about the matters of dress that they had discussed, but Margaret felt the look of her criticism in her eyes almost as if it had been in words. Aunt Carlotta knew she was dealing with a very sensitive nature, and confidently expected to win by this silent steady look of disapproval. The girl felt it was very hard to bear. It wore on her young nerves like salt in a wound.

Oh, they differed on so many things. On dress, on smoking and drinking, on amusements. But most of all they differed about Bailey Wicke. Aunt Carlotta had quite set her heart on making sure of the Wicke millions for her niece, and Margaret didn't enjoy the young man's company in the least. Neither did she like the idea of being parceled out to anybody as if she were a possession. She had thoughts of love and marriage in life, and not in trying to find a life companion. She was still little-girl enough to want to put off the day of grown-up things, and to desire to remain young awhile longer, learning and enjoying, not scheming for the future. It seemed a sordid thing to do, and repelled her rather than interesting her. She loved nature, liked to take long walks and see new sights, loved exercise of all sorts, and was quite proficient in many simple things. She liked housework, too, but there was none of that to be had in her aunt's quite perfect bungalow. There were servants to perform all those menial tasks.

Margaret loved to read and study, but there seemed so little opportunity. There was always a bunch of giddy young people around, most of them utterly uncongenial to her.

They seldom read anything but a movie magazine, and they never studied, not if they could help it. And most of them could. Margaret suspected strongly that the real reason they made much of her was in order to enjoy as much as possible of her aunt's generous hospitality.

As the summer drew to a close, and the fall was coming on, the school that Margaret had hoped to find was not forthcoming, not in the community where her aunt lived. There were a couple of "finishing" schools near by, fashionable schools where the wealthy girls went, taking dancing lessons and riding lessons and studying French and a smattering of other things. And there was a high school. But Margaret had finished high school before she came away, that is all but graduating. She had done some extra work in the spring, having in mind her migration to the west, and had certificates that would stand her in place of a diploma, and help her in college entrance, so there would be no advantage in going back over her high school work.

"But why should you *want* to go to school any more, my dear?" asked her aunt when Margaret would question her about colleges. "It seems to me your brains are pretty well stocked with all the information you'll need. And college courses are very expensive, aren't they? I don't believe I'd waste my time and money that way. It really isn't so awfully necessary nowadays, do you think? I mean, you'll easily be considered smart without it. And you'll find this place is very lively in the winter. Even if there were a college here you wouldn't have much time to study seriously after the season opens."

Margaret looked at her in utter dismay, and was thankful in her heart that Aunt Carlotta was not her guardian, and had no legal jurisdiction over her actions. Her real guardian was an elderly friend of her father's, who took care of her very small heritage, and sent her a remittance from time to time. Otherwise he was a kind adviser merely, feeling that she was wise enough generally to arrange her own life as she wanted it. He was always willing to help or advise if she asked it, which she seldom did. She could see from her summer's experience how different her life would be if he were like her aunt.

For Aunt Carlotta did not seem in the least troubled that the girl was not in school and had no plans for her winter except to stay with her and have a gay time. For her own pride's sake she wanted her niece to be what she called "a success," socially, and she was happy indeed that Margaret should be in receipt almost daily of gay invitations to house parties, and also little affairs here and there. But they all involved a letting down of certain standards that her mother had taught her and her conscience approved, or else the alternative of sitting as a wallflower and getting a lot of criticism and plenty of sneers. She didn't mind the criticism nor the sneers so much, but she felt that she should not be there. She did not belong among such things.

As often as she could she found some excuse to stay away from some festivity but every time she refused an invitation she had her aunt to deal with, and the days grew more and more uncomfortable.

She did not enjoy being with people who drank so much they were stupid and silly. She did not enjoy being laughed at for refusing cocktails, and yet she was again and again thrust into a situation where there was no avoiding it.

There were plenty of nice pleasant girls and boys among the crowd that infested her aunt's house, but they were all tied up in the same activities, and not one of them seemed to be interested in breaking away from the rest and doing something really worth while. Margaret tried them all out, one by one, and found they were thoroughly intrigued by the life they were living, and had no desire for higher things. Even their conversation was of silly doings. They knew all the night clubs and the movie stars. They could talk of the last plays, but they did not care whether they read any books or not, and they were always rushing off to see a horse race, or taking chances in some questionable operation.

Some of the girls were a little jealous of her because the young millionaire was so attentive to her, and her greatest distress was that the young man Bailey Wicke continued to consider her as his exclusive property, and would come over sometimes in the morning and just park at the house, encouraged to the limit by Aunt Carlotta who apparently was very fond of him.

Margaret would avoid him as long as she could, staying in her room till a late hour, or running away to see some one of the girls sometimes, but it could not be done all the time without bringing down condemnation from Aunt Carlotta. A young man worth millions, it seemed, could not be avoided.

Sometimes he would demand that she play tennis all the morning. Well, that wasn't bad if he would only play, instead of mooning around in the summer house, or on the rustic benches, talking and flirting, saying nothings, about the beauty of her eyes, and the power of her voice over his heart to stir it to unbelievable depths, things that Margaret abominated. She always strove to get some other girls to be around when he came, but somehow that did no good for he managed to drive them away before another day and have the field to himself again. He spent a great deal of time in trying to coax her to go off dancing, to night clubs and various places that Margaret did not like nor approve, and sometimes she was almost in tears before she would finally get rid of him.

So one day she took advantage of a drive to the city offered by a friend who was going shopping, and while the friend shopped she went to the university and inquired into things. She reasoned that if Revel could arrange to work his way through a college perhaps she could, and so get away from her present environment, and not be losing this time entirely.

She found that there were classes she could enter, at a rate not too enormous for her modest pocketbook.

She had carried with her a letter from her high school superintendent, and certificates of the work she had been doing, and was most fortunate in finding the dean in his office, and a pleasant reception. He allowed her to take one important examination at once, and gave her assurance that if she passed the test they would welcome her into the university.

She went back to her aunt's that night and told them what she had done. Bailey Wicke was there as usual, and several of the other girls and boys, and she told it very casually in answer to her aunt's question about where she had been that day.

"Why, I went to the university and took an entrance examination," she said. "I have to go in day after tomorrow for another, and two more next week, and if I pass I'm entering the university for regular work the first of the month."

The room was very still for a moment and then a great uproar of protest broke forth.

"Why, my *dear!*" said her aunt quite severely, "I certainly don't approve of that at all! That's ab*surd!* You haven't time for studies. This is going to be a gay winter and you won't be able to study here with all that will be going on."

"Oh," said Margaret quietly, "*I* shall not be here. I have selected a room in the dormitory, and I expect to do a lot of hard work. You know I came out here to go to school!"

"Like fun you did!" said Bailey Wicke suddenly rising up and stalking over to stand in front of her. "You came out here to marry me, and you're going to do that little thing just as soon as I come of age and come into my property. That won't be long now. And I don't want you educated! I don't care for awfully educated women. They think they know too much and they're hard to get along with. I like you better the way you are. You make a good appearance, and you talk as well as anybody, and that's all that's necessary for *my wife!* A wife as rich as you'll be won't have any need to know a whole lot. You'd be foolish to spend time in *learning.* You can have more fun without it, and I don't approve of it. No sir! We can have a better time without any more schooling. And believe me we are going to have the time of our life when we get married, so cut that idea out and don't speak of it again."

The other girls looked at him in astonishment, and caught their breath softly, but Margaret just laughed merrily.

"Oh Bailey!" she said gaily, "how funny you are! Who crowned you? I never had the slightest intention of marrying you, so get *that* thoroughly out of your head, and don't mention it again. I wouldn't marry you if you were the last bridegroom left in the world. Besides, I don't want to get married! I'd rather have an education!"

But Bailey paid no heed to her. He went on declaiming against education. He said *he* hadn't been to college, and didn't intend to go, it was far too much trouble, and why should he? And besides, Margaret knew enough now.

"There's not a thing in the world you need to learn," he said arrogantly, "except how to use make-up, and how to get a little more peppy clothes. Oh, yes, and how to dance. But I'm going to teach you that myself. We'll begin tomorrow evening."

"Oh *yes?*" said Margaret, still laughing, "well, you've got another guess coming. I have other plans for tomorrow evening."

The other girls stared at her that she could so coolly turn down that sweeping proposal of marriage, even though only in fun, even though it was publicly made. Not one of them would have said no to those millions.

Aunt Carlotta regarded her with cold disfavor, and prepared to give her niece a severe lecture after the others were gone, but Margaret was suddenly feeling the freedom of having taken the initiative in this matter and smiled gaily on, saying bright nothings and being her own sunny self, as she hadn't been during the last troubled days.

While the ices and drinks were being brought in she

slipped away for a few minutes to her aunt's telephone and
sent a day letter to her guardian in the east.

> Have entered university here. Need several hundred
> dollars immediately. Please see check is honored when
> it comes. Don't worry. Being very careful. Sure this is
> wise. Thanks.

> Margaret

Having dispatched her telegram she ran back again and
arrived on the scene just in time to be presented with a glass
of ginger ale by Bailey, while he lifted a glass of champagne
and said with a flourish: "To my future wife!"

Margaret stared at him a second and them broke into a
smile of mischief.

"Oh, *lovely!*" she cried. "I hope she'll be a beautiful
blonde with golden curls and eyes like star sapphires." And
then amid the loud laughter that followed Margaret drained
her glass to the last drop, tossing back her own dark hair, and
twinkling her dark eyes at the discomfited Bailey.

She was gay as a bird all the next day, helping her aunt to
prepare for a bridge luncheon that was on her program, and
there was no time till late that night for the lecture that Aunt
Carlotta had meant to give her.

By that time Margaret had received assurance from her
guardian that the money for her matriculation at the university would be forthcoming, when wanted, and she was happy as a lark.

She was glad that she had arranged for the examinations
to begin at once, for she felt mortally sure by the way her
announcement had been received last night, that some insur-
mountable obstacle would surely be put in her way if there
were the slightest delay.

All day, whenever she was not needed, she had been quietly packing, so that her actual going tomorrow could be
quickly accomplished. She had told the young people she

wouldn't have any time to see them that day because she was helping her aunt with her luncheon, but they went straight to her aunt and announced their intention of coming over immediately after dinner for the evening as usual, and she had not said them nay, so they arrived promptly.

It was not until very late that evening when they were all gone that Aunt Carlotta had opportunity to talk with Margaret about what she called her "crazy scheme."

"Oh, my dear!" she said as Margaret stopped at her room, "I'll just have to put off our talk until the morning, I'm so utterly worn out with that bridge party and all. Tomorrow morning right after breakfast we'll go out on the side terrace under the trees and have a real talk. I'll go into things quite fully, and help you to understand just where you stand. We'll say ten o'clock. I don't think anybody will be over as early as that, and we'll have the terrace all to ourselves. I have some things to tell you that I think will surprise you."

Margaret looked troubled.

"I'm sorry, Aunt Carlotta! I really couldn't be here then. I have to leave on the early train to get to my examinations. They begin at ten o'clock. Perhaps some day when you are to be free and have plenty of time you can send me word and I can come out and have a talk with you, and then *I'll* have a lot of things to tell *you* myself, I hope."

"Oh, but my dear! You can't go tomorrow. Didn't I tell you Bailey's mother is giving a party in your honor, and it would be very rude of you to go away that very day. Didn't I tell you about it? She asked me last week to make you keep that day free, and she has sent out a lot of invitations."

"Why, I'm sorry you let her do that, Aunt Carlotta, because anyway I wouldn't want to go to a party given in my honor. It would look as if there was really something between me and Bailey, and of course there isn't, and never will be."

"My dear! You shouldn't say anything rash like that. You are going and you don't really know what you might do later."

"No, Aunt Carlotta, that's impossible. I should never care to marry Bailey, and he does not even appeal to me as a friend, just an acquaintance. I'm sorry if this is going to mortify you at all but if you had told me before I would have made it plain to you that I could *never* go to that house as a special guest, especially not to a party given in my honor. It would give a wrong impression, and I would hate it. Besides, I couldn't possibly change my plans now. I have already arranged for this examination. The teacher is coming down from his summer home in the mountains to meet me at the university."

"Oh, you could easily phone him that you couldn't come."

"No, I don't think I could. Not honorably. He has put off something he was intending to do in order to meet me tomorrow and let me get done in time to start in with my classes when they begin the first of next week."

"Oh, my *dear!* My poor foolish little girl! Do you have any idea what you are getting into? Don't you know that a university course is going to cost you *terribly?* You couldn't possibly afford it. Just where do you expect to get the money? I'm sorry, but *I* can't help you out any. I really can't. I have all I can do to keep my expenses down to my income now."

"Oh, Aunt Carlotta, I wouldn't think of expecting you to help me. I wouldn't accept it even if you offered it. I have my own little money, you know. It isn't a lot, but it's enough for that, and I have asked my guardian to see that it is ready for me in the city bank tomorrow. He expected to do that when I came out here. I was to send him word when I had decided on a college, and he is all ready for me."

"Oh!" said the aunt, bleakly. "I didn't know you had any money, Margaret. Surely it is only a pittance!"

"It is not a great deal of course," said Margaret reservedly, "but it was left by my father for that purpose, for my education, so you see I shall not need to trouble anybody to help me out!"

"But my dear, why be so prodigal of it? Going to the university? I should think it would be so much wiser to save it to buy your wedding trousseau. You know if you marry somebody worthwhile you will be ashamed to go to them without a suitable wedding outfit."

Margaret laughed, a real gay little ripple.

"You know, Aunt Carlotta, I shouldn't mind getting married with only a few clothes, such as I always get every so often, and I've always had enough for that. Besides if I didn't I could always make over some old ones I am sure. Mother taught me to sew, and I like to make clothes. I'd much rather go with a small outfit for my poor brains. I should really be ashamed of that, if I had had the opportunity to get them cultivated. Sorry, dear, but you'll have to take me as I am for I guess I don't make over very easily. Now, you go to bed. You look so very tired. And I'll just kiss you good-by with my good night, so I won't disturb you in the morning, for I shall be gone when you wake up. And I thank you so very much for all you've done for me since I've been here, and the nice times you've planned for me. I'm awfully sorry I was such a disappointment to you, and didn't fit in to your plans. Good-night! And *good-by!*"

Margaret reached up and gave her aunt two hearty kisses and then slipped into her room. And Aunt Carlotta, puzzled beyond expression, looked despairingly after her.

14

THE first night that Margaret was alone in her new dormitory she felt suddenly very desolate. Not that she wished herself back in Crystal Beach, for she was conscious of great relief to be away from there, but this was an utterly new experience to be in a strange city, with not a soul in all its wide reaches whom she knew. Even the professors were away tonight attending some gathering of interest to educators. Not many students had as yet arrived, for the classes did not open until the following Monday.

Margaret had been taking examinations all day long. She was very tired.

It was her own fault that she had worked so hard. She was anxious to have it done, and know her standing, anxious to begin real work and feel as if she were getting somewhere. She was a bright student and loved to study, and the last three months had been a weariness to her because so much of the time was spent on vapid idle conversation that didn't interest her. Now she was brought up against loneliness. Of course she would not feel it long, not after she got to know other students, and was interested in her studies. But as she lay down on the strange bed in that strange room, unexpectedly her thoughts turned to Revel Radcliffe.

She hadn't written to him lately, for she saw by his letters that he was interested in his work, and had little time for just letter writing, and she did not want to be a burden to him. But now she suddenly wished she could talk to him for a few minutes. She felt that he would understand why she had come away, and what it was that made it so impossible for her to stay at her aunt's. Perhaps it might even be that his prayers had helped to influence her move. Who knew?

Margaret had not been thinking much of Revel the past few weeks. He had not seemed to fit with the atmosphere in which she had found herself. Yet now tonight her thoughts turned toward him. Almost she was moved to write him another letter. Yet she did not owe him one. And the last letter he had written had closed with the words "I'll be letting you know if anything new turns up." That sort of closed the communication from his end, didn't it? And if there were anything she despised it was a girl who tagged after a boy and forced herself upon him. After all, their friendship was only casual, and it was his place to write if he wanted to hear from her again. Of course if he wrote to Crystal Beach his letter would be forwarded to her. Better not write again yet. Give him time to write if he wanted to. But she *would* like to see him a few minutes. So after a moment she went and got out Revel's letters and read them over, just to get the companionable atmosphere, and make herself feel that she had had a pleasant talk with him.

And it worked. She really felt refreshed and not so lonely after she had read those friendly boy-letters, and gone over in her mind their brief contacts.

Over in her window there stood a little flower pot, set in a small jardiniere of twisted white china lattice. The small plants that lifted their heads from the pot looked brave and well-intentioned. She had dug them up very early that morning, and slid them carefully into the pot, concealing the pot among her baggage, and guarding them at every move.

She was hoping that they would live through the winter till she could find a way and a place to plant them again. How queer it was that she should feel so much more at home with this stranger-boy who had given them to her, than with the other young people she had met since. Thinking back over that one evening she had met him, she drifted off into pleasant sleep, with a memory of Revel's warm lips upon hers in that quick farewell in the dark beside the bushes. How different that was from the kind of kisses Bailey Wicke had tried to force upon her, and never quite succeeded! How glad she was to have escaped from him. Or had she?

And the very next day Bailey Wicke came traveling up to the city in a handsome automobile belonging to his father, to take her a-riding and a-dining.

But Margaret did not go with him. Instead she met him down in a small reception room of the university and dismissed him with a smiling thanks, told him she had arranged an appointment with one of her professors, and she couldn't tell how long it was going to take her. Wouldn't she set another time or day when she could go, he asked. No, she would not. She had not come to the university to spend her time going out with friends. She had come here to study, and much as he thought women should not improve their minds he would have to understand that there was one girl who *intended* to get all the culture she could. It was all very gay and laughing, but it was so definite that he finally left, promising however that he would return.

And return he did, not only once but many times, until Margaret would fain have invented excuses not to see him, so much annoyed she was. So one day she sat down pleasantly beside him in the reception room and told him carefully and gently that she wished he would not come to see her any more. That she was only a very young girl, and had no desire to be taken out away from her work on any pretext. She told him she would think much better of him as a friend if he would stop trying to make her go out with him.

"But I love you, Margaret," he said blandly, as if that settled it.

"Oh, no, you don't, Bailey. You just *think* you do. You're too young to love anybody that way, and so am I. Besides I don't *want* to. And *you'll* get over it."

So then the next time he came he enlisted Aunt Carlotta and brought her along.

"Your aunt was getting homesick to see you," he said persuasively, "and so I offered to bring her up. She wants to see you and have a nice little quiet talk with you, and there's no place where you can talk as well without interruption as in the back seat of my car. So come on. Get your togs on, Margaret, and I'll show you some of the sights of the town."

And there seemed nothing for Margaret to do but go, for Aunt Carlotta was as pleased as a child at the arrangement. She had plans for a Christmas party that she wanted to talk over with Margaret, because she insisted that she couldn't have a Christmas party without her dear niece, that the young people would never come just for an old woman.

So there was that to be done. She had to do of course.

But there was this about it, Bailey Wicke was much more tractable since her serious talk with him than he had been before, and less possessive.

But Margaret did not go to her aunt's for Christmas as she had expected she must. Instead a holiday job suddenly dropped into her lap, which might promise more afterward if she proved satisfactory, and she felt she must take it. One of the professors had an invitation for himself and his wife to take a trip during the holiday vacation, and in looking about to find someone to look after their three children and grandmother, and make them have a pleasant time, they pitched upon Margaret as the most likely entertainer for both the young ones and the old lady, so Margaret stayed in the city and had Christmas with the children. There was a servant so she had no housework to do, and it really was a nice rest for her.

She selected a charming little ivory figurine for her aunt,

and some lovely Christmas cards for the young people she knew. Her aunt had promised to forward any mail that should come for her, but day after day went by and nothing came, and Margaret found a growing disappointment that there was no word of any sort from Revel. In vain she reflected that Revel was only a boy, and a boy in college with lots of interests and lots of hard work. Besides he would not be lonely any more as he was when she first knew him, and he would not be needing word from her to keep up his spirits. It was ridiculous of course that she should think anything about him. It showed how lonely she was that she should miss a thing like this.

In due time there came a reproachful letter briefly from her aunt. It seemed very rude to her that Margaret should be willing to do a favor for one of the faculty when her own aunt was expecting her there, and had invited guests to meet her. As for a job, what little pay she would get for telling stories to children wouldn't be worth mentioning. She thanked her for her gift, though she said she was sorry she wasted her money on it if she was so hard up she had to work. And yes, of course she would forward any mail that came. She didn't think that anything had come so far except a sort of a circular. It seemed to be a circular about some college, but of course she knew Margaret wouldn't want that now since she was already in a college, so she threw it in the waste basket. It was a rather disheartening letter and after she read it she curled up on the bed and had a good cry. It seemed as if there was nobody anywhere that remembered her or cared.

Even Bailey Wicke failed to appear, a new blonde having arrived in Crystal Beach and absorbed his attention for the time being. But Margaret was only glad of that. It was a great relief. Though of course she didn't know about the blonde. But that would not have bothered her in the least.

It was not a very happy Christmas that Margaret spent, doing her best to make the three little children under her care have a good time. And yet she was, with it all, relieved not to be in her aunt's gay house. It didn't seem like Christmas there. It seemed like a world that didn't know what Christmas meant.

Katie, Aunt Carlotta's maid, came to her mistress several days before Christmas with a small package addressed to Margaret.

"Will you be sending it on by mail, madam?" she asked. "Or shall I be putting it away in her bureau drawer for her?"

"Oh no, Katie. She'll be here herself in a few days," said Aunt Carlotta. But that was before they had the letter from Margaret saying she would not be coming.

So Katie had put the package safely in the upper bureau drawer and thought no more about it, naturally supposing that her mistress would send on the package herself when she discovered the girl was not coming. But as Aunt Carlotta seldom went through the bureau drawers of her guest rooms, Revel's lovely gift of a simple bracelet with settings of rose quartz did not reach Margaret in time for Christmas, and neither did the letter that accompanied it, for Revel had put the letter inside the box with the bracelet and no one knew there was a letter.

Then the sad lonely Christmas was over, and the New Year, and Margaret started on to work harder than ever. Certainly she must get all she could out of this winter's work, for it was costing more in money than she had ever expected to pay for a single year, and she *must* get her money's worth of knowledge. She did some really brilliant work in several classes and was greatly commended.

But she had definitely decided now not to remain there another year, and had sent for catalogues of various colleges. She did not include Linwood College however, for much as she would have enjoyed life in such a college as Revel had described, she was deeply hurt that he had not written, and she certainly could not force herself to his notice when he had apparently dropped her. Well, of course they had been nothing but kids, and now he must be growing up and having other girl friends. He couldn't be tied to her friendship always just because he thought she had been kind to him once.

So she carefully put away thoughts of the stranger boy who had come into her life in passing, and had made such a pleasant interlude. She was a young woman now, not a child, and she must not be silly.

Resolutely she forced herself to get acquainted with her fellow students, especially those who seemed alone, or aloof, and tried to make others have a good time. Her mother had told her when she was but a child that when a person could not have what he wanted for himself, the next best thing was to try and get something pleasant for someone else. So she went to work trying out the rule in real earnest, and found that it did bring a certain thrill, though it was different from the thrill of having one's heart's desire.

So, the winter went on, and the spring came, and still there was no word from Revel, though she asked her aunt every time she wrote if she was sure there had been no mail for her. Always she received that vague message. "Why, no, I think not."

Then Bailey's blonde went back east, and Bailey returned, to her great annoyance, and began to pester her again. He had thought she would have recovered or changed her mind by this time, but he found her more determined than ever not to go riding with him, nor dancing, nor dining, nor anything else. She was deep into her studies now, and really enjoying them.

Aunt Carlotta was still a bit cross at Margaret that she had not come to her party at Christmas, and so she did not invite her to come for the summer. In fact she was going on a trip to Alaska herself and it would not be convenient to have her.

But Margaret got a job for the summer and could not have gone if she had been invited. The job was looking after children again, with another old lady thrown in, and it was

located in a lovely house with handsome grounds and myri-
ads of flowers, and occasionally there were excursions, by
boat, or plane or rail, which made a pleasant change for her,
and took her mind away from her own loneliness. Though
sometimes she would fancy telling Revel about some of the
things she saw, and pleased herself by imagining that he
would have enjoyed seeing some of the places she saw. So
she was growing in wisdom and knowledge and experience,
and also her pocketbook was better filled. She began to feel
that perhaps it was just as well for her to remain another year
in the university, rather than to undertake an unknown
quantity in the shape of a strange college in a new quarter,
and have it turn out a disappointment perhaps, and waste
money in railroad fare.

So back to the university she went again, and undertook a
still heavier schedule than the year before, with little expec-
tation of any relief in the way of a good time.

Once her uncle Mr. Devereaux brought his wife, her other aunt, to call upon her when they were in the city on a
shopping expedition, but this aunt did not seem to be much
better than the other one. Her sole interest seemed to be in
bridge, and when she found Margaret did not play she
seemed to dismiss her as a hopeless case.

And so the second winter passed without a word from
Revel, and the spring began to come again.

One day when Margaret was walking in the park she saw
some little wild flowers growing in the grass and they reminded her of her own, which had long ago pined away and
died an unhappy death at the hand of the strange chambermaid
in the dormitory, who was taking the place of the regular
maid. She had promised Margaret to care for the flowers
while she was away, and then had forgotten them, till they
were dead, so she dashed them out the window into the
court below. Margaret mourned for her flowers, and resolved that some day she would go back to Sumter Hills,
walk up into that woods again, and replace her flowers. But

she couldn't go now of course. She hadn't money enough to go running all over the country after a whim.

But as she thought about her little flowers, and the boy who had so kindly got them for her, and how he had been utterly silent all this time, she could not understand it. He had not seemed as if he would be like that. Perhaps he had been sick, or been in an accident, maybe even been killed, and perhaps she would never find out about it. Was there any way that she could inquire without seeming to be running after him? He was getting older now, and would perhaps think she was a fool if she would write and ask what had become of her old friend. Oh, she wished she knew where he was, and whether his father had made him leave his grandfather and his wonderful college that he thought so much of, and perhaps go to the university of his father's choice.

She thought about it a great deal, and one day she ventured to call up her Aunt Carlotta and ask if she was *sure* there had been no mail at all since she left. But Aunt Carlotta was quite cross about it and asked her if she thought she was *stealing* her mail, and what mail of great value did she have anyway, that she should spend the money to telephone about it?

And so that was that, and Margaret decided she would likely never hear anything more of Revel Radcliffe. Because he had promised definitely to let her know if anything more happened, and it did seem as if, if he were still alive, he would certainly have kept that promise.

15

IT was at Ladies' Aid they discussed the latest scandal in Sumter Hills again, and it was Mrs. Hopkins who brought the news this time, although she lived the farthest off, and nobody understood how she always heard these questionable things before any of the rest did. Some said she went by intuition. But it always turned out afterward to be true. At least in some respects.

She always waited and timed her opening sentences till Mrs. Martin had arrived and was within hearing distance. She loved to watch Mrs. Martin's face to find out if her news *was* a surprise to her, although Mrs. Martin was an accomplished actress and could veil surprise almost better than any other emotion.

"Well, I suppose you've heard the latest about Lady Radcliffe, haven't you?"

"What?" said Mrs. Green on the alert at once.

"Why her husband's suing her for divorce! I never thought it would go that far, did you? A man of such in*tegri*ty and good *prin*ciples. It seems too bad for him, to have lost one wife, and have the other turn out good-for-nothing!" Mrs. Hopkins was shaking her head lugubriously. "Mrs.

Martin, does this dress get short sleeves or wrist length? Oh, just caps? Well that's easy. Yes, as I was saying I never thought she'd let it go that far. She seemed kind of a comely person, if she hadn't been so sort of high-hat and all, and I should have thought she'd have been a little careful, this being her second husband, and he being such a fine man as some say. *Say*! Was her first husband divorced, or did he die, Joanna Bitterman? You said you used to hear of her through some cousins who lived in Rochester, New York, where she came from didn't you? Do you happen to remember if he *died* or was *divorced?*"

"Oh, yes, he died," said Joanna importantly. "My cousin went to his funeral. He used to sell him socks sometimes. He was in the hosiery business, and he went to the funeral. Yes, he died all right. Seems 'zif she didn't have very good luck with her husbands, did she?"

"Good *luck!*" said Mrs. Martin with a sniff. "If you ask me I'd say she had better luck than she deserved. Mr. Radcliffe is a saint on earth if there ever was one. Always kindly and affectionate to his first wife, although I never felt she was worth much either. And then to think he was to be dragged through the divorce court! I declare, women are getting beyond all belief, to think a woman would go and break up a lovely home like that after only a little over two years! I think that man has had more than his share. First his wife dies, and then an ungrateful son wouldn't even come to his father's wedding, and brought all that disgrace and humiliation on him, and now his second wife goes back on him! She couldn't have been a decent woman. Oh, I know it's fashionable nowadays to get fond of some other man besides your husband, but I think women like that ought to be strung up. I never did like her anyway. Bleached hair on a woman of that age! And lipstick thick enough to paint a boat. And her finger nails! Mercy! They made me shudder whenever I came near her. They actually *clatter*ed! Didn't you ever hear them?"

"Well, it beats me how he ever chose a woman with all that make-up on her," said quiet little Mrs. Bowen. "If he's such a fine man I should have thought he would have been more careful choosing a second wife. It isn't as if he was an impulsive kid."

"Well, he's rid of her now, if what you hear is true," said Mrs. Hopkins. "They say she went to Reno six weeks ago! Funny we haven't heard about it before. But she was such a gad-about, always running down to Miami, or over to Los Angeles or somewhere. When she went to Reno no one took notice of her."

"Well, how did *you* learn about it, Mrs. Hopkins," asked Mrs. Martin curiously. "Since I happen to know they tried to keep it quiet I shouldn't think *you* would get it soon, living away off up there so near the woods."

"Who, me? Why I was over to Chenango to visit my daughter last week, just got back this morning, and my daughter heard it from her husband's cousin who lives out in Reno. They said her name was published in the paper and he noticed 'Sumter Hills,' and that's how he came to pay attention to it."

"Well, it certainly isn't going to make much difference in *our* lives, having her go divorcée on us, is it?" laughed Mrs. Martin. "She certainly was the biggest bluff, with her high chin, and her patronizing airs. She seemed to consider the people of the town weren't worth speaking to, and she never came near church, nor any of our meetings. She didn't even come when she was invited to dinner or anything. I know for I invited her. Poor man! I thought he'd feel it if none of us ever came near her. We always were fairly friendly with his first wife, even if she was so sorrowful looking, and did have a perfect rat of a son!"

"Where is that son? I don't seem to see him around anywhere, do you?" asked Mrs. Green.

"No, he hasn't been around home since his father married," said Mrs. Grant pinning the seam she was overcasting to her knee. "Some say his father sent him off, and some say he ran away. Dear knows what he had done, little reprobate!"

"Well, he ain't so little now any more," said old Mrs. Crittenden thoughtfully. "I remember he was born two days after my Cassie, and she's goin' on twenty. It won't be long before he's of age. I heard he went to live with his grandfather. Did the old man die, or did he get well?"

"Oh, he got well! I think that was just a big bluff of the boy wanting to get away and do as he pleased," said Mrs. Martin.

"But I heard he went to college. I think he is in college now, Mrs. Martin," said the minister's wife protestingly. "I'm quite sure Rose said he was in college. He used to be in her class in high school, you know, and the young people keep informed about their classmates."

"Well, if he's in college yet I'll eat my hat," said Mrs. Martin. "You can't tell me that that rapscallion of a boy could settle down to stay in college all this time. What college is it, do you know, Mrs. Castor?"

"Why, I believe it's some small college up there in New York or New England somewhere, where his grandfather lives," said Mrs. Castor.

"It probably was the only college his father could get to accept him, a boy like that!" snorted Mrs. Martin. "Juliana Green, did you remember to set that kettle of soup where it would keep hot without scorching? Seems 'zif I smelt scorched meat."

"Yes, I put it on the simmerer," said Mrs. Green offendedly.

"Well, say, what is all this about Mrs. Radcliffe?" asked Mrs. Brown who had been away all winter and had just got back home. "What did she do that she had to be divorced? Is she getting a lot of alimony?"

"Not she," said Mrs. Hopkins. "I tell you it's *he* that's getting the divorce, and he claims she—"

"Ssh!" said Mrs. Perkins. "Here comes the minister, and don't you mind how he preached on gossiping last Sunday?"

There was a dead silence in the room as the minister entered. His wife was in the kitchen looking after the soup, and hadn't heard the last words.

"Well," said Mrs. Martin, setting her needle firmly where she intended to take the next stitch, "of course I don't believe in gossip nor in carrying tales, but where people are actually *wrong*, where they are a menace to the general public, I do think people ought to be warned about them, don't you? Now that boy for instance. I felt I ought to tell that sweet little guest of mine just what she was taking up with."

"By the way," said Mrs. Green hurriedly, watching the minister to see if he had heard Mrs. Martin, "whatever became of that girl? She was such a sweet little unsophisticated child. I did admire her so much."

"Yes, she was sweet," conceded Mrs. Martin. "Why, she went out west to her aunt's to go to school or college or something. I haven't heard from her, except a nice little bread-and-butter letter the day after she left. You see she isn't staying with her aunt I know, she's with another side of the family. The Devereaux are the relatives I know, and Mr. Devereaux just drove her out when she went. He was a half brother of her father, and the other aunt was a sister of her mother. I certainly hope she is a good woman and carries a firm hand, for I would hate to see that child go wrong. There are so many scalawags going around nowadays, like the one I was talking about, and she deserves a good husband. She had fine people. And that's half for a good start always."

"Oh, did you know her mother?" asked Mrs. Green.

"Well, no, not personally, but I've always heard a lot about her father. He was a dear good man, one of the salt of the earth. It would be a shame to have anything happen to his pretty little daughter."

"Oh, do you think she kept up her acquaintance with that young man?" asked Mrs. Green eagerly. "Maybe that's where he's gone, out west somewhere."

"Dear knows," said Mrs. Martin. "I haven't kept track of any of them. I thought it wasn't my business, though I did my best to make Mr. Devereaux understand about the boy before they left here. But girls nowadays do hang on to every man they get hold of. I wouldn't be at all surprised but what they correspond, at least. Things are so informal in this age. And of course girls do go crazy over a fine head of hair and big eyes. If you admire that type. Personally I never did. I like a man to be plain and dependable looking. When they think they are handsome it just sticks out all over them. But, where did you say you heard this about the divorce, Mrs. Hopkins? You know that wasn't supposed to be told. That's why they kept it so quiet. That poor man. He only told a very few, those who absolutely *had* to be in the secret. He didn't want talk. He hates talk. He only confided in the few he knew he could trust. He wouldn't be the successful business man he is if he couldn't keep his mouth shut. Of course I suppose it will be known after a little, when all the formalities are concluded, but if I were you I'd say as little about it as I could if you want to be well thought of. I think Mr. Radcliffe is depending on the best people in the community to stand by him and not talk. That's been *my* policy."

"Oh," said Mrs. Hopkins, somewhat deflated, "when did *you* know about it, Mrs. Martin? I supposed it was news to everybody."

"Well, I'm not saying when I was told," said the indomitable Martin. "There! Elva Griggs, there's that apron all ready for you to hem. If you work fast I should think you'd be done before lunch."

Then the minister came back from the kitchen where he had been interviewing his wife about some matters, and drifted around among the members of his church, talking pleasantly, and the voice of criticism and gossip ceased for the time being.

But the story had started on its way, and was not likely to be forgotten. Each one of those women went home to tell all about it at the supper table, with embellishments, and it was not long before it had gone around the neighborhood at least twice, and each time with additions. And yet no one knew just who had given the first information.

"I think," said Mrs. Martin on the way home in her old jalopy wherein she had stowed an astonished Mrs. Hopkins who wasn't used to being asked to ride home because she lived at the top of the hill opposite the woods. "I really *think,* Mrs. Hopkins, that it is important for *you* to tell whoever told you that story about the Radcliffes, that it is to be kept *strictly quiet* until some regular announcement is made. As a friend of the family *I* feel justified in asking *you* to do that. And not to tell *another living soul* at present! Who was it you said told you?"

"Why, it was my daughter over in Chenango. Her husband's cousin who lives out in Reno was visiting there, and he remarked that they had one of Sumter Hills' best citizens out there getting a divorce, and of course we asked who it was. Then afterwards he hunted up the paper he had seen it in and sent it to my daughter, and she sent it to me."

"Well, if I was you I'd hide it, and I wouldn't give out another word of it. I think too, that you ought to ask your daughter to tell her husband's cousin *not* to tell it again around here! And when you get home I think you should go straight to the telephone and call all those women that you told this afternoon that you aren't just sure about the story, and you think they better not say anything about it yet. Not till some public announcement is made. Tell them you didn't understand that it wasn't something that ought not to be talked about. It might not come off you know, and then how would *you* feel. You know we ought to be *awfully* careful what we tell. You heard Rev. Castor's sermon yesterday, didn't you?"

"Why, yes, but what's that got to do with it? Mr. Radcliffe doesn't even *go* to our church. Besides, if I heard it I certainly have a right to tell it."

"Look here, Emmeline Hopkins, if you aren't willing to go around and stop tongues after you've cast out a story that wasn't supposed to be told—or not yet anyway—then *I* shall feel it my bounden duty to tell Mr. Radcliffe what you're doing, the story you're spreading, and what'll that do to your brother who works for Radcliffe, do you think?"

"Oh, my soul!" said Mrs. Hopkins blanching. "Now how did I know *you* was a friend of the Radcliffes and would get sore because I told something that was in a paper. I saw the paper myself."

"Well, all the same if you want to keep your brother in with Mr. Radcliffe I think you better not talk about it. I really mean it. I shouldn't feel it right not to let him know who was trying to undermine his privacy."

Mrs. Hopkins sat sulkily until she reached the corner of her lane and then she said:

"You can let me out here. I like to walk up the lane this time of night. Yes, I *mean* it. But honestly, Mrs. Martin, I can't see what the difference is between the way I was telling a few facts about that woman that none of us liked, and the way you was lambastin' her stepson. If you ask me I think he was the better one of the two, just a young sprig, with his own mother gone, and not a soul to care whether he lived or died except a pair of servants. Of course they *were* devoted as far as that goes, but that ain't bein' properly taught by a mother."

"You forget," said Mrs. Martin severely, "that he had a *wonder*ful father. He had the advantage of his upright example, and the advice such a father is able to give."

"Oh *yeah?*" said Mrs. Hopkins. "If *you* had him holding a mortgage over *your* little home, and seen him refuse to wait even one single month for your last payment, when you gave him *proof* the money would be there *for sure* the day you said, and if *you* had lost your home just through his greediness, you wouldn't think his 'upright example' was so keen for any boy to copy. If that Revel don't turn out to be a better man than his father, then I'll miss my guess. You may be an intimate friend of the family for all I know, although I never heard you were before this, but you don't know all there is to know about that family by a long shot! But *I* know, for that's the reason I happen to be living up this ratty old lane in a whitewashed shanty that isn't even whitewashed, instead of in my nice little white cottage with green blinds and vines over the porch, down on Robins Road. And that after my man slaved and slaved to get the money to buy it, and all, and *trusted* that old reprobate with *all he had!* You may feel inclined to go and tell your friend Hiram Radcliffe all I've said, I don't know, and you may think it'll lose my brother his job, but you're *mistaken* this once! It *won't!* Because my brother has *already* lost his job. He gave it up on his own free will yesterday, just because he couldn't stand it any longer to be doing old Hiram's dirty work, serving notices on other people like us who were too trustful, and were losing all they had! Thanks awfully for the ride, Mrs. Martin, and if I ever get a car, which I don't expect to, I'll return the favor. But if you want anybody called up about the news I gave, you better do it yourself. For I wasn't giving any false alarm, and I've got just as much right to talk about one person as you have to talk about twenty. *You*'re supposed to be a Christian, and I'm not. I'm only a Ladies-Aider, but I don't see that you're any better than I am, and I guess I'll stand my chance with you in the long run. Good-by, Mrs. Martin. I'm pretty plain-spoken, but I guess I've told the truth, and if they don't like it they'll have to do the other thing." And Mrs. Hopkins turned loftily and marched up the hill in the setting sunlight, with her chin up and her shoulders held high. She had always ached to tell Mrs. Martin just where to get off, and now she'd done it! She was glad! People posing as such wonderful Christians, always doing a lot of church work, and going around saying the rottenest kind of things about a boy that was a mere child! She didn't know anything about Revel Radcliffe herself, but she'd defend him if she could, just because Mrs. Martin was scandalized by everything he did, and because he had such a whale of a mean old father.

And Mrs. Martin, silenced for the moment, sat staring after the determined figure as it marched up the hill sturdily toward the unwhitewashed shanty without a waver, and wondered.

16

BUT Revel *had* written another letter to Margaret, telling her how he was making good in college, reporting Grand's general improvement in health, and saying that the doctor was greatly delighted, as of course he was.

The letter had been hurriedly written because he had an examination to study for that night, but he had a longing to let her know that as yet he had not been remanded home.

He had expressed the opinion that the reason for this was probably because his father's wife did not care to be bothered with him in her vicinity, and he supposed he ought to be very grateful for that. He had asked Margaret to continue to pray for him, because he had come to have great faith in prayer, and he felt that she knew the rules for answered prayer better than he did, and perhaps had more faith.

Then he enclosed his letter in one of the new college catalogues, with little arrows and scribbled notes to explain some of the pictures, such as "The president of our Fellowship," "The guy that helped us to put our football team on the map," "The prof I like the best," "The field I walk across every day to get to college quickly." He had also slipped in a little snapshot of Grandfather Revel, and the dear old farmhouse where he lived.

He put his letter into the envelope that belonged with the catalogue, and sealed it up, paying full letter postage, and mailed it on his way to college next morning. Then he waited. And he wondered. Why didn't Margaret write and tell what she thought of the catalogue, and especially the house, and most of all, Grand? He couldn't understand it. She hadn't ever waited so long before. Could his mail have miscarried? Not possible of course. She must be busy, or maybe sick. Still she hadn't looked like a girl who was sickly. And it wasn't a bit like her to wait so long. She had really seemed so interested in his Fellowship.

The college catalogue had long ago found its way from the waste basket to Aunt Carlotta's incinerator, and disappeared in flames, but of course no one, not even Aunt Carlotta knew that. She had merely cast aside that which seemed of no value whatever. The snapshots might have saved it if they had come to light, but Revel had slipped them firmly back in the crease of the book and they did not come out easily.

Revel waited, week after week, being sure that Margaret would write him soon, now and again tormenting himself lest she was sick or suffering, not able to write. Till at last he concluded the she didn't *want* to write him any more, or was bored with his hurried letters, and then his natural pride asserted itself. Still he kept on waiting.

But when the autumn was past and Christmas time was approaching he began to think about sending her some gift.

The last time he had been in the city he had stopped in front of a jewelry store and looked at the lovely things displayed. The article that interested him most was a slender bangle bracelet of platinum with little drops of rose quartz the color of a rose petal dropping from it at intervals. They looked like dew, or raindrops with the light of sunrise in their depths. And because the wild rose color reminded him of the soft color in Margaret's cheeks after she had been running with him across the meadow, and also of the two tiny bows that held her lovely brown hair away from her face, he had bought it. He wasn't at all sure when he bought it that he intended to give it to her. It seemed presumptuous. Though there had been no one to tell him that well brought up young girls did not accept jewelry, at least expensive jewelry, from young men, it seemed the most fitting thing he could give her. It seemed as if it was like her. And just in case she should write again before Christmas it would be nice to have it on hand to send.

He carried it home with him and hid it in his treasure box, and now and again he would take it out and look at it. And once he prayed: "Dear God, do you think I ought to send it to her when she hasn't written to me for so long? Please help me to know what to do about it."

He was half ashamed to pray about a thing like that. It seemed almost too trivial. And yet in a way it affected his whole relationship to this new friend whom God had seemed to send to him in his need, and therefore it was really important.

So, after waiting many days, and Christmas not far away, he put it carefully in its pretty box, wrote a card:

> Dear Margaret: This seemed like you so I am sending it to you and wishing you a happy Christmas and a glad New Year.
>
> Yours,
> Revel

and he sent it on its way. And so it found its way into the top drawer of the green guest room where Margaret had roomed when she was staying with Aunt Carlotta, and was utterly forgotten.

Then more days went by for the two who were distressed about this state of things, but thought they must not do anything more about it.

The boy grew serious these days and his grandfather

watched him with troubled eyes, asked leading questions that might give him an inkling of the trouble, Revel was silent, answering only in monosyllables. At last one day his grandfather asked him point blank:

"Boy, have you had some word from your father that is troubling you?"

Revel looked up clear-eyed.

"Oh no," he said, surprised. "No word since the ultimatum. He is waiting for me to fail and get to the end of my rope and come crawling. I know him well enough to know he won't make any move until that happens. He can hold hate a long time, and strike with venom when he is ready."

The grandfather puffed out his lips sorrowfully.

"Boy! That's a hard thing to say against one's own father!" There was no reproof in his tone, only sadness that such a thing had to be.

"Yes, isn't it?" said the boy, his voice, too, sorrowful. "But it's true, Grand. I don't think he ever has really cared much for me, if he cared at all."

"Did you ever try *loving* him?"

Revel was silent a minute, then he said gravely:

"Yes, I did. When I was a little kid. I used to run to him when he came home and ask to be taken up. I can remember it distinctly. I used to be really glad when I saw him coming. But he would greet me with a gruff hello, and brush me aside, and either go into the house and shut himself in his den, or else come and scold my mother for something he thought she ought to have done. I've seen so much of that, Grand! Can you blame me for not having much love for a father like that?"

"No," said the old man with a sorrowful sigh. "And yet, we are told to love our enemies, and to pray for them that despitefully use us and persecute us. Have you ever tried *praying* for him, Revel?"

"No," said the boy, thoughtfully, "I don't think I have. I've prayed sometimes a protective prayer for mother *against* him, but I don't think I every prayed *for* him. I don't believe I *wanted* him to be helped."

"Yes, I can see that, boy, but perhaps you could pray that he might be made different. You wouldn't dislike that, would you?"

"No," said Revel, "I wouldn't dislike it. I'd like it, of course. I'm afraid my trouble would be that I wouldn't have faith to believe that could ever happen."

"I see, of course. But boy, that would be doubting God. God *is able*. He *can* do all things!"

"You said once He wouldn't overstep a man's own free will and force him to yield. I don't think my father would ever yield to God. I think he would want to do everything himself. He wouldn't want God to be God. He would want to be God himself."

"Yes, that was Satan's sin of course. He wanted to be God, and wouldn't yield. Read about that. But son, God has ways of His own, and He knows if this thing should be done. I guess you'll have to let Him show you what He will do. Of course His object for us all, His purpose in making us, is that we should be conformed to the image of His Son. And if a man deliberately won't let himself be made to conform, God will not insist. You'll just have to work that one with God, and see."

"I'll think about it," said Revel.

But the days passed and the cloud over Revel's brow did not lift. It was more a puzzled, hurt look than a troubled one, but he did not confide in his grandfather. It somehow seemed to be too sacred to confide to anybody, even Grand, not anybody but God. And maybe God thought he ought not to worry about a *girl*. He had never thought about girls before, nor worried whether they even noticed him or not, why should he worry about this one?

But somehow she hadn't been just a girl, she had been a real friend. She had been something more than he had ever had before till he got Grand, and it depressed him. Perhaps he ought not to care. To heck with her and let him get his education! Nothing else mattered. He was a college student, and they didn't need girls.

Yet what had he done to lose the friendship of this wonderful girl? For she had been wonderful. Why, even those girls in that girls' fellowship in the college were kind of silly creatures. They were always giggling and making eyes. They were Christians, yes, and they could even pray very well when they had a joint meeting of the two groups now and then, but they hadn't been like Margaret. Had he been silly to feel that way about her?

Well, Grand had said the other day that if you wanted something that God felt was not good for you, you shouldn't insist. That if God wanted you to have it, and felt it was best for you, He would eventually give it, but not till his own best time.

So that night when Revel prayed he said:

"God, if you please, I'd like to put this thing that troubles me into your hands entirely to straighten it out. Make it your best for me."

He got up from his knees and went and stood staring out the window into the starry darkness for a moment, and then he went back and knelt again and prayed:

"Dear God, make it please the best for Margaret, too."

The next morning his grandfather looked him over quietly, seriously, and nodded as if he was satisfied.

"Well, boy, you've put whatever was troubling you over into God's hands fully, haven't you? Am I right?"

Revel gave him a quick look, and then dropped his gaze, a faint flush coming over his cheeks. Then he said in a low husky voice:

"Yes sir, I guess I have."

"I thought so. And now you're happier. Am I right?"

"Yes sir, I think I am," said Revel lifting his clear gaze now with a smile.

The grandfather smiled tenderly.

"You looked like your little mother Emily then, boy. That's the way she used to do. That's the way she used to answer."

The light in the boy's eyes blazed out now with joy.

"I'm glad!" he said.

"And so am I," said the old man. "You know there is nothing like that in the whole world for giving joy and peace. Just trusting things to Him. For after all He who made the world and us, knows far better than we do what is best. And there is nobody can bring to pass like God. Just take Him into your confidence and then let Him do the rest. It'll all come right. And don't get impatient!"

"Okay, Grand," said Revel with a smile. "I guess it will. When it comes right I'll maybe tell you all about it. Or anyway *some*time I think I'll tell you."

"Okay," smiled the grandfather. "Take your time, boy, I can wait. And I'll pray about it, too."

"Even if you don't know what it is?"

"Yes, even if I don't know what it is, because I know my Father knows, and He'll understand, so He'll know what I'm talking about even if I don't and that's enough for me."

"Grand," said the boy, "you're wonderful! You've been next to God in my life. I think even if everything went wrong sometimes I'd have to believe, because of the way God let your letter that your nurse wrote, answer my prayer when I didn't know what to do."

It was two days later that a letter came from Margaret, but Revel was not there.

17

FOR some unexplained reason Aunt Carlotta got a spell of conscience. She decided that she wasn't seeing enough of her only sister's only child, and so she sent a most urgent letter to Margaret, begging that she would spend the summer with her, and enclosing a check (generous for her) which she supposed would cover the largest amount that her niece could possibly earn for the summer. Somehow there seemed to be an underlying appeal in the letter that made Margaret think twice before she answered it.

Her natural impulse would have been to decline, and to go on and take a job, for there were several she could have had, but there was one little phrase in the letter that made her wonder if she was right in doing so, if this were not perhaps something that her mother would have wished her to do.

"You are my only niece," she had written, "and I'm terribly disappointed not to be seeing more of you." Then farther on she added, "besides, there's a question or two I'd like to ask you about something you said once. It sounded like your mother, as she used to talk. I'm getting old now, you know, and there are things that people should know I suppose, when they haven't much longer to live."

So Margaret wrote that she would come.

And yet Aunt Carlotta didn't seem much changed when she got there. She was as flippant as ever, and she began to plan about having some young folks over very soon so that Margaret would feel at home. Of course Margaret never had felt at home with that particular set of young people, but she had come prepared to accept happily whatever came, and so she smiled and greeted them all like long-lost brothers and sisters, even including Bailey's returned ash-blonde who stared at her as if she were an interloper.

So Margaret came back to Crystal Beach, and went to her own room. In due time she opened the upper bureau drawer and saw a package addressed to herself in a familiar handwriting.

She caught her breath, and her heart gave a little leap, actual tears springing to her eyes. Why, when did this come? Was it something she had left behind when she went away? But no, that could not be. And it was not an empty box. The string was still uncut. She looked at the postmark and suddenly sat down weakly in the nearest chair. It was Christmas, a year ago. The first Christmas after she went to the university! Oh, had it been here ever since? How could Aunt Carlotta do that to her? Oh, surely she hadn't been told it was there. It must have been the blundering act of some servant.

But she had not time to let her temper boil over now. She was too eager to see what was in the box. Besides, she had been sent to get ready for dinner, and there was company coming. Some of them had already arrived.

She cut the string of the package and opened it, finding another box beneath with a card bearing a message. A message from Revel! Then he had written and it had been lying here all this time, unanswered, too, and he probably had thought it strange of her not to write.

She read the little card eagerly. It was a very short message, just to accompany the gift, but it sounded so like him, casual, yet real, as he had been always since she knew him. She studied the words through a blurring of tears.

Dear Margaret: This seemed like you so I am sending it to you and wishing you a happy Christmas and a glad New Year.

Yours,
Revel

She put her face down and touched it with her tear-wet eyes, and then touched it gently with her lips. Dear Revel! Was it wrong for her even to think that of him? She had so few real friends!

Then suddenly she was consumed with a desire to see what he thought seemed like her, and she opened the spring of the little leather box and there was the bracelet. Such a lovely thing! She exclaimed aloud over it. And she had been all this time without thanking him for it, and thinking he had forgotten her. She closed her eyes in a quick prayer of thankfulness. She slipped the bracelet over her hand, and watched the rosy stones twinkle in the light. What a beautiful gift and how happy it had made her. Then she heard the distant tinkle of a bell and knew that dinner was ready.

She sprang up quickly, pushed the boxes and paper back in the drawer and hurried over to her suitcase.

She chose a simple white jersey dress to wear, clipped the two little rosy bows in her hair, the bows she had kept for remembrance since ever that day she had met Revel, and with a glance down at her bracelet hurried to the dining room.

They noticed the bracelet almost at once, it was such a lovely thing, and so unique!

"Oh, where did you get a thing like that? What is it?" the girls asked.

"Why, that is rose quartz," said Aunt Carlotta. "Was that something of your mother's? I didn't know she ran to jewelry. And it looks like platinum. It certainly is quaint. Was it hers?"

"No, Aunt Carlotta, it was a Christmas present from a friend."

"A friend? Mmmmm!" said one of the girls, "I told you, Mrs. Gurlie, she would have found someone quite absorbing in that university. Who is he, Margaret? Why didn't you bring him down with you? Call him up and make him come. We want to see your friend!"

"Sorry," said Margaret smiling quite coolly. "It isn't from anyone in the university, it comes from the east, and I didn't say it was from a man. You certainly jump to conclusions. Aunt Carlotta, why didn't you tell me that package was here? I even called you up to see if there wasn't some mail for me, and here it's been all this time. It was sent me a year ago last Christmas!" Margaret covered the appalling treachery of her aunt's indifference by a merry smile, as if it were somehow a pleasant joke.

"Why, what do you mean, Margaret? Where did you find the bracelet? I never saw it before, I am sure."

"I found it in the upper bureau drawer, and the postmark was quite plain on it, so I know it came long ago. The thing I mind most is that I should seem to be so ungrateful, not sending a thank you for it."

"Oh, my dear!" said Aunt Carlotta, the slow red stealing dully up under her rouge, "I'm sure you must be mistaken. I really don't remember any mail coming for you. Probably one of the maids took it from the postman and put it away for you. Wasn't that the time we were expecting you to come for Christmas holidays? Yes, that was it, and so you see nobody was to blame. It was just one of those things that happen sometimes. I'm really sorry, but I should think you could easily explain."

"I suppose so," said Margaret quietly, and no more was said but Margaret's mind was roving off from the gay company, thinking what she would say to Revel, and how she could explain, tell him of her sorrow without showing her heart too much. Two years! It seemed awful. And how foolish she had been not to have written him a pleasant little note sometime and told him where she was. She should not have been so shy, as if it would matter to him so much what she was doing.

Well, it was done now, and she could explain the whole thing. Perhaps already he had forgotten her. But at least she must explain and apologize.

When they were all gone she kissed her aunt good night and asked to be excused.

"I'm rather tired," she said with a smile. "You won't mind, will you?"

"Why no, my dear, of course not. You're going to stay all summer of course and we'll have lots of chances to talk. And oh, by the way, I'm terribly sorry about that bracelet. Katie says I told her to put that box in the drawer, and of course I forgot it and she thought I had sent it to you. Was he a very special friend?"

Margaret's eyes looked past her, very far away. Then she smiled a bit sadly.

"Yes, rather, Aunt Carlotta. But don't worry about it. I'll try to explain, if it isn't too late." Then she hurried into her room to stop the downfall of tears she knew were quite near the surface, and her aunt looked after her puzzled.

"A very queer little girl," she decided. "Now, I wonder what she meant by that? 'If it isn't too late?' How could it be too late, a little trinket like that? Does she think somebody else may have stolen some country lover away during her absence?"

But that night before she slept, and tired as she was, Margaret wrote her letter to Revel.

Crystal Beach

Dear Revel:

I don't know what you think of me, perhaps the same thing I have been trying not to think of you, that I didn't want to write to you any more. Please don't think that. It isn't so.

You see I went away from Crystal Beach. I couldn't

stand the worldliness here, and there was no suitable school or college. So I went to the university. I'm sending you a circular so you can see what it's like. Not that I got into a particularly heavenly atmosphere, for it wasn't, but it was the best I could do for the small amount of money I could spend, and it didn't cost much to go there.

I left word that my mail was to be forwarded and every little while I would write to my aunt to know if there wasn't *any* mail, and once she said no, nothing but a college catalogue, which she threw in the waste basket because she knew I already had a college. I have since wondered if you might have sent one of your catalogues to me. But it is gone now so I have no means of knowing.

I haven't been back here since I left until today. My aunt wrote she wanted to talk to me, and she said it in such a way that I thought maybe I should come. So I'm here again, at least for the summer, and I shall never again trust to having anybody forward my mail. For when I went up to my room and opened the bureau drawer there I found a wonderful package from you. I was so happy I almost cried, for I really have been very lonely, and have missed your pleasant friendliness, but my mother taught me a girl should never run after a boy, nor tag onto him, and I knew you were busy, and thought probably you felt you had no time to write letters to girls, and besides, now you had your grandfather and your college, I didn't think you would need me for a friend any more. So that's why I didn't write. I know that was silly. I should have written to say where I was, or I might have sent you a Christmas card or something, but maybe I was a little too proud. Anyway I didn't, and now I am ashamed. To think this lovely wonderful bracelet has been here almost two years and I never saw it, nor had a chance to tell you how I loved it, and how I thank you for it. It is the prettiest bracelet I ever saw, and I'm enjoying it a lot. Can't you hear the little rosy balls tinkling as I write? They make a lovely sound. Oh, Revel, it was such a beautiful thing for you to give me, and it breaks my heart that I couldn't have thanked you for it right away. Can you ever forgive me, and take me on for a friend again?

There followed a brief account of her work in the university, and then she went on.

I have not had much time for anything but study for I was taking a very stiff course and had to work hard. So I didn't make a lot of friends, and I was pretty lonesome. And two summers I have been a sort of nursery governess for three little girls when their parents were on vacation. But now my aunt has begged me to come for the summer, so I'm back here, and if I hadn't come I never would have found my bracelet, nor known that it was my fault and not yours that I didn't hear from you any more. I'm so *very* glad I came.

Now I want to know if Grand is all right, and whether you have had further trouble about your father and the stepmother? Oh, I hope not! I do hope the college has proved as nice as you thought it would be in the beginning.

Please let me know about yourself right away, and whether you will ever forgive me. I shall be miserable about that until I hear from you.

> Your old friend, the girl of the woods,
> Margaret

When Margaret got into bed at last she lay down very happy, happier than she had been for many months.

It was the next day that her aunt got around to talking with her.

"Sit down there in that big chair, Margaret. I want to ask you a few questions. You see I haven't been very well, and I have been sort of uneasy."

"Oh, I'm sorry, Aunt Carlotta."

"Well, I presume it's nothing. Just a little high blood pressure I guess, and of course that pulls on the heart. I really don't suppose it's anything at all, and the doctor is unduly alarmed, but it seemed to me that now while I'm a little upset about my state, would be the time to get a few things settled that will make me feel fully prepared for anything. I wanted to ask you, Margaret, if you were around your mother much during the last days of her life."

"Oh yes indeed," said the girl with a tender accent. "I was with her as much as I could be during the last weeks of her illness. I wouldn't have been away from her for anything."

"Well, I thought you would likely do that," said the aunt with satisfaction. "You are such a conscientious child. Was it a very gruesome, unpleasant experience for you, to be near a person who was slowly dying?"

"Unpleasant? Gruesome? Why no, Aunt Carlotta, it was like being just outside the gates of Heaven and watching to be sure to catch a glimpse of the glory when the gates opened to let her in. It was beautiful!"

The aunt watched her closely.

"Well, was your mother very unhappy? Did she cry about having to die?"

"Why no, she was glad to go. She was very happy about it. Sometimes she would smile so sweetly!"

"Well, she always was a sunny little thing, but not everybody has a nature like that. Most people are afraid to die."

"Oh, my mother wasn't afraid to die. She said she was going Home to be with the Lord Jesus. And sometimes she would waken from a little sleep and say she thought she had

had a glimpse of His glory in her sleep, and it was going to be even more beautiful than she had dreamed."

"Oh yes," sighed the aunt, yawning a little, "she always was a most imaginative child. But I never could be like that. I never had any imagination at all."

"Oh, but Aunt Carlotta, it wasn't imagination! Mother loved the Lord and belonged to Him. She had always longed to see Him, and she was happy to go."

"Happy to go away and leave you, her pretty little daughter, all alone for years and years in a wicked world?"

"Why, of course she was sorry to leave me, but she knew I would come to her by and by. And she wasn't leaving me alone, she was leaving me with God. She knew I was saved, and that I would be taken care of. She trusted me to God's care. Besides she was going to see father and my baby brother who died when he was only a year old, and grandmother, and her dear father, and a lot of others."

"Oh yes, I know that story. I was brought up on it," said Aunt Carlotta impatiently. "But somehow it never appealed to me to sit down and imagine a lot of things and try to work myself up to the point where I could believe it all. You needn't tell me that everyone is alive. I really couldn't get any comfort out of all that. I'd have to see to believe it."

Margaret looked at her aunt thoughtfully, with a tender little smile. She was learning other reasons now for her coming back to Crystal Beach besides the bracelet. She was finding out that God had some work for her, a message to pass on to another soul, and her heart was crying so softly, "Dear God, teach me how to answer her."

Then she lifted up sweet eyes to the questioner and said:

"But all that would be quite different if you were saved. If you really knew the Lord Jesus."

"Saved! *Saved!* There's that horrid old phrase that I used to hear so much at home when I was a girl. It always used to make me shudder. I didn't want to be saved! I didn't need saving! I hadn't done anything!"

"Oh, but you *do* need saving," said Margaret quietly. "It's that that makes you so unhappy at the thought of death. You won't own you need saving, and yet you know you do. You won't do anything about it because you don't wish to acknowledge that there was any sin or wrong in your life."

"Well now, what sin have I committed, I should like to know? I have always been kind to everybody, I have never overworked my servants, nor underpaid them, and I've always given to good charitable causes—"

Margaret caught her breath. She could not help but remember the words of the Pharisee, "I fast twice in the week, I give tithes of all that I possess." But the shrill complaining voice went on. "I've even been to church often, although I never liked it, it bored me terribly, and I never was unkind to my husband's relatives, although they were sometimes very unkind to me."

"But it isn't things like that that save you," Margaret said earnestly.

"No? Well, what does then?"

"Why, accepting God's Son Jesus Christ as your sinbearer, your Saviour."

"Well, how for mercy's sake could you do that? I don't know what you mean anyway, and I never could believe that. I don't believe that anybody else can save me. I think you have to save yourself. It sounds like nonsense to me."

"But it isn't nonsense, Aunt Carlotta. God says that to go to Heaven we must have righteousness and no sin. And we have only sin and no *real* righteousness. But God really wanted us to come to Heaven with Him, so He came down—His Son Jesus Christ died—and took all our sin. God says He piled all the sin of all the world on Christ, and He gives us all His righteousness, if we'll take it. Don't you see that under these conditions you couldn't save yourself, any more than a man in the old days could get himself out of debtor's prison for owing money when he hadn't anything to pay with? If you were bankrupt and couldn't get out till you paid your debts, how *could* you ever get out unless someone else paid them for you? That's what the Lord Jesus Christ did for us. If you would only believe that He has, you would see. And He brings such peace and joy when once you put your trust in Him."

"How do *you* know?" said the aunt unbelievingly. "You're scarcely more than a child."

"I know because I've accepted Him, and I *know* Him. He lives in my heart and makes it possible for me to live and be happy even when things are very hard."

Her aunt looked at her curiously, studying her face to try and make it out, and just then the lunch bell rang and there was no more opportunity to talk.

For several days Aunt Carlotta seemed to avoid talking any more about it, but Margaret thought a great deal, wondering if she had said the right thing, and praying for her aunt with all her heart. Perhaps God was going to use her to help her aunt to know Him, but oh, she needed wisdom. She must ask to be taught. So far she had only been telling the simple truths her mother had taught her. Now she began to spend more time with her Bible.

18

THE new mistress had not been in Radcliffe House many days before she told Irving and Mandy that she would not be needing them any longer, and sent them on their way into a world that had not been theirs for many years, for they had been with Mr. Radcliffe since before Revel was born.

She chose a time when Hiram Radcliffe was off on one of his business trips for two or three days, and when he returned he found that his old retainers had departed.

"They were simply impossible!" declared the new Mrs. Radcliffe. "As soon as you left they both became so impertinent that it was out of the question to let them stay even until your return. I can't understand how you have endured them all these years. But of course you two poor dears were alone here and men don't know how to hire new servants."

As a matter of fact Hiram had hired Irving and Mandy himself and forced them on his gentle first wife. Then he had withstood her every attempt to make any kind of a change from the order he himself had established.

Hiram was somewhat dismayed at the announcement, and drew his brows in an old-time frown, but his wife touched his forehead lightly with the tips of her velvet fingers and smoothed out the frown.

"But what shall we do?" he asked. "It isn't so easy to get such servants nowadays, and it takes years to train them in the ways of a household."

"Then change the ways of the household," smiled the new mistress. "You know you had gotten into terribly old-fashioned ways. Why, I would have been ashamed to invite any of my friends out here, the way things were being run."

Astonishment dawned on Hiram's hard face. No one had dared to speak in that way to him for years. He resembled a much petted family cat who has had its ears severely boxed for the first time.

"Well, but I thought you would be so delighted with my household regime. I thought Mandy was such a fine cook. You won't find another cook who can equal her."

"Oh, yes, I will. I have one now. Wait until you see. Hurry and get ready for dinner. We've a couple of guests, old friends of mine from New York. They were passing through the town and stopped to call. I simply made them stay. I knew you'd be crazy to see them. You don't know half my old friends."

Hiram frowned heavily.

"Well, I'm not keen on unexpected company. When I come home I'm tired as a dog, and I don't want to get togged up and talk nonsense all the evening."

"Oh, now, Hi, that's ridiculous! What did you want me to marry you for if we weren't going to have a grand time together? And here I've got up a lovely surprise for you and you begin to pout and growl like a naughty little boy!"

"I thought you said these people just *happened* to stop here, and now you're saying you got this up," roared Hiram.

"Well, of course I did indicate to them when I heard them saying they were coming this way, that we would be delighted to have them drop in."

"Oh, you *did!* Yes, I see!"

"But Hi, don't you want me to be happy here?"

"Why yes—of course. But why should you drag in a lot of other people? This is our home, and I want you all to myself!"

"Oh, you silly old fellow," laughed the new wife. "You'll appreciate me all the more when you see me around with other people! Come, now, Hi, don't let's waste any more time. I don't like to give my new servants the impression that we're not prompt. Servants do get such a quick prejudice if everything isn't just as they want it at the very first. And you know it isn't easy to get really trained servants to come away out in the sticks like this and *stay*. And I do want these to stay, at least till we can sell this place and move nearer to the city."

"*Move?*" exclaimed Hiram looking at her aghast. "*Sell* this place that I've spent my life getting the money together to build! Certainly I have no intention of selling, and I am sure you understood that before we were married, Natalie."

"Well, don't let's discuss it now. I tell you dinner is ready and our guests are waiting downstairs. This is awful!"

"Guests be hanged!" asserted Hiram angrily. "*I* didn't invite them. Let them wait! I want this thing understood at once, and settled for good and all. I do *not* intend to sell this place *ever!* I built it for a permanent home! And if the servants you have hired don't like it they can *go*, right *now*, before they serve dinner, and the guests can *go hungry!* This is *my* house and I am *master* of it."

Hiram was getting worked up to a good fit of temper, such as he had dished out to his first wife early and late, if ever she ventured to differ from him in any smallest matter. But Natalie Radcliffe had never seen a hint of this characteristic in him. She stared at him in horror, then quickly changed her tactics. She was a clever lady, else she would never have snared Hiram Radcliffe.

"There, now, Hi dear! Think of all the pleasant peace and quietness you are spoiling with this display of temper. You shouldn't waste your energy! Energy is the same as any other possession, it needs to be economized. And just because I was having a little joke you took me in earnest and got all worked up. Of course we won't sell the house if you are attached to it. I was only using that as a little illustration to show how careful we ought to be with these new servants—"

"Well, I never had to be careful with Mandy and Irving!" roared Hiram, still furious with the idea that she should have dared to venture to upset his regime.

"Yes?" said the new wife in a soothing tone. "Well, we shall see. In the meantime let's try to make the best impression possible on the new servants, and then you can properly judge just what you really like."

Then came a knock at the door and one of the new servants carried on a low-toned conversation.

"Yes, that's right, Lucile. Suppose you tap at their door and tell them that dinner will be served in ten minutes. Yes, Mr. Radcliffe will be ready by that time. Yes, that will be all right, and don't forget what I told you about the wines."

These last words were spoken so low that Hiram didn't hear them. He had never been in the habit of serving liquor in his house, though not from any inherent conviction about it, just that it was an expensive habit which one who was trying to accumulate wealth would do well to avoid.

The subject had not come up between them at all but the new Mrs. Radcliffe did not intend it should. She was planning to produce the liquor at her dinner and let it come as a matter of course.

So for the first time Hiram went down to dinner in his own house and found a great change had come upon the place while he had been absent for a few days.

He was not a man who accepted anything against his will easily. His wife had counted without knowledge of him when she dared to make innovations in the house without telling him, expecting that the presence of strangers would keep him from demurring. Hiram had never abstained from demurring in his life if he felt like it, no matter who was present. He therefore sat him down solemnly at his table and surveyed the whole arrangement. To begin with there were new dishes. Dishes he had never seen before. Had she been buying new dishes without consulting him? That fact alone was sufficient to make him glower. He resolved that those dishes, if they had been bought on any charge account of his, should go straight back to the store the next morning.

So the dinner began with a glowering host, who said very little to his unwanted guests, and went on from bad to worse. Whatever talking there was, was done by the guests, and the laughter, of which there was a good deal, was performed by his wife. She carried the evening off in fine style and appeared to be entirely satisfied, and much amused at her angry husband.

As a result of the disaffection of the master of the house the guests took themselves off soon after dinner instead of staying all night, which was exactly what Hiram had intended they would do. It was a method he had effectually used on his first wife's friends.

But before they left and while the dinner was in progress, two or three times he thundered orders to the new servants, just as he had been in the habit of ordering Irving and Mandy about. But they only looked at him haughtily, and finally ignored his orders entirely, carrying out instead the orders of his wife. At last he roared at them that they might do as he said or leave the house at once. So the lofty butler, and the waitress who had been added to the menage, with heads held stiffly high, marched solemnly out of the room and remained out of sight till the main part of the meal was concluded.

But the new mistress was clever. She did not intend to let her dinner be spoiled nor her husband be misjudged. She would teach him later the amenities of life, but just at present she would create the idea that all this had been planned. She smiled upon her guests and said:

"Well, now we're going into the other room for the dessert. I thought it would be pleasant if we ate it sitting around the fire," and she gave the signal to rise, touching the bell by her place as if it were a prearranged plan.

Nothing happened about the bell, but she led the way toward the big living room, saying in a silvery voice:

"I know you will excuse my poor husband. He has been working so hard on his trip, and didn't sleep at all last night in the sleeper. He has come home simply worn out. I told him he might go and lie down and take a little sleep. I was sure you would excuse him." Then at the door she waved her guests into the living room and slid back into the kitchen to whisper to the waitress, who was standing with haughty chin and curling lips by the pantry door.

"Don't mind what he said. He is half sick. Serve the dessert in the living room."

Hiram stood there by his table place in his own house and looked uncertainly around. Was it possible that anyone had dared to treat him like that? A mere wife? Who did she think she was?

And then she was gone, on into the living room with her guests, and he was left standing alone, free to follow, or to escape.

He escaped.

He went to his own room and paced the floor back and forth, and well for his wife's peace of mind that his room was not over the living room, for he made a thunderous noise, flinging chairs about and stamping around the room like a crazy person.

So the guests sat silently in the living room and ate their lovely ices, served by disapproving angry servants with pursed lips and fine intentions of leaving early in the morning. As soon as the guests could make their excuses they left, watched from the master's window with satisfaction. This was the method by which he had subdued his first wife so effectually.

But the new Mrs. Radcliffe was of sterner stuff than her predecessor, and she had her plans well laid. When her guests were gone she went swiftly into the kitchen where the glowering servants were reviling her and her husband together, and did a fine little placating apology act.

"You know," she said with a charming smile, the smile that had won their consent to working in the country when she hired them, "I'm depending on you all to help me." Then she told them with a gentle voice how ill her husband had been when he came home and how he could hardly hold up his head, and had been upset that there were guests when he was feeling so badly. So she hoped they would pass over any little irregularities in his conduct and just simply forget them. He would be all right in the morning she was sure, and wouldn't in the least realize what he had done to upset them. She begged them to forget it all and go to bed, get a good rest, and in another day or two things would become adjusted and they would like the country.

She did her act so well that the servants were actually placated, and relented, promising that they would give the master of the house another chance.

So the new lady, with a bewildering smile of gratitude went on her way to endeavor to placate her new lord now. She did not anticipate it would be a very difficult task.

But Mrs. Radcliffe had reckoned this time without knowledge of her bridegroom. He wheeled on her when she entered their room and gave her a choice arrangement of very definite language calculated to show her his exact feelings with regard to her high-handed dismissal of the family servants, and family arrangements, and her audacity in purchasing new dishes and the like. He called it unforgivable waste.

He had placed himself where the light would show up his severity, and where he could see her quail and quiver, as his first wife had done when he delivered his ultimatum to her. But there was no quivering nor quailing in Natalie. She was of different fiber. She stood watching him icily for a moment as he went ranting on, giving her his first husbandly homily on economy and good taste, and then her attractive delicate chin lifted almost imperceptibly, until it was both severe and haughty. And in an interval when he paused to select a more fitting and cutting word for his purpose she spoke, with a voice like an icicle:

"Hiram! You forget yourself! Remember you are speaking to a lady! To your wife! That will be about all I care to hear from you tonight," and then she sailed majestically out of the room, closing the door with a finality the like of which he had never had administered to him before. He stood still, amazed, there by the window, and stared at the door through which she had passed, feeling stunned and helpless. Emily had never treated him this way. What did it mean? Emily had always yielded quickly and sorrowfully to his outrageous tirades, and never spoken of the subject of his harangue again, only grown sadder and meeker with every day that passed, and quivered when he found a new subject to scold her about. But now this lady had turned haughty on him, and how was he to manage a temperament like that? He must not give in to her. And yet how charming and imperious she had looked as she stood there coldly and surveyed him. Well, she had to learn of course. He couldn't have her carrying things with a high hand that way, and forcing obnoxious company upon him every time she took a notion. But how charming she had been with her head held high. How fitting a lady to manage his handsome house and meet his guests! Of course he could afford to be a little lenient with her, after she thoroughly understood what he would have and what he would not. He would forgive her, and have a charming time doing it, melt her out of that icy mask into which she had retired at his first word of fault finding. But those servants would have to go, and those dishes would have to be returned to the people who inveigled her into buying them. He wouldn't have dishes like that when he already had handsome dishes that were plenty good enough for anything, and she certainly must have a good strong lesson on economy. She needn't think she could run out and buy new house furnishings without consulting him. There must be an end of that.

Then when she thoroughly understood, he would forgive her of course, and buy her some trinket to make her forget her anger. Perhaps he would give her one of the sets of jewelry he had given Emily, and which she had never worn. They were reposing in a vault in the bank now. The emeralds, perhaps, or the set of pearls.

He waited for some time for Natalie to return and beg his forgiveness, and he would forgive her of course when she got humble enough. But somehow the time got longer and longer and she did not return.

At last he opened the door noiselessly and looked down the hall, but all was quite silent. She had probably gone to one of the guest rooms. So he tiptoed down the hall and tried the door of one but found it locked. His face grew stony with anger, but again he turned the knob and then tapped with the tips of his fingers.

"Natalie!" in a stern demand.

Another silence and then he tried again more gently:

"Natalie!"

Still no answer.

At last, "Natalie, my *dear!*" but only silence answered him.

It was a long time before he gave up and tiptoed back to his room, leaving the door ajar, hoping she would repent and come back, but the night went on and she did not come, and in the morning she was cold and unconquered. And though he tried in a polite way to say something again about the subject matter of their difference, he got nowhere with her. She only looked past him and managed to make him feel that she did not see him.

It was the first time that anyone in close relation to him had ever tried that, and he didn't quite know what to make of it, that she should *dare*. Why, she was his *wife*, and she had no *right* to act that way!

That was the start of their trouble, and it went on from there. It was not till evening that she relented and condescended to speak to him, telling him plainly how uncomfortable he had made her, how ashamed she had been *of him!*

19

IT was some time before Hiram really realized that he was up against someone who would not take his sharp words and sulks and criticisms the way Emily had done, and by the time he got to the point where he knew that if he protested against any of her arrangements he had to look forward to hours, perhaps days, of being ignored, or reproved in a cold sarcastic tone, he was almost beside himself, for he had never controlled his temper in his life, and it did not come easily now. There were days when he sat in his office boiling over with rage at some little word of Natalie's at the breakfast table. He began to see that his work was suffering, and that the home he had planned with a view to utter contentment was really a hotbed of contention. She kept him so occupied in protesting everything she was doing that he had little time to think of anything else, least of all of his son. Whenever his thoughts did turn toward Revel and the way he was continually frustrating all his plans for him, it seemed so trivial a matter beside his own disappointments that he passed it over. He could attend to the boy afterward when he got his own life straightened out. Surely, surely no woman could keep this up, trying to change everything that he liked and make over his home.

But she did. And whenever she relaxed in her unpleasant campaign and condescended to smile upon him again, he presently learned that it was only a presage to a definite plan for something more that she wanted. She desired new furniture, and when he demurred she even went so far as to purchase what she wanted herself, charging it to her husband, in places where he had never had a charge account before. And she gave away some of the old things. In vain he stormed and glowered, and declared he would return everything she had bought. She managed calmly and smilingly, sometimes even contemptuously, to conquer. She kept what she wanted always, whether it had to be gained by battle, or by wheedling and coaxing, and a brief period of sweetness.

What she bought was all modern stuff, furniture without normal legs, straight and square, bookcases in sections of square cubby holes, cabinets that looked like boxes, nothing sensible and beautiful according to old-fashioned lines. Not that Hiram was a connoisseur in art or beauty, but he hated all this stuff that she had bought, and he had to pay for. And he hated it worse when the bills came in. There was a storm and a tempest in the house every time when a new and unexpected bill was discovered to him. Then the lady went about with a haughty abused look on her delicate face, until Hiram wondered why he had ever had the idea of marrying her. There was no pleasure to be found with a woman who looked that way.

But it was when Natalie began to demand that the house be built over, with an extensive addition to its already impressive proportions, that the real fight was on. Hiram put his foot down with all the force of former years, and Natalie tried all her wiles on him without effect.

All this time there had been frequent battles about the servants. Hiram detested the French maids and the butler who had been established in the house. He longed for the accustomed deference of Irving and Mandy, and he saw no sense in having four servants where two had been all that were necessary. He told Natalie that they were all sly, and were always snooping around to spy on him. He occasionally lost his temper with one or another of them and roared at them, and then these special servants of his wife carried their heads high and ignored him. That he could not brook.

And always there was company, guests who sometimes stayed a week or more. Ladies and men, a married couple now and then. And Hiram did not like any of them. He did not like the men she brought there, and the women did not attract him. Oh, he was getting his eyes open to a great many things, almost open to some of his own faults, though that of course he never would own.

So when Natalie declared she couldn't stand the restrictions of this country house that Hiram had once thought so stately and palatial, and began to tell what additions she wanted, how there should be dressing rooms, and bathrooms for every bedroom, and there should be sun porches, sleeping porches, a game room with billiard table and other accommodations for entertaining her guests, Hiram began to swear roundly.

He had never had occasion before to swear in his own home, for the women who had been around him had always done his bidding. He had scolded them and roared at them, but he had not sworn. He hadn't *had* to swear to get his wishes carried out, but now this wife was obdurate. She wanted what she wanted *at once!* And she even went so far as to say that she had been to the city to see an architect, and had secured prices on what she wanted.

That finally finished Hiram. He roared at her so that the servants came hastily from different parts of the house where their duties called them, and peered furtively at him.

"What in the name of all that's unholy do you want all that room for, I'd like to know? Are you planning on taking in boarders? You might as well, I suppose, for we are never alone now. It might be a little profitable. I don't know why I have to feed such hordes of strangers, who just come and park on us continually. I used to think I would be a rich man some day, but you are trying to spend every cent I had saved as fast as you can. I think the time has come to call a halt."

"Call a *halt?*" said the lady of the house lifting well groomed eyebrows. "I should think the time had come for *you* to call a halt on *yourself.* You are making yourself a by-word in the kitchen and among my friends. Don't roar so! You can be heard all the way out to the street."

Hiram's reaction to that was to roar a little louder.

"I shall speak as I like in my own house!" he thundered. "And I want a halt called on the strangers that are coming here in a continual stream. There is one man in particular that I don't want to have darken these doors again, and that is that lily of a fool who hovers around *you* every minute when he is here. I mean that creature you call 'Herbert doll-ing!' If he comes here again I shall certainly have him ar-rested or thrown out or something. You might tell him, to avoid trouble. And I'm just about fed up with all these guests. If you have any more coming just cancel them. I *mean* that! I want to find my house to myself this evening when I get home. If I find any guests here I'll send for taxis to take them home, and I'll tell them I don't want them to come again. Those are *orders!*"

"But Hiram—"

"No 'but-Hirams'! I mean what I have said. I want a little peace and rest. I did want the company of my wife in a com-fortable home, till you opened the doors for the whole world to come in and eat and drink and be merry. And now I'm *done.* I don't want to see strangers smirking around occu-pying my rooms, and playing bridge and running their ex-cruciating jazz and swing on your radio. I don't want to hear another radio as long as I live! And no, I *won't* build this house over! It's going to stay just as it was when you married me, and told me it was the most adorable house you ever saw. I want to get rid of all these queer-shaped things you call furniture in the place where my fine antiques used to be, and I want to get rid of your high and mighty creatures you call servants. I'm going out in the kitchen and fire them this minute, and I'm going to town to hunt up Mandy and Irving. I want them back, and we won't have any comfort till they get here. I'm sick of these stylish messes your servants get up for food and I won't have another meal in this house until I get Mandy back to cook it! Now, if you don't like that you can *go too!* For now I'm the head of this house, and you'll do as I say if you want to stay here."

"But Hiram! Hi *dear!*" Natalie was crying prettily now.

"No! You needn't try any Hi-dears on me either. I'm done with that nonsense. If you want to stay here you've got to quit this sloppy business, calling everybody 'dolling' and trying to make my honorable name of Hiram into a fool modern contraction!"

"But—but—I thought you *liked* me to call you by a special pet name that was all our own," she pleaded, her large eyes filling with great effective tears that were trained to fall just at the proper moment down a well made-up cheek.

"Yes, that was all very well when you first came and were a well-behaved wife, as you ought to be, before you began to upset the whole regime here, and fire my servants I had had for years, and put out my furniture, and bring in your pestiferous friends. Then I used to think it was cute and you were very attractive. But now I've found you out, and I don't want to hear it again! I heard that baboon of a Herbert yelling it all over the place, 'Hi! Oh, *Hi!* I say where are you, Hi? I want another bottle of wine. Will you tell the sehvant to bring it in?' "

Hiram in his extreme rage imitated the man Herbert's tone to perfection. The servants listening in had a great laugh over it. It was as if a mad dog should stop in his wild career to put on a little lap-poodle's act.

But Natalie was very angry. Her eyes were flashing now. She stiffened visibly.

"That will be enough!" she said in her severest tone.

"When you take to caricaturing my friends I think we have reached the limit."

"I agree with you," said Hiram. "I have reached the limit! If you can behave like a decent woman, and put off this social act and live at home quietly with your husband, and be guided by my wishes, well and good. I will agree to put aside and forget what you have done. Otherwise you can get out and stay out! I want no more to do with you!"

Hiram turned and stamped across the dining room to the door of the butler's pantry. He could hear the scuttling of quick feet as the servants fled before his coming, and Natalie caught her breath. She was not ready for this turn of events. Things had been going on this way for almost two years now, since they were married, and she had managed to stave off their coming to a head before the time was ripe. Never before had Hiram gone quite so far. He had made threats, but he had not actually put them into action. Actually carrying the war into the kitchen! And those foreign servants of hers wouldn't stand for his high-tempered nonsense. They would resent it. And it did not suit her purposes to have them dismissed just now. They were discreet. In case of real difficulty of some sort they would be excellent witnesses for her if any real trouble arose. She knew their testimony would be all for herself. She had been working toward that end, if at any time her purposes did not carry out, and she got into trouble.

Natalie turned deadly white as she followed cautiously after her husband, near enough to hear without being seen.

So she heard Hiram announce to the discreet-looking waitress in the pantry who was demurely putting away dishes on the pantry shelves that she might go to her room and pack her things at once. She was *done* working here, and a taxi would be at the door within a half hour to take them all to the station. He would see that she had her wages.

Natalie looking through the crack of the swing door was able to see the sneer on the maid's face, and hear her contemptuous laugh as she went on with her work as much as to say that she did not take her orders from him.

But Hiram did not stay to argue with her. He stalked on into the kitchen, and out to the back door whither the butler had vanished, and gave the same orders to him and the other maids in a very final tone.

It was the butler, standing on the back steps, who dared to answer him in a most disrespectful way.

"It was the lady who hired us," he said. "We have nothing to do with you, sir!"

"Yes," said Hiram, "it was the lady who hired you, but it was I who paid your wages. Now *go,* and be quick about it!" and he turned and went back into the house with a look on his face that boded no good to anyone who crossed him.

He went straight to the telephone and ordered a taxi to be there in exactly half an hour to take four people to the station for the next train, in a tone so loud that they could not fail to hear every word he said. Then he slammed down the receiver and hunted up his wife who was weeping very effectively in the library, and ordered her to tell her servants to hurry and get out. He would give her checks for each of them, and he wanted to have the matter finished as quickly as possible.

He wrote the four checks at high speed, as if he were hastening the departure of the hated servants, and then went to the telephone again, and called a henchman in his office. This message too was easily heard all over the house as it was delivered in stentorian tones:

"That you, Jim? I want you to get ready to go to the city in my car and find Mandy and Irving. You know where they used to live. They probably have gone back there. If they are not there find out where they are, and go get them. Bring them out to my house with you tonight! If they are working some other place tell them I'll make it well worth their while to give it up and come back to me. Tell Irving those are *orders.*"

The click that came as Hiram hung up the receiver seemed to reverberate through the whole house, even to the third story, where now the packing of the departing crew became accelerated. The master had evidently come into his own, and meant business. The lady had just been up with evidences of weeping on her face and given them their checks, arranging an address where she could contact them if circumstances should change and she wanted them back again, or she needed them to stand by her.

Then the taxi arrived and the lady retired to her locked room to see what she should do next, while the master of the house saw the whole menage speedily into the coach, and watched them depart with a grim look on his face. He had never made it his business to keep tabs on the amount of liquor that was brought into the house, so he did not know that quite a number of bottles departed with the servants. But his first act after he came back into the house was to investigate the sideboard, pantries, and store closets in the cellar, and gather all refreshments of that sort together, putting it under lock and key. It wasn't that he wanted it for himself, for he did not have the habit of drinking. He was too frugal of nature for that. But he desired to put out of the house all that contributed to the constant stream of wild guests who seemed to be satellites of this wife of his. If her guests came again they would not stay long if she had nothing to give them to drink, he reasoned.

Next he called up all the stores in the village where he had charge accounts and asked for an itemized statement of what he owed, and told them to send all further orders C.O.D. and not to charge anything more until further notice from him. He said he wanted to straighten out his accounts, for he had just discharged some servants and he wanted to check up on what they had been doing.

When Natalie heard that she was furious, and resolved somehow to get even with him. But before she could formulate any plans Hiram had stamped out of the house and slammed the door behind him. Then she heard his car go out the drive and she knew that she was alone in the house, with only her problems to consider, for which she would probably have the whole day. Hiram would not likely return until late in the evening. That had come to be a habit with him when there had been discord in the morning before he went away.

She went to the telephone and called up a few of her friends. She had to do something before Hiram got home. It wouldn't do for him to come back tonight and find them all here as usual. And yet of course she didn't want to tell them too much, for there had been many a storm of tempers in that house during the past two years, and they had passed. Perhaps this too would pass.

She was safe of course during the daytime, and after consideration she called Herbert Grandison. After all, why hadn't she married Herbert? He was fairly wealthy, and not the least bit stingy, as Hiram was beginning to show that he was. Of course Herbert was devoted, and dressed charmingly, always so well groomed, which, now that their honeymoon was over, could not often be said of Hiram. But she adored big men and Hiram was big and broad shouldered and strong. That was really why she had chosen him after all. Well, he had been devoted for a time, and perhaps that was all one could expect of any human being—devotion for a time.

So with a smile and a sigh for glories past that had not lasted she betook herself to the telephone. She arranged for an evening with one of her women friends, dinner at her house, with a round of night clubs afterwards. She said of her husband that he was busy and couldn't possibly go, and of course they would invite "dolling Herbie" to be her escort.

It was all comfortably arranged at last, and she settled down to rest a little after the exciting morning she had passed, to rest and to get a bite of something to eat and *drink*. But lo, she found the sideboard and all the places where liquor could be, locked! How out*rage*ous! She prowled around and had to be satisfied with a few fancy cakes and some icewater. She wouldn't even make coffee. Hiram should see how destitute he had left her when he came home and went the rounds to try and find something to eat himself. He could take a little of his own punishment. It was he who had sent four most efficient servants away! And of course he would not be able to get his old Mandy and Irving. Well, let him suffer. She didn't intend to get his breakfast for him. She would let him see the consequences of his own act. And she would keep it up for weeks if necessary. She could always run into the city and get a good meal for herself if she got hungry, and for a time she would return some of her guests' visits.

Early in the afternoon she arrayed herself in an attractive negligee and awaited Herbert. And he was not long in coming.

He came in with a smiling face, a glint of triumph in his eyes. This was the time for which he had been waiting. Natalie had sent for him herself, had told him that she would be alone.

He came forward into the room, his hands extended, and took her hands in both of his. He drew her close and looked down into her eyes.

"Dolling Natalie!" he said effulgently. "We are free from the angry mob at last! I have you to myself. Let's sit down here Natalie, my dear," and he drew her down beside him on a love seat that was placed diagonally across in front of the fireplace. Natalie had started a gentle blaze that the maids had arranged for early that morning. All Natalie had to do was to touch a match to the kindling as soon as she heard her Herbert ring the bell, and then fly to open the door.

She sank gently down on the sofa, his arm about her, and looked up into his eyes.

"Oh, this is like heaven, to rest with your arm about me," she murmured. "I've had such a terrible day!"

"Well, forget it, and let us just enjoy this time together,

my sweet. Then tonight you'll meet me somewhere, and we'll go dancing, or to the opera—"

"Not tonight," she said sadly. "I've already promised Neeta to come there to dinner and go places. I guess I can't get out of that."

"Oh, well, I'll go there too. She asked me. I said I wasn't sure, but how about tomorrow night? You'll give me that, surely?"

"Oh yes," said Natalie, "that will be sweet. I'll give you that of course."

"And *I* will give *you tonight!*" said Hiram, suddenly stepping up behind them and laying a strong hand on "dolling Herbie's" neck. He slid his fingers under Herbert's collar and lifted the other man bodily from the couch with a mighty grip, lifted him *over* the couch, set his feet on the floor and propelled him choking and gulping and strangling from the room. On the front steps he paused, then giving his man a swift and efficient kick he sent him sprawling down the steps and onto the walk.

"Now," said Hiram, "get out and go practice your fascinations on some other man's wife!"

Then he went and faced his wife.

"Well," he said grimly, "so that's the game you're playing! Well, you needn't play it any longer in my house! Do you want to go *with* him, or shall I send for a taxi in half an hour for you? I'll give you as much time as your maids had to pack. Take whatever you can in that limited time, for when you go I'm *done* with you!"

"Oh, Hi dear," she began piteously. "Don't talk that way to me. It wasn't my fault. It really wasn't!"

"Shut up!" said Hiram roughly. "It was *all* your fault from start to finish. You were putting the works on that man just as you did on me. That doesn't excuse him, but it certainly doesn't let you out! Get *up!* Go upstairs and get ready to go. Put something decent on in place of that flimflam, and get what you need tonight, for that's about all you'll get.

Now scram! Oh, I blamed my son for not wanting a step-mother, but if I had known what I was getting when I got you, he certainly should have had the right to blame me! That's all! I'm *done* with you!"

"But Hi! You can't send me away this way—!"

"Can't I? Just watch me! Perhaps you'd like an escort of police. I'll get them if you delay much longer."

Natalie turned a frightened look at him, and fairly flew up the stairs on her trembling limbs. She flung on garments without regard to suitability. She dragged her two big suit-cases out and stuffed her best beloved and most expensive garments in with trembling hands. She flung a handful of jewels in one corner, a couple of hats atop, some shoes be-side them, and came hurrying downstairs with her latest pur-chase, a handsome fur coat turned inside out over her arm, not to attract attention to its gorgeous quality. But Hiram reached out and took it from her. "You'll not need that," he said dryly. "This is spring time. Had you forgotten? This can go back to the store where you purchased it. Now, the taxi is out there. I'll take your baggage. But first give me your house key. I want no stealing back and coming in on me. I'm *done*, I tell you, entirely done!"

She opened her purse, shaking with sobs, and handed him the key.

"Now GO!" he thundered.

"Why—where do you want me to go?"

"That's entirely up to you. Go just where you please. I shall never try to tell you what to do again!" and he picked up the baggage and carried it down the steps, she followed sorrowfully behind.

He put the baggage into the front seat, handed the driver some money and turned back, running up the steps and slamming the door.

An hour later another car drew up at the door and Irving and Mandy got out. No one answered their ring so they opened the door and walked in and they found the master lying crumpled in a heap as he had fallen, his face all twisted into an ugly grimace, his hands clinched and rigid, his limbs stiff and unable to move. He opened wild eyes and looked at them, and Irving thought he recognized him.

They picked him up most tenderly and bore him to his bed. They sent for the doctor, and the two faithful souls ministered to him as best they could, Mandy still with her funny spring hat mounted atop her gray bobbed head, and cocked over her right eye, a wide white rubber band like a bandage holding it in place behind above a billow of stiff straight gray hair. Somehow in spite of all the years of his unfairness and almost cruel faultfinding, there seemed to be tears in Mandy's eyes. As she looked down piteously into the poor twisted face, and at the powerless paralyzed body, Mandy couldn't help feeling sorry for him. The thin drawn lips, the sharp tongue that could no longer utter a word, they were all quiet now, and at the mercy of herself and Irving.

There he lay utterly paralyzed from head to foot, whether from shock that his lady love had turned out to be a traitor, or because he had found someone he could not bend to his own will, who shall say?

20

WHEN Irving and Mandy had been dismissed by the new lady of the house during the absence of her husband, they had questioned whether they ought to go before his return. They had not been at all happy staying here since the advent of the new mistress, but it didn't seem quite ethical to Irving just to disappear before the man who had been his mind and conscience as it were for the last two decades returned to set his seal upon his wife's orders. But Mandy had stubbornly said "I'm *goin'*. Irvin' Potter, ef you wants to stay and serve a man whose woman doesn't want you here, you ken stay *alone*. I'm goin' ta git out while the goin's good. Ef you don't know when you got the gate, *I do!*"

Irving lost no time in getting everything he owned packed and ready to go. In fact they had begun to pack before they were dismissed, for they wanted to be ready to leave at a moment's notice. So it had not taken them long.

On the train, en route to the city, they discussed where they would go.

"I think we'd better go where the Boss can find us if he ever wants us again," said Irving. "I feel mighty sure he'll be shouting for us before long."

"I wouldn't wonder," agreed Mandy, "What if we see if your brother Henry knows of any place near him? The Boss knows Henry."

And so it turned out they went to Henry's, left most of their goods in boxes in Henry's attic, and settled down to wait.

Irving got himself a job as head waiter in a restaurant. It wasn't a very notable restaurant, but it paid fairly well, and it was not far away from their rooms which were in the other half of brother Henry's house, so that a messenger could easily round the two up and get them ready to go at a moment's notice in case the "home folks" ever sent for them.

Mandy got up a little business of her own, going out to cook dinners for people who couldn't afford to get the expensive caterers. So both these good people were busy, keeping their minds from dwelling too sadly on the people who had almost become their children, so long they had been waiting on their needs.

And yet, when there was a little let-up in the long day's work, or in the morning when Mandy had time to put her own rooms in order and do any mending she had, she was continually thinking of young Revel, and wondering how he was and what he was doing.

She had written him a letter, poor of penmanship and worse of spelling, when he first reached his grandfather's house, and he had written her back telling her his grandfather was better but that he was staying out there and going to college. So on the strength of that news she lived and wove her romances about him. But often she wished she might be somewhere near him so that she could make a tasty pie or cake now and then to hearten him.

And often in the early mornings before Irving had to go to his restaurant the two would sit together by a forlorn little back-street window and talk about the changes that had come into their lives since the little "Mrs. Emily" went to Heaven. They talked about the "new missus" as they called her, too, and they could not say enough against her, for even during those few days before she took her courage in her hands and dismissed them, she had shown a great many qualities that they could not admire, and many more that they could but despise. So the days went on but there came no summons to the old house where they had worked so long.

Once Mandy said, "Irving, you reckon you could drive any automobile?"

Irving gave her a withering look.

"Why of course, Mandy, what do you think I am? A moron to forget a thing like that so soon?"

"Well," sighed Mandy, "why couldn't you borrow Henry's car? He don't use it every day, and you get a day off sometimes. Why couldn't we take a vacation and go up to that Grandfather Revel's and find that boy? I'd like to see if he don't look kinda peeked, or mebbe his socks aren't darned right and hurt his feet. Or mebbe they don't give him the right things ta eat."

"Oh, now, Mandy, quit your fretting. You know you aren't the only one who can darn a sock without a lump in the heel or toe, and you aren't the only one who can cook. Just you stop your fretting. When it comes time for us to do something for Mister Revel we'll know it. Besides, Mandy, you know we can't take vacations and expect our jobs to just sit around waiting for us to get back. We are mighty lucky to get jobs while we're waiting, so I guess we'd better stick by them till something better turns up."

"Yes, I s'pose so," sighed Mandy, "but sometimes I get wearyin' about that boy. You know I promised his little mother—Mrs. Em'ly—I'd look after him, an' I can't seem ta think she'll think I'm doin' it."

"Now look here, Mandy, you haven't anything at all to do with it. You've got to wait till the time comes. It'll come. It surely will."

And so when at last the summons did come, it didn't take

long for those two faithful souls to resign their work, pack a few hurried necessities, and get into the old car to be taken "home."

The doctor came hastily at Irving's summons and shook his head. When he came out from the sick room he asked where Revel was. So Mandy got herself together and wrote her second letter to Revel.

> Dear Mister Revel,
>   This is to tell you we are back in the old hous taken care of yur daddy agen. We found him alone on the hall floor, parlized. The doctor says he don't know how long he will last, and we should let you know. You better come at once!
>   So no more at present,
>
>   Your devoted servant,
>   Mandy

Mandy went out in the dark and mailed her letter in the nearest post box, and when she got back she found that Irving had sent a telegram to the young master, neither of which he received for two days because he had gone with his debating team to an intercollegiate debate.

But in the meantime Grand had been getting some side lines of gossip from various sources, and had learned that there had been trouble between Hiram and his second wife, and she had left him, or he had turned her out, according to the various gossip mongers who brought the word to town. They had got it in the village paper, just because they thought it would be interesting news, since Revel was very popular in the town and college. And so hard things were coming Revel's way again, testing to try him out. "For the perfection of the saints" quoted Grandfather Revel to himself as he thought what he had to tell Revel. Then he got out his very best smile that hinted glory somewhere behind its lines, for the moment that his dear boy should arrive.

So Revel came in on the light of that smile, and saw at once there was something graver behind it. And there was the letter and the telegram awaiting him on the table beside the old man, and neither of them were from Margaret. With premonition in his eyes he tore open the telegram. It was brief and to the point. "Your father has had a bad stroke. Come at once. Irving."

"Grand, what shall I do?" He handed over the telegram. The old man read it, and then with that grave smile of self-abnegation he handed it back.

"You'll have to go, of course, son. He's your father."

"But, Grand, that woman will be there."

"Well, son, duty is duty."

"But she didn't send for me. Perhaps she doesn't want me now."

"What has that to do with it? He is your father. He may be dying."

"Yes, I know," said the boy with white lips. "Of course I'll go. But would he want me?"

"He is still your father."

"Yes."

Then Revel saw the letter and picked it up, studying it. The address was peculiar to say the least. Then he saw the postmark and tore the envelope quickly.

"Oh!" he said, and handed the letter over, saying, "Yes, of course I must go, Grand. I'll hurry. There's a train down to New York in half an hour. I'll try to get that. Will you be all right while I'm gone? I don't suppose I'll be wanted long."

"You can't tell, Revel. You'll stay as long as you are needed, and don't think of me. There are people enough here to look out for me. You'll maybe have some message for your father's soul before he is called away. There may be a chance he would understand. I'll be praying you know, boy."

Revel looked startled.

"I can't think that any message would ever reach him," said the boy.

"Don't limit your Lord," said the grandfather.

"I won't, Grand. And thank you for the prayers. I'll be watching for the chance."

So Revel went away from the things he counted dear into an atmosphere of horror and sorrow and mystery. But he knew that he went God-led.

Margaret's letter reached Linwood the afternoon that Revel left for Arleth, and was forwarded the next morning by his grandfather. It brought great relief and joy to Revel who was having a sorrowful time in the great house that had once been his home, and now no longer seemed to have anything to do with him.

He had been met at the station by Irving, who had met every train since he sent his telegram, and Mandy came to the door with smiling solemnity. Both the old servants felt that they were entertaining death in the house, and went about their duties with great awe upon them.

The doctor had sent a nurse, and they were now serving her, as if she had been an angel, while they waited for Revel whom they looked upon as the real master of the house. They escorted Revel up to his father's room and waited outside the door with tears running down their old faces, tears for the master and tears for his son.

A strange thing it was that nobody had thought at all about the second wife, nor knew where she was, to send word if they had. It was not until the doctor brought word of Mr. Radcliffe's condition that the news began to drift about the town, and Natalie's friends began to wonder, and to ask questions of one another with bated breath.

Natalie and Herbert had gone to the dinner at Neeta's, and had gone the rounds afterwards, though Herbert looked badly shaken up and had a cut on his forehead, and a sprained wrist. He had told them he had had a bad fall, and let it go at that. They had gone away together, he and

Natalie, saying that they could not join the company the next night as they both had engagements. Natalie had driven away in Herbert's car, but no one had seen either of them since. And no one in the Radcliffe house had thought to miss Natalie.

Revel had walked quietly into his father's room and stood by the bed looking sadly down at him. Suddenly he saw his father's eyes open, and he was looking straight at him, a look of recognition.

The nurse had tiptoed out of the room leaving the two alone for the moment, and the startled son was standing there as if he were seeing his father, the real father, for the first time. Then without realizing that his father could not talk, could not even hear, perhaps, he spoke:

"Father, I'm *sorry!*" and he brushed his fingers over his eyes to flick away the tears that came.

A quick contortion of muscles came upon the twisted face, a look of utmost agony, and the eyes closed quickly. For an instant Revel wondered if perhaps this might be death, and he was glad he had spoken tenderly. He was wholly without preparation to meet this emergency of his life. But had that little word of his brought death? Maybe he should not have spoken, though the nurse had given him no warning not to.

Then as he watched he saw a slow tear make its way out from under the closed eyelid, and trickle down the hard cheek, and suddenly something happened to himself. The alienation of the years seemed bridged, and he felt a deep sympathy for the father who lay there locked and still as if he were dead. Tears! It had never occurred to him as a child that his father *could* have tears. And a silent tongue! When he had always had plenty of scathing words to visit upon everybody. And now he was here, silent, and quiet, locked in a living death.

"Father, I'm *sorry!*" He murmured again, more softly now, and slid down upon his knees beside the bed, his hand on his father's motionless one. Then he stooped his tall head and kissed his father's forehead. He couldn't remember to have done that since he was almost a baby, and had been rudely thrust aside.

But now the anger and the hatred were gone out of his heart. All the resentment! He hadn't ever thought that that could be. He had suffered so much through the years, all alone! But it was as if it had never been. He felt a great sympathy, a sorrow for his father. A strange belated love, where love had never been welcome before.

After that he sat for a long time beside the bed and held his father's hand, praying in his heart. And he found a great longing that he might be able to do something for him. If he could only bring a message that would reach his heart. If he could only make him know the love of Christ, and what it had been to his lonely boy! But how to bring that about. That was the problem. God would have to do it, not he.

It was the next day that Margaret's letter reached him and brought that great relief and joy to his heart. It shone in his face, so that when the eyes from the bed opened and looked at him again, they saw it, and the father continued to look with a kind of wonder growing in his gaze. He did not remember his son to have had that light in his face. What was it?

Then the eyes looked toward the book Revel was holding. His *Bible!* The eyes lingered with a growing wonder, and looked from the book to the boy's face, and down to the book again. They didn't seem actually to move, and yet Revel was sure they focused on himself, then on the book, and he gave his dazzling smile, as if it were somehow light that could reach down into his father's soul and touch it. A point of contact.

There was no answering smile, no change of expression, just that wondering look.

"Would you like me to read some to you, father?" he asked suddenly as if an angel had suddenly suggested the idea to him.

And so, taking up the Bible where he had been reading, with his finger in the pages, he began to read in a low, steady, clear voice, not realizing what the selection was to be as he began, only that it was the place where he had left off reading yesterday.

> For the preaching of the cross is to them that perish foolishness; but unto us which are saved it is the power of God.
>
> For it is written, I will destroy the wisdom of the wise and will bring to nothing the understanding of the prudent.
>
> Where is the wise? Where is the scribe? Where is the disputer of this world? hath not God made foolish the wisdom of this world?
>
> For after that in the wisdom of God the world by wisdom knew not God, it pleased God by the foolishness of preaching to save them that believe.

What was this he was reading to a man who had never listened to things of this sort? Was there any message in it for him? His father rarely went to church, nor heard preaching. He had heard him sneer at preaching! And would he think—if indeed the poor locked mind was able to think— would he think that he was trying to mock him for the past? Oh, that must not be. Quickly he turned to a familiar passage that seemed the foundation of all faith.

> For God so loved the world, that He gave His only begotten Son, that whosoever believeth in Him should not perish, but have everlasting life.
>
> For God sent not His Son into the world to condemn the world, but that the world through Him might be saved.
>
> He that believeth on Him is not condemned: but he that believeth not is condemned already, because he

hath not believed in the name of the only begotten Son of God.

And this is the condemnation, that light is come into the world, and men loved darkness rather than light, because their deeds were evil.

Again Revel turned the pages and read a verse he had marked a little while ago. Perhaps not one he would have chosen if he had given much thought to what would be the best. But he read smoothly:

But if our gospel be hid, it is hid to them that are lost: In whom the god of this world hath blinded the minds of them that believe not, lest the light of the glorious gospel of Christ, who is the image of God, should shine unto them.

The searching, steady, listening eyes were still open, upon him, and Revel turned to another verse:

But we all, with open face beholding as in a glass the glory of the Lord, are changed into the same image from glory to glory, even as by the Spirit of the Lord.

And again another:

While we look not at the things which are seen, but at the things which are not seen: for the things which are seen are temporal; but the things which are not seen are eternal.

The doctor came in just then and looked curiously at Revel, and then keenly at his patient.

"Will it hurt him for me to read?" Revel asked a little later when the doctor had gone out in the hall and was telling him about something to order at the drugstore.

"No, I think not," said the doctor lifting his eyebrows casually. "But I doubt if he understands much. Of course, at that, he may. I don't know! Go on. Read him anything you think he would be interested in. He might not be keen on the Bible. But do as you think best. I doubt if it matters much."

The doctor went away, and Revel went to his knees and asked for direction, and his father had a longer, steadier, more natural sleep than he had had since he was taken.

Revel's heart was lighter that night than it had been since he came. He had put the matter of his father into the hands of the Lord. And now he could allow himself to be glad about that letter from Margaret.

What a woman that aunt must be, that she would let a package lie in a drawer for two whole years without delivering it, or even remembering it!

Revel didn't understand why he cared so much about this, but it was a happy thing to get his girl of the woods back again, and he was going to have grand times writing to her.

So that night he sat in his room writing Margaret a letter.

Dear Margaret:

Don't be surprised at the postmark. I've come home to be with my father while he needs me. He has had a stroke and is entirely paralyzed. His wife is not here. I don't know yet what happened, nor where she is, so we won't talk about it tonight. Let's just talk about *us*.

I don't think you can know how greatly pleased I was when I got your letter. I have been looking so long for one, and it didn't come, and it didn't come, and then I thought you were done with me, and didn't want to bother writing any more. So I got proud too, and said I wouldn't write till you did. I'm sorry now. I could have spared myself a lot of worry and pain, and maybe even have found your package for you sooner.

But now it's over, and I am all kinds of glad. Because you're the nicest girl I ever met, and I didn't want to lose you for a friend. Besides I felt as if we were sort of pals, and that means a lot to a fellow who hasn't got any mother living down here. I guess you know what I mean. Of course I've got Grand now, and that is great, but I wanted you too.

I'm glad you liked the bracelet. I thought it was pretty and looked like you. I'd like to see it on your wrist. You have pretty hands to carry off a thing like that. But you see I've thought so long that you didn't like my sending it to you, that I'm kind of daffy about it now, to find out you are pleased. But please don't let's get separated again. You won't let that happen again, will you? Promise? So do I. No little old pride is going to stop me writing even if you do stop.

Now I've got a pretty sad proposition on hand. I'll write you more about it when I know more. My father is lying like a dead man, except for his eyes which open and shut. And sometimes I find him looking at me with the saddest look you ever saw.

Grand told me before I came away that I must remember there might be a chance for me to bring him a message, but I couldn't see how. It doesn't seem to me possible that my father as I knew him would ever stand for any kind of a message. But Grand said I musn't limit God, so I'm putting it up to my Heavenly Father to show me the way if he wants me to do or say anything. Won't you help me pray that I may know how, if there is any chance?

Today, though, I was sitting in his room reading my Bible and I looked up and found his eyes on me. Then he seemed to be looking at my Bible, so I began to read aloud. I didn't have any special selection, I just read where I had opened the book, and he kept watching me.

I don't know what's become of the step lady. Mandy thinks she may have gone to Reno, but Mandy is only surmising. Mandy doesn't like her one little bit. I presume some explanation will come soon. At present it is like reading the end of a serial story without the beginning. *Something* must have happened to make father have a stroke. But my job is to help him to know God. You'll pray, won't you?

> Good night, Girl of the woods, I'm so glad I have you again as a friend.
> Revel

21

THEN into the midst of the dreary monotony of those sad days there came an announcement in the paper of an accident on a highway out toward the west, in which a number of people were killed and several severely injured. Among the dead was listed the name of Mrs. Hiram Radcliffe. Later down the column it said that one of the smashed cars was owned by Herbert W. Grandison.

It was Irving who brought in the paper that morning and who was the first to read the news. Appalled he hesitated whether to tell anyone about it, even Mandy. They had trouble enough in that house. But as he thought it over he saw that it must eventually be told and it would be his part to talk it over with Revel and decide what to do, before the world should get hold of the story and give it a lurid aspect.

So he went with the paper to Revel. Poor Revel! How he wished for his dear Grand to give advice. But gradually as he thought it over and asked questions about the people he did not himself know, he came to the conclusion that it was up to him to do something about this. She was his father's wife at least. "Wasn't she?" he asked Irving. "There hadn't been a divorce or anything, had there?"

"No, Mister Revel. Not that I ever heard, and I always read the newspapers. But I have heard that there was talk of her going to Reno, though I couldn't say rightly who told that. One thing is certain, she and your father never got along together, not even while Mandy and I were here. She wanted to build the house over, and she bought a lot of new dishes and furniture that your father didn't like. She wanted to sell the house and move away, and they had words all the time. Then she had those drinking carousing people here every night almost, till he was wild. He couldn't abide them. Oh, yes, there was plenty reason for those two to get a divorce, but they hadn't done it yet, not to my knowledge."

"Well, then," said Revel, "I think it must be my duty to go out and attend to this. But—how could I know—how would I identify her, Irving? I never saw her."

"I'd have to go, Mister Revel. I could identify her all right."

"Yes," said Revel, "but that wouldn't do. For my father's honor it should be one of the family. There would be a lot of arrangements to make too. I'd have to be there to say what."

"Then I better go with you, Mister Revel," said Irving.

"Do you think we could be spared here?" asked Revel.

"You go ask the doctor," said the old servant. "He'll know what to do."

So Revel gravely went to ask the doctor.

"Well, of course you'll have to go," said the doctor. "Sure, you can be spared. I doubt if your father'll know you're gone. And I'll be right on the job. I'll come in oftener and look after everything till you get back."

So Irving got his brother Henry to come up from the city and take his place while they were gone, and Revel talked to his grandfather over the telephone and got his advice. "Yes, go, Revel, boy! That's your job of course."

The two caught the next plane and went to the tragic duty.

It was not a long task. It was over in a day, and the two were on their way back, but Revel felt that it had been ages since he started. He felt like an old old man with the griefs of the world upon him.

But his father was too ill to know what had happened. He would never likely know this side of death.

Revel had decided that for the present at least, it would be better to lay the crushed body in a simple grave in the little town where it had met its death. There seemed to be no near relatives. At least Mandy said "the missus" had told her she had no one left in her family, and Revel had no data by which to trace any. So the home coming was very quiet and not noised abroad much. Revel allowed the undertaker to put a notice of Natalie's death in the paper, and beyond that there was nothing to do but nurse the sick man and await the outcome. He would probably never be any better, and the end might come at any time.

But little by little the town came to know something about it all, and there were a few callers. Hiram hadn't many close friends. He wasn't a man who made friends. Emily Revel's old minister called, but saw only Revel. Then one day Mrs. Martin arrived, pompously, in her old jalopy.

Mandy let her in and greeted her sourly. She knew the bitter tongue the woman wielded.

"I would like to see Mr. Radcliffe," she said sweetly. "I'm an old friend and well-wisher," she added.

Mandy glared at her and her eyes said plainly, "Oh, yeah?" She opened her mouth to say that Mr. Radcliffe was too ill to see anybody and the doctor did not allow visitors, no matter how old friends they might be. But a sudden thought came to her.

"Sit down," she said, and turned to go upstairs. "I'll see if he can come."

"Oh," said the caller, "I understood that he was confined to his bed. I can just as well go upstairs. I'm not one who has to save herself."

"Sit down!" commanded Mandy, and padded off to mount the backstairs and call Revel.

"There's a woman downstairs wants to see yeh," she announced, and then slid on down the backstairs again.

Revel was tired. He was resting and trying to write an account of things in a very few words to Margaret, but he arose with a sigh. There seemed to be so many new things required of him since he had come to man's estate, for he was within only a few days of his majority now.

He went downstairs slowly and into the living room. Then he paused as he recognized his old enemy.

"You wanted to see me?" he asked politely, hoping she wouldn't recognize him as the little boy he used to be who had so offended her about a poor dead fish that wasn't hers at all.

Mrs. Martin arose and faced him, and then her countenance changed.

"Oh, it's you again, is it? No, I didn't want to see you at all. I *never* want to see you! It was your father I came to see. I want to express my sympathy to him in the death of his wife!"

"Oh," said Revel, "I'm sorry. I suppose you have not heard. My father is not able to see anyone. He is too ill even to be told that his wife has died."

There was a certain dignity about Revel's bearing that astonished Mrs. Martin. She looked at him again.

"Well," she said firmly after an instant's pause, "I think you're making a very grave mistake not to tell him. He has a right to know."

"Yes?" said Revel. "Well, the doctor thinks otherwise. Besides, I doubt if he would understand."

"What do you mean? I think you are taking a great deal on yourself to decide a matter like that. Why don't you ask him if he wants to know what has happened?"

"Mrs. Martin, you evidently don't know my father is unable to move or speak, and is much of the time unconscious. He has had a stroke."

"Yes? And who but yourself is responsible for that? A son who wouldn't come to his father's wedding, and made him go through the shame of having that known. Dragging him through the muck of common gossip."

"I'm sorry, Mrs. Martin, you evidently have been misinformed about a good many things. I was staying with my grandfather who was at death's door at the time of the wedding. My father and his wife were aware of the facts. That was all that was necessary."

"Yes, well, when you keep facts so close they are apt to get twisted. Suppose you answer a few questions for me, and I'll try to do your father the favor of seeing that the truth goes out instead of lies."

"The truth?" said Revel.

"Yes, the truth, the whole truth and nothing but the truth. That is the only thing that can prevent wild stories going around that can so easily injure a good man's name and character. Suppose you tell me first, was Mrs. Radcliffe on her way to Reno to get a divorce when she was killed?"

Revel quivered with anger but kept his voice steady as he answered:

"Not that I know of, Mrs. Martin. But I cannot see how that concerns you or any of the townspeople."

"You *can't*? You can't understand that it would bring reproach upon your father to have it known that she was intending to get a divorce from that good man?"

"Mrs. Martin, you'll have to excuse me from any further discussion of this subject. I am quite sure that if my father were able to know about this he would consider your questions an impertinence."

"H'm!" said Mrs. Martin, pressing her thin lips together. "I see you still have an impudent tongue, even if you have grown up, and gone away to college as some *suppose*. But it is quite plain that your stepmother was on her way to Reno to get a divorce or you would deny it at once, and I shall see that people understand it is a fact. You have as good as said so."

"No," said Revel coolly, "I said nothing of the sort. I do not know anything about Mrs. Radcliffe's intentions, and I think that is a matter with which we have nothing to do. That is between her and the Lord."

"Oh! The *Lord!*" sniffed the caller. "I call that blasphemous, talking about the Lord in that flippant way! Well, I suppose that was to be expected, too, with all the rest. And now, if you'll tell me one more thing I'll go. I want to know where your stepmother is buried."

"Well, that is a matter with which neither you nor the neighbors have anything to do!" said Revel with dignity, and he bowed the woman out gravely, then closed and locked the front door.

Mr. Radcliffe's condition continued about the same for weeks. Sometimes the vise that seemed to hold his muscles bound tight would relax a little and there would be less contortion in the twisted face, less anguish in the tortured eyes and sometimes, almost, it would seem he was making an effort to speak, or to move one hand a trifle, a motion almost of protest or beseeching. Then the next day his face would be a set mask again, worse than ever, and the doctor would say he had had another slight stroke in the night.

One night after this had happened, Revel was holding his father's hand and the stiffened fingers feebly tried to press on his, to cling. There came a slight sound of great urgency, as born of a deep desire for something, a cry for mercy!

Then Revel dropped upon his knees, the inert hand still held close in his, till his own hand's warmth seemed to bring a warmth almost of life in the other one. He bowed his head, closed his eyes, and prayed aloud.

"Oh, my Heavenly Father, please make my earthly father understand that You love him. Help him to accept Your Son as his own Saviour, and get ready to go Home to live with You and mother and all of us forever. Please do this for my father, and forgive his sins in Jesus' name and for His sake, Amen."

A long time he knelt thus, with that other hand warm in his, until at last he heard the labored regular breathing and knew that the man was asleep.

Letters were a great comfort to Revel in these days. Margaret's were deep with sympathy, warm with heartfelt wishes, and the two young souls grew closer as the days went by.

And Grand's letters, though they were brief, were full of loving advice, and trust in God and his grandson.

And then, almost nine months after the stroke had laid him low Hiram passed gently into another world in the night, after an evening in which Revel had been near him all the time, talking quietly to him, begging him to call in his heart on Jesus. And who shall say but that the imprisoned soul had heard God's call and answered it? God does hear prayer, Revel was sure of that.

The simple service with which they laid Hiram Radcliffe to rest was filled with trust and hope for any listening ones who would take Christ as their Saviour.

There were only a few present. The old servants, Revel, the faithful Jim from the front office, a few others who had worked for Hiram. There were none of those unwelcome guests that used to swarm to that house in the lifetime of its second mistress, for most of them had gotten out of town as soon as possible after the accident. They shuddered and spoke to one another about their hitherto unwilling host with haughty contempt, and said they thought that this strange death must be a judgment upon him for the way he treated his pretty wife, and spoiled all her pleasures.

But none of them would have understood why the son had hope for his father for another life, or why he should want to have hope for him.

So Revel went back to his grandfather and told him everything. Also he took out all of Margaret's letters and made the old man read them one by one as he told the story of his acquaintance with the girl of the woods.

Revel watched the sweet old face glow with pleasure as Grand read the letters, and listened to Revel's account, and studied the photograph of the lovely girl his boy had found, and his pulse quickened with joy.

Grand asked a few questions, and when he finally handed back the letters he said with a smile and a sigh of content:

"Well, that's one big burden off my mind. I was afraid of what kind of a girl you might take up with. You know I lived through a lot of sorrow for your dear mother, my little girl Em'ly. But I'm satisfied you've picked the right girl. Now go get her, boy! Make it sure that she is yours before any other fellow steps in and takes her. There aren't so many of her kind around. May the Lord go with you, boy, and give you success."

Revel's face blazed with joy.

"Then you don't think, Grand, that I ought to wait till I graduate before I say anything to her?"

"No, lad. Don't wait! Go out and find out if she loves you. But don't take any chances on that. If you know she loves you, you can both wait better if you have the comfort of knowing that you belong to each other. You know it is a long time since you have looked into each other's faces, and you need to catch up!"

22

A telegram had come to Margaret in the university to say that her aunt had died in the sanitarium where she had been taking treatment for several weeks, and sadly she hurried back to Crystal Beach for the funeral service.

It was the nurse from the sanitarium who had come down for the funeral, who told her of her aunt's last days.

"Pretty near the last thing she said was, 'Tell my niece Margaret that I decided to take her advice, so it's all right with me.' She didn't explain what she meant. She said you would understand." Margaret lifted sweet eyes filled with joy as she said: "Yes, I understand."

Margaret did not return to the university at once, for there were many little things in her aunt's house that needed her attention. She had to see to packing some of her aunt's things that had been left to various people, a few to herself, and it must be done at once. The house itself would go to a nephew of her dead uncle, but the aunt had left her a small sum of money, and a number of things in the house that she knew the girl admired, so there was plenty to be done, and she was hard at work every day. She had written of course to Revel to tell him what had happened, but her letter did not reach Linwood until after he had left, and so Revel went first to the university.

He was greatly dismayed when he found she was not there. He had been counting every minute until he should see her face, and hear her well-remembered voice, and now it was a great disappointment not to see her at once.

He had not sent her word that he was coming. He wanted to come upon her unaware, and get her first reaction to the sight of him. He had studied it out that way so he would be able to find out whether she really cared for him—*yet*. If she didn't he meant to stay until he had *made* her care—if he *could*. Revel was never one to think too highly of himself, and he had not taken account of stock and reckoned greatly on his own assets. She was a friend, yes, he knew that surely, and could never be made to doubt it again, but would she be willing to take him for a lover?

He stood at the desk and frowned at the girl who had said that Margaret Weldon was not there.

"Oh no," said the girl, "she's just gone down to Crystal Beach. Her aunt died and she had to go to the funeral. No, I can't say when she's coming back. She talked to somebody over the phone yesterday. She said she had some things to do and she couldn't tell just when she would be done."

So Revel turned and hastened away to find a train to Crystal Beach.

It was midafternoon when Revel reached the Gurlie house and Katie had gone out to the store for something she needed in her dinner preparations. Margaret went to the door herself, and her face as it dawned with amazement written over it was all he had dreamed it would be, only she seemed even lovelier.

"Margaret!" he said, as he put down the luggage he was carrying and put out his arms. *"My Margaret!"* and then he laid his lips down on hers and kissed her, as he folded his eager arms about her and held her close. "Oh, Margaret, my sweet, I love you so!" It wasn't at all what he had meant to do.

He came to himself long enough to kick the door shut behind him and then he held her very close again, thrilled to his soul.

He forgot that he had been going to go at this matter very cautiously. He knew nothing but that her nearness was the most precious thing he had ever known, as his hungry arms drew her closer and closer till her sweet head was on his breast and her little pink ear was close to his lips. Then he whispered, "Oh, Margaret, my darling, I love you with my whole soul. Can you ever love me? I've come all the way out here because I couldn't stand it another day without you. I want you for my own. Will you marry me?"

Margaret lifted her lovely head and looked at him with a glory in her eyes, and then her arms came softly about his neck and drew his head down till her lips could meet his own.

"Oh, Revel dear!" she whispered. *"Love* you? Of *course* I love you. I've loved you ever since I saw you in the woods. I've often dreamed of your lips on mine when you kissed me good-by. I thought I was wrong and silly to do it. We were just children then, but I couldn't forget you, and I *loved* you."

They went and sat down on the couch, his arm about her, her head resting on his shoulder, and now and then they would stop talking and their lips would steal together again. It was the happiest reunion that ever could be!

And so for a time they just sat and talked together, his arm still about her, drawing her closer now and again.

He told her all about his father's death, and what he hoped for him, for he had only had time to write the briefest facts before he left, and as she had left before it got to the university she had not seen it yet. He thrilled again to see how her face lighted with sympathy. How she entered into his very innermost thoughts and hopes and fears.

"I think he may have been saved," he said reverently. "I don't know whether I have the right to believe that or not, but I somehow feel it. There was a look in his face at the last when I read to him. A softer look, if you know what I mean."

"Yes," said Margaret. "I think you can believe that. We prayed, with promises. I think we can always trust that those promises of God will be performed. I'm sure we shall meet him in Heaven and be glad together. Your mother will be glad, and my mother will be glad too. She was like that, glad in others' joys. Perhaps our mothers know each other now."

"You *dear!*" said Revel, touching her eyelids with his lips, and gently smoothing her silky fingers.

"I shall love your mother," said Revel thoughtfully. "She will be my mother too, then, and mine will be yours!"

Something went singing then in Margaret's heart and she reached up and kissed him tenderly.

Then Margaret began to talk about her aunt, telling what the nurse had said.

"And so she is saved too," said Revel, "for that must be what she means."

"Yes," said the girl happily. "I think so. And just to think, I wanted to get away from her! I didn't want to stay with her worldly crew, and all the time God was wanting me to bring her a message for Him! And suppose I hadn't done it? It seems He just had to keep my lovely bracelet away from me for awhile to bring me back here before I could have it, because He had some work for me to do for Him here. Strange, it never occurred to me that I could help a self-sufficient worldly woman, who half despised me for a little Puritan, and did her best to try and make me over into her kind."

"And when she found she couldn't do it, you got her goat!" said Revel. "That's where you got your opening. She saw you had something she didn't have, and after a while she saw she needed it."

Margaret smiled half shamedly.

"Yes, but how much time I wasted! All that first summer I was here I was so unhappy."

"Well, probably the time hadn't come yet when God wanted you to work. It might not have reached her then. She had to test your witness out first."

"Perhaps," said Margaret. "But Revel, do you know what she said? She said if I went on this way and didn't learn to smoke and drink and do as others did, and didn't dance nor anything, that I would never be a success. And when I asked what she meant by being a success, she said she meant make a brilliant marriage! Oh, I wish she could look down now for just a few minutes and see what a wonderful man I'm going to marry!"

"Well, maybe she can see now, I don't know. We'll have to ask Grand about that. He knows a lot about Heaven and things. But it's certain she wouldn't have thought this was a grand marriage if it had dawned on her then. She wasn't in a state to think so you know. I'm not much."

Then Katie came back from the store, surprised to find there was company to dinner, and while they were eating they talked of practical things.

"Can't we be married right away, tonight, or tomorrow, and you go back with me?" asked Revel eagerly.

Margaret shook her head.

"That would be lovely," she said, "but I don't believe we should. I know my dear old guardian would be terribly hurt. He made me promise when I came away that I would come back to him for my wedding. He said it was going to be his wedding gift, my wedding. And Grand should be there of course. We haven't got so many people left in our families that we can afford to ignore them. Besides, I have to stay here till everything is settled up, they told me; and you'll be needing to get back and round up a lot of things yourself, you know. Grand will live with us, won't he, while he's spared to us?"

Revel drew her close again.

"What a girl!" he said reverently and kissed her softly. "You anticipate all the problems and take the problem out of them. I'd love it and he'll want to, I know. But if you don't like it we can arrange for him, of course."

"I'll like it, I know. I love him already."

"There's a Bible verse that comes to mind," he said, drawing her more tenderly close. " 'Delight thyself also in the Lord and He shall give thee the desires of thine heart.' What more could my heart desire than you, my precious? But, dearest, I don't like to go away and leave you here alone."

"I'm not here alone. God is here just as He has been all these two-three years, and I've got work to do. I should go back to the university and get my credits. I don't suppose it will ever matter whether I have credits of that sort now or not, but anyway I'd better get them. And I've a lot of things there to gather up and pack. I can do that after I finish up here, and then when I get my things started I'll go right to my guardian's in New York and you can come and see me as much as you like until I get a few bibs and tuckers ready for a trousseau."

"You don't need any bibs and tuckers," he said with a smile, "it shall be *my pleasure* to get them *for* you. Grand thinks that I should go right into my father's business, though I'm not sure I shall carry it on always. But there'll be enough to keep us from want, anyway. And now, since you insist you won't get married tonight, I think I'd better take the late train to the city. I've some business to transact for a friend of father's, some oil-well stock to inquire about, and I'd better do that the first thing in the morning. It might take a couple of days, but I can run out here for the afternoons and evenings, and then when it's done I'll take the night plane home. If I'm going to be a sober married man I've a lot of things to attend to myself."

So they marched happily through the hours, dreading the brief separation that was ahead of them, yet trusting God to bring it all out right in the end.

And one day not many weeks later, in a stately old church

in New York where her guardian was a member, Margaret walked down the flower-decked aisle, wearing a dress her mother had worn years ago, white and soft and lovely, decked with rare old lace, and in her dark hair the same wreath of orange blossoms her mother had worn. With head high and shining eyes she went forward to meet her bridegroom standing tall and handsome with a college chum for best man, and a look in his eyes as if he were about to be crowned.

Down in the audience there sat a few old friends of Margaret's mother, and a few of her own childhood friends who were still living in the vicinity of New York, and her guardian's wife. And away at the back sat Bailey Wicke and his ash-blonde wife, looking sullen and disappointed. "There never was anybody like her," he mumbled.

"Well, she's getting a stunningly handsome man," said his wife.

Over on the groom's side, sat Grand in the place Revel's father might have occupied if he had been living, and behind a fine array of college students. The fellowship and the debating team, and the football team and all the others who could possibly get to New York, for Revel was a great favorite, and they all were glad for him. They knew what a hard time he had been having during the long months of his father's illness.

"Say, that's a pip of a girl Rev is marrying, Walt," said one called Sam, "where do you suppose he got her? You don't see many like that nowadays."

"I asked him that same thing once," said the man named Walter, "and what do you think he answered? He said, 'I found her in the woods, man, one day when I went to pick wild flowers.' "

"H'm!" said the other fellow, "I wonder if there are any more like that. If I thought there were I'd take to picking wild flowers myself."

About the Author

Grace Livingston Hill is well-known as one of the most prolific writers of romantic fiction. Her personal life was fraught with joys and sorrows not unlike those experienced by many of her fictional heroines.

Born in Wellsville, New York, Grace nearly died during the first hours of life. But her loving parents and friends turned to God in prayer. She survived miraculously, thus her thankful father named her Grace.

Grace was always close to her father, a Presbyterian minister, and her mother, a published writer. It was from them that she learned the art of storytelling. When Grace was twelve, a close aunt surprised her with a hardbound, illustrated copy of one of Grace's stories. This was the beginning of Grace's journey into being a published author.

In 1892 Grace married Fred Hill, a young minister, and they soon had two lovely young daughters. Then came 1901, a difficult year for Grace—the year when, within months of each other, both her father and husband died. Suddenly Grace had to find a new place to live (her home was owned by the church where her husband had been pastor). It was a struggle for Grace to raise her young daughters alone, but through everything she kept writing. In 1902 she produced *The Angel of His Presence, The Story of a Whim,* and *An Unwilling Guest.* In 1903 her two books *According to the Pattern* and *Because of Stephen* were published.

It wasn't long before Grace was a well-known author, but she wanted to go beyond just entertaining her readers. She soon included the message of God's salvation through Jesus Christ in each of her books. For Grace, the most important thing she did was not write books but share the message of salvation, a message she felt God wanted her to share through the abilities he had given her.

In all, Grace Livingston Hill wrote more than one hundred books, all of which have sold thousands of copies and have touched the lives of readers around the world with their message of "enduring love" and the true way to lasting happiness: a relationship with God through his Son, Jesus Christ.

In an interview shortly before her death, Grace's devotion to her Lord still shone clear. She commented that whatever she had accomplished had been God's doing. She was only his servant, one who had tried to follow his teaching in all her thoughts and writing.

Don't miss these Grace Livingston Hill romance novels!